DALIAN CRYSTALS

Chronicles of the Imperial Rangers

BARBARA J. ROBERTSON

DALIAN CRYSTALS - Chronicles of the Imperial Rangers

Copyright © 2019 by Barbara J. Robertson

DEDICATION

The "Chronicles of the Imperial Rangers" series is dedicated to the men and women of the United States Marines, Navy, Army, Air Force, and Coast Guard, whose hard work and sacrifice continues to provide us with the freedoms we enjoy, and hold so dear.
Thank you for your service!

ACKNOWLEDGMENTS

Many thanks are owed to my close friends, sisters, and advisors:
To RMCM Marie Vellis, for her support for this project. Her leadership and dedication to duty during an exemplary 30-year career in the US Navy helped open the doors for women to achieve ranks and careers previously not available to them. Thank you for your friendship.
To Bonnie Copeland for reading my works, and providing commentary and gentle criticism during the creation process. Thank you, thank you!
To Denise Robertson, RN, and Debbie Hilst, RN, my sisters, for patiently providing medical advice during the creation of this book, and for reading the finished work. Love You!
To Mara Kalcheim, for her encouragement, and for holding my feet to the fire. Thank you!
To Roe Andersen, my proofreader, for her excellent skill and constructive criticism.
To Bettina Moss, for helping drill down to the essence of our heroes. Time in conversation with you was priceless.
To John Lenzi, for his encouragement, friendship, and humor. Thank you, always.
To Rosalie Bruce, for your invaluable advice and assistance during the publishing process.
To the many veterans who shared their memories of military service and battles with me. You are a priceless resource. As you requested, your names have not been disclosed. But your stories of victories and defeats in battle will stay alive.

PROLOGUE

Located in the far corner of the T'Cetyl galaxy is the solar system known as "R'Genra." Four inhabited planets orbit their sun: Ban'Ti, the jungle planet, third from the sun; M'Wati, the planet of islands, with only two large continental masses and thousands of islands; Home World, the center of the Empire, with eight billion calling the beautiful planet home; and massive K'Halon Prime, the source of human life in the R'Genra system. For nearly 2,500 years, the Empire has ruled K'Halon Prime and Home World, and later M'Wati. Ban'Ti was populated last, being on the inside of the asteroid-filled White Belt.

An unidentified catastrophe over 2,500 years ago was blamed for the current state of K'Halon Prime. The source of the devastation is known only to the Emperor and his highest scientists, and Keeper of the Imperial Records. One side of the planet is densely forested, with two billion people, and even more large mammals, birds, and many other animals. The other side of K'Halon Prime is barren desert, sparse fresh water sources, and thus, absent diversity of plant and animal life. Only vermin, reptiles, vultures, and poisonous insects call the desert side home.

Prior to the catastrophe, humans lived only on K'Halon Prime. The chilly forest planet was divided among many kings, who warred against each other for land, riches, and power. After the catastrophic devastation, surviving kings formed the Empire, and peace and order were established. A great awakening of knowledge occurred during the next centuries. Fantastic technological advances in flight enabled the people to reach beyond the realm of K'Halon Prime to its beautiful neighbor, which they named Home World.

The climate of Home World was mildly temperate, and its soil was very fertile, with many lakes and rivers providing fresh water. Its oceans were dotted with large and small islands, making trade easy and abundant. Its diverse array of plants, land mammals, fish, and birds provided food for the settlers. The human population grew rapidly. The orbit of Home World took one year, whereas K'Halon Prime spent 2.65 years orbiting around the sun. The people relocated to Home World in transport after transport, seeking more favorable living conditions, and much milder winters.

Rapid advancements were made in science and technology during the next millennium, and ships sent out for exploration discovered the planet of islands, M'Wati, and eventually, the little jungle planet of Ban'Ti. The Empire expanded to include the four inhabited planets and beyond, to the outer reaches of the R'Genra system. A thriving arrangement of trade and commerce developed rapidly. Six space bases were established within the system to provide protection for the four worlds and their interdependent commerce.

Minor uprisings had occurred throughout the 2,500 years of the Empire, but were quickly and soundly defeated. The last twenty years of the reign of the Great Benevolent Emperor P'Lau have witnessed the rise and expansion of the Rebellion. Many blamed the very generosity and benevolence of Emperor P'Lau for the growth of the Rebellion, led by his half-brother, Duma Wat. The Rebellion was growing in scope and size, and seemingly unrelated events were coordinated to rally more wealthy supporters to its cause. For the first time in its existence, the security of the Empire was being threatened.

From the first days of the Empire, the Imperial Class System has been the social system for all peoples of the R'Genra system. The Warrior Class has held the uppermost tier of the Imperial Class System. Since the beginning of the Empire, all emperors and empresses have come directly from the Warrior Class, and the same bloodline as Emperor P'Lau. The highest-ranking warriors are the Rangers, sworn by blood oath to the Emperor for their service, will, and their lives. The males are the Borgund Rangers, and the females are the Shi'Lon Rangers. The Rangers are sworn to obey and enforce the will of the Emperor.

Herein begins the first of the Chronicles of the Borgund and Shi'Lon Rangers.

I

The courtyard of the Royal Palace of Home World was very festive on this New Year's Eve. Hanging lanterns of all colors swayed in the light breeze, illuminating the entire courtyard and its beautiful displays of twinkling light crystals, colorful pennants, and holiday figurines. For 800 years, the Royal Palace and its surrounding buildings within the thick, ancient stone walls was home for the Emperor and his Rangers, since the first days of the Palace's construction. Modern holiday lighting decorated every building, giving a fairy-tale glow to the entire Palace complex. It was a glorious place tonight; almost magical.

The tall Borgund Ranger Commander Steph'N slowed his pace to enjoy the evening inside the courtyard for a moment. The night blooming jasmine was so fragrant tonight, competing with the roses' familiar scent. He could have enjoyed the peaceful, delightful courtyard for hours. But in a few minutes, the Royal Palace Guards would open the courtyard gates, letting people enter for the holiday festivities, and the later fireworks. The musicians were setting up to play. Soon, loud conversations, music, and laughter would completely shatter the peaceful quiet.

Breathing in deeply for a last intoxicating fragrance high, Commander Steph'N savored the peace and quiet for one moment longer. Then he jogged to the entrance doors of the Palace Main Court. It would not reflect well on Steph'N or his Commander Superior Vu'Duc if he arrived late for the Honors Banquet.

Running steps behind him let Steph'N know he was not the last Borgund Ranger to join their formation, thankfully. The women Shi'Lon Rangers were in perfect formation, each one impeccably dressed in their formal red uniforms. One hundred-fifty Imperial Guards dressed in their purple cloaks and uniforms flanked the Rangers. The trumpets sounded, and twenty Imperial Guards escorted the Great Emperor P'Lau to the golden stairs leading up to his magnificent, levitating throne. When the Emperor turned to face his Rangers and Imperial Guards, they all knelt before him on their right knees. Vu'Duc called, "Draw swords!" The Rangers drew their fiery white plasma swords and held them high with both hands. Then they pulled their swords down to their left breastplates in the Royal Salute, saying, "Long live Emperor P'Lau!" They replaced their fiery swords into their backplates.

"Rise, my Beloved Daughters and Faithful Sons," the Emperor said. The Imperial Guards, Borgund and Shi'Lon Rangers stood at attention. The Honors Banquet was primarily a formal ceremony to honor the Imperial Guards, and the one hundred-fifty Borgund and fifty Shi'Lon Rangers. Unlike the Army, Navy, Air Corps, and Space Cadre, the Rangers and Imperial Guardsmen never wore medals of any kind, merely rank insignia at the uniform collars. Their awards and commendations were announced in the secluded setting of their Honors Banquet, and notated in their service records. Being a Ranger was the ultimate honor in itself; they were the highest tier of the Warrior Class. The Imperial Guards ranked directly below the Rangers.

Each award winner knelt before the Emperor, thanked him, and silently rejoined the ranks. Steph'N made a mental note of the Ranger awards; many more than years past. The Rebellion was spreading, and its battles and Rangers' secret assignments multiplying. Six Borgunds and two Shi'Lons gave their lives protecting Emperor P'Lau, or during dangerous assignments this year. Their parents, life partners, or nearest relative received their awards.

Most of the Rangers were sent on missions alone, or in small teams of two or three. The Shi'Lon Rangers were the Emissaries of the Emperor, his Beloved Daughters, and were usually sent as the "Last Chance" Imperial negotiators. They were fully prepared for either a peaceful or hostile end to the negotiations. The Shi'Lon Rangers and the Borgund Rangers were trained together for two and one-half years, in Phase 1, Phase 2 and Phase 3 Training. Both types of Rangers were master fighters, highly-trained killers, disciplined, and dedicated their lives to serve the Emperor, and to obey and enforce his will.

But the Borgund Rangers were also trained as deadly assassins. Whereas the Shi'Lons were trained in negotiations, body language interpretation, and contract bargaining in Phase 3 Training, the Borgunds were trained to infiltrate, "neutralize" their target, and disappear without a trace. Steph'N was excellent at disappearing after accomplishing his mission. He successfully completed two high-risk missions this year for the Emperor.

Commander Steph'N received an award and a bonus for "Mission Success under Duress," a nebulous term for the living hell he endured for five weeks on the jungle planet, Ban'Ti, during its oppressively scorching summer. He lived with the silent monks in their caves, awaiting the optimum time to neutralize his target. He slept fully clothed, with his pant legs tucked into his boots, and the fabric at his wrists and collar snugly tied closed. He also used ear plugs. Bugs were everywhere in Ban'Ti. He hated the fleas, earwigs, and roaches. They were food for the poisonous centipedes, spiders, and scorpions. Steph'N got used to the snakes, lizards, rats, and shrews, but not the insects. He shuttered again, recalling his experience on Ban'Ti.

A fabulous banquet followed the awards. The Emperor honored his Rangers and Imperial Guards with the best food and fine wine from all four planets in the solar system. After an exotic dessert of honeyed wine and snow-ice, most of the Rangers and Imperial Guards marched out of the Main Court to enjoy a couple of weeks off during the holiday with family and friends. But not Steph'N.

He was ordered into the private Royal Court of Emperor P'Lau immediately after the banquet by his Commander Superior Vu'Duc. Two Space Cadre Admirals he'd never met watched him walk up to the gold line between the gold pillars, and they all knelt before the Emperor. "Rise. Please, all of you rise, and be seated," P'Lau said impatiently.

An Admiral approached the Emperor, and was given leave to speak. "Your Majesty, Commanders Superior Vu'Duc and Bette are correct. He looks just like the Major, Sire," the Admiral said, staring at Steph'N. The other officer agreed, both officers now staring at Steph'N. His feelings of success and reverie evaporated as Commander Superior Bette approached, and studied him closely.

Shi'Lon Commander Superior Bette was a tough old bird, and made Vu'Duc seem like a pussycat. "Great Emperor P'Lau, your Borgund Ranger could be the traitor's twin," she surmised while staring at Steph'N. "The resemblance is remarkable. Only their eyes and hair length are different, Sire."

Emperor P'Lau called Steph'N to come forward, and stood directly in front of him. It was the closest he'd ever been to his Emperor, with his painted white face and red lips. P'Lau walked around Steph'N, and then turned his head from side to side while holding his chin. "My Faithful Son, have you ever met or heard of Major S'Loc?" He asked.

"Major S'Loc? No, Sire. I know of no such person, my Emperor," Steph'N replied nervously. "Sire, we Borgund Rangers are not good at being the center of attention. May I be permitted to enquire what exactly is transpiring, my Liege?" C.S. Vu'Duc immediately stood next to Steph'N, glaring at him for being so bold, and addressing the Emperor directly.

The Emperor said, "It's all right, Vu'Duc. My Ranger has been unfairly treated as an object here, and not given the proper respect one of my Faithful Sons deserves. Let us dispense with the drama, then. I will cut to the heart of the matter. My Faithful Son Commander Steph'N, you bear an uncanny resemblance to the very recently uncovered traitor Major S'Loc. Word of his death has not left this Royal Court," the Emperor said, and moved his arm to the right.

Imperial Guards parted to reveal the body of Major S'Loc on the floor. Steph'N walked over to the dead body. The dead Major was white and lifeless, but did indeed look just like him. It was bone-chilling; a harbinger of immense foreboding. The white foam around his mouth clearly showed S'Loc committed suicide by cyanide capsule.

"Your Emperor must ask a near-impossible task of his Borgund Ranger Commander Steph'N: will you assume the life of Major S'Loc, a confessed traitor to the Empire, and a Rebel? Will you agree to infiltrate the senior ranks of the Rebels as an undercover agent for your Emperor? The risk is very great. I will not sugar-coat the situation, Steph'N. It would mean deep immersion, perhaps for more than a year or two. But the opportunity presents itself. Right now," P'Lau said, standing next to Steph'N.

Commander Steph'N looked his Emperor in the eyes for the first time, and then answered, "I swore my service, my will, and my life to you five years ago, Sire. Nothing has changed. I am yours to command, Great Emperor P'Lau," he answered firmly, and knelt before the Emperor with his head bowed.

Emperor P'Lau touched Steph'N's shoulder, sighed heavily, and quickly walked back to his throne. He said, "Then I command my Faithful Son Commander Steph'N to assume the life of the traitor Major S'Loc immediately. You are now a Rebel senior officer. You will be hunted by the Empire for S'Loc's crimes. Your deep immersion status is known only to those present. You will report only to Commander Superior Vu'Duc or your Emperor. Your objective is to become a confidant of the Rebel Leader, the Traitor, Duma Wat. Your mission begins immediately after your briefing from these two Admirals and Commander Superior Vu'Duc. May the Creator bless my Faithful Son Steph'N!"

Steph'N's deep immersion briefing with the two Admirals from the Space Cadre and C.S. Vu'Duc lasted two hours. The Admirals spent an hour describing Major S'Loc's experience and current duties to Comm. Steph'N, and his recently discovered subterfuge for the Rebellion. The Major was the Chief Engineering Officer for his battleship, and a real taskmaster, according to the reports from his fellow officers. He was very disciplined, a workaholic, and prided himself on having the best crews in the fleet. No one suspected he harbored a grudge against the Space Cadre and the Empire, and had turned traitor several years ago. Since he socialized infrequently onboard ship, no one paid attention to his after-work activities, or really cared what he did, as long as the Major wasn't after them.

The Major was the only surviving member of his family. The Admirals said his parents and siblings were all killed three years ago while traveling from Home World to K'Halon Prime to celebrate S'Loc's big promotion to Major, and making Chief Engineer of his battleship. The passenger transport's life support system malfunctioned, and the stored oxygen onboard flooded the engine compartment. A Space Cadre rescue ship was en route to the disabled transport, but did not make it in time. The transport exploded in a fireball, killing everyone on board. S'Loc buried his feelings, hiding his resentment from everyone, and threw himself into his work. Later, he joined the Rebels to take out his revenge against the Space Cadre.

S'Loc's traitorous activities were discovered by chance. He volunteered to stay aboard the brand-new, docked battleship during the holiday vacations, supposedly to conduct inventories of the spare engine parts, tools, and other engineering department equipment. But he was secretly committing sabotage, intentionally disabling the new battleship before its maiden mission. His goal was to leave the new battleship adrift and without any functioning weaponry, for the Rebel Leader Duma Wat to commandeer. The Ship's Captain returned to the battleship to surprise his Chief Engineer with a New Year's gift, feeling sorry for the man without a family - and caught him in the act of sabotaging the weapons control system.

The Admiral said, "Only the Ship's Captain and those with you in the Emperor's Royal Court know of S'Loc's confession and his deeds. It is unfortunate that several security crewmen and officers were involved in his capture and incarceration. It would've been best if you could have assumed his duties, but that is not possible."

"Now, you must escape to the Rebels from a prison transport," C.S. Vu'Duc said, "an awkward situation. We have communicated with our assets already undercover with the Rebels, and have made arrangements for your getaway and delivery to the second-in-command officer of the Rebels forces, Colonel Vas. He is former Imperial Army. All S'Loc's personal belongings were confiscated upon his arrest, of course. He maintained no residence other than his ship. He does have a nephew, D'Wayn, with whom he stays whenever he is on Home World. You will be virtually bankrupt, Commander Steph'N," his Commander Superior cautioned. "On your own, with nary a credit in your pockets. Understand, Ranger?" Steph'N nodded in understanding. "Good. We have another asset currently with Colonel Vas, but he will not reveal himself to you, interact with you on board, or disclose his true identity. You will leave shortly."

Steph'N asked, "May I be permitted to call my family and let them know I won't be coming home for the holidays? They are expecting my arrival tomorrow, sir."

Vu'Duc looked at his Ranger, and slowly shook his head. "I'm afraid not, Steph'N. You must change into S'Loc's uniform and leave within the next few minutes. The time schedule is very tight. The prison transport is awaiting delivery of a high-profile prisoner now. We cannot afford to bring any undue attention to you by forcing the prison shuttle to hold departure," he explained. "Everything is in place. The clock is ticking, Commander Steph'N."

Steph'N had to change into the dirty, soiled uniform of Major S'Loc with Vu'Duc watching. His wallet, Ranger uniform, cloak, boots, and his armor, the breastplate and backplate, were taken by Vu'Duc, and he promised to leave his assigned quarters and belongings under lock and key for the duration of his mission. A barber was brought into his office, and Steph'N's long hair was cut in Space Cadre regulation style, short and non-descript. Then the Royal Physician spent a few minutes showing him how to insert and remove his new eye contacts. Steph'N had blue eyes, and the Major's eyes were brown. At least they would last for one week, and he wouldn't have to change them out every day.

He looked at himself in the mirror as Major S'Loc. If his uniform had been clean, he would've looked good. It was a perfect fit. Vu'Duc checked him out, and approved. Then he said, "One more thing, Commander Steph'N. A technicality, really, but important: Major S'Loc was homosexual. He had a penchant for teenage boys, but never approached anyone on board during his assignments. We think "Nephew D'Wayn," is really his lover, perhaps one of several. We don't know for certain. S'Loc was very private and discreet."

A technicality? A big one. Steph'N bristled, and remarked, "I trust the Emperor does not expect me to perform any sexual acts with a man. I'm not homosexual, sir. I have never refused his orders, and hope I don't have to do so now, sir."

His Commander Superior said, "It's up to you, Commander Steph'N. I would feel the same, truthfully. Here is our new, secret comm link number. Memorize it. Try to call me every few days, and at least weekly. We will have one of our Rangers answer as "D'Wayn," to keep up appearances, but either I or the Emperor himself will be listening to each of your calls. Good luck, and may the Creator bless you, Commander Steph'N."

He saluted Vu'Duc, and was then cuffed and escorted by Space Cadre security to the waiting prison transport, destination Ban'Ti Military Prison. He was thrown into a tight Top Security holding cell, restrained, and strapped into his transport seat roughly by the security guards, one of whom blew him a kiss when he clanked the door shut. Bloody hell. The Major's gay reputation was going along for the ride with him. The transport was launched quickly, and they were on their way to Ban'Ti, a two-week trip in this transport. Fine. Steph'N would rather deal with snakes and vermin than homosexual prison guards. He hoped they wouldn't try anything with him.

Sitting in a dead traitor's dirty uniform with empty pockets, cuffed and restrained in a prison transport. *Happy bloody New Year to me*, he thought. Vu'Duc said this was a two-year deep immersion assignment. *Probably longer*, he smirked. His entire life would change. No one would know what happened to him, other than the Emperor, Vu'Duc, and those two Space Cadre Admirals. He had heard tales of some men sent into deep immersion who never came back. Every ounce of training, meditation and concentration would be needed to carry out this mission, and make sure he survived.

Steph'N leaned his head back and thought of his original plans for the New Year's Holiday, a full two weeks off duty. He had planned to spend tonight with his girlfriend Va'Pal, a Shi'Lon Commander. She was such fun to be around, with her wicked sense of humor, and her love for him. Would C.S. Vu'Duc tell Va'Pal he was sent away on a deep immersion mission for up to two years? Probably not. She would think he had abandoned her, and eventually find another man. His family would think he ran off with a woman for the holiday and ditched them. The prison guard who blew him a kiss came around just then, and stuck his disgusting tongue out at him. Bloody hell. It would be a long night. No way was he falling asleep.

The third day of his trip, the prison transport was attacked, stopped dead in space, and quickly boarded by Rebels. They took him and four other men with them on board their old, rusty destroyer. No wonder Duma Wat wanted the new battleship the Major was sabotaging. He soon developed ample respect for the Rebels who kept the ancient destroyer running. They gave him officer's quarters, new Rebel uniforms, and a debriefing. He was ordered to clean up, eat in the chow hall, rest for a day, and then his new duty would begin. He felt good to be clean, and he looked good in the Rebel officer uniform. But his masquerade was only beginning.

Someone hid ear buds under his pillow, with a small player and recorded crystal. He inserted the ear buds into his ears, played the crystal, and heard recorded files on the Major. His service record, his friends, and his habits; it was the Major's whole life, as the Space Cadre knew it. He listened all night, learning how to become the traitor Major S'Loc.

II

The High Priest and High Priestess said prayers and offered sacrifices in the ancient religious language on the large, wide fire dish sitting on the platform above the main stage. The audience was respectfully quiet during the Blessing of the Graduates, everyone uncomfortable in the sweltering summer heat. The ceremony had already lasted two hours. When the incense was placed on the fire, it erupted in dancing silver and blue flames, and then smoke filled the air with its strange, spicy fragrance. The High Priest and High Priestess turned to the graduates, moved their arms and hands in the "Great Spiral" religious blessing, and bowed. The audience erupted in cheers when the graduates of the Royal Academy stood. The graduates walked off the stage to join their friends and families.

"The graduation ceremony was beautiful this year," Master Commander Javette said to her approaching son, Dan'L. "But I am prejudiced, of course, since my Son was graduating!" Mother and Son clasped forearms and kissed each other's cheek in joy. Little sister K'Rissa happily hugged her big brother.

Dan'L excitedly told her, "Mother, I have invited my best friend Kayla to join our celebration this afternoon. Kayla, this is my Mother, Master Commander Javette, and my little sister, K'Rissa," he proudly said, introducing them. Kayla, also a graduate, bowed her head slightly to show respect to Shi'Lon Master Commander Javette.

Javette said, "The best friend of my Son is welcome to join us anytime. Come now, and let's politely mingle with the other Warrior Class members. You don't want to begin your career offending anyone," she sarcastically said to the new graduates. "Save that for after Phase 3, and your Confirmation," she laughed. They socialized for a respectful amount of time, meeting, mingling, and talking with the Warrior Class parents and friends of the new graduates.

For ten years, Kayla and Dan'L attended the Imperial Royal Academy on Home World. The Warrior Class children were taken from their parents around age five, and brought to the Royal Academy for study, training, and indoctrination to the laws and customs of the Empire. All children of the Warrior Class belonged to the Emperor. It was a proud tradition for more than fifteen hundred years. The Warrior Class was the highest tier in the Imperial Class System, with the most powerful and loyal members. Each warrior swore a blood oath to the Emperor, whose bloodline came directly from their own class.

The celebration with Dan'L, M.C. Javette, their family and friends was fun. Kayla appreciated her friend Dan'L including her in the festivities. Kayla's father, Borgund Ranger Master Commander Tom'S, was killed just seven months ago fighting against the Rebels. Her Shi'Lon Master Commander Mother Rosa died two years ago, in a heroic battle defeating a Rebel insurgent force on Space Base Orioc, in the Outer Rim. Kayla's only living relative was her brother Olm, and he was serving aboard a Space Cadre battleship in the Central Core. She would have spent the day alone, if not for Dan'L and his kindness. She went to bed and rose early the next day, in eager anticipation of her newest adventure, Phase 1 Training.

The new graduates who were invited to Phase 1 Training were told to pack only their toiletries and personal items, and leave their Royal Academy and Court clothing behind for their journey. They were traveling to the third moon of K'Halon Prime, called "Xau," for Phase 1 Training. A small travel case was given to each trainee, and they could take no more than what fit inside the travel case. Kayla boarded the huge transport, looking for Dan'L. They sat together and chatted excitedly about the upcoming training, and their four-day transport trip.

Most Royal Academy graduates chose to pursue their studies at a university, if they were not invited for Phase 1 training. They had to be in prime physical shape, mentally focused, and the child of a Warrior Class parent to receive an invitation to Phase 1 Training. Although aristocrats also sent their children to the Royal Academy, those graduates did not receive invitations to Phase 1 training, like Kayla and Dan'L. And their aristocrat parents had to pay tuition for their children's education, room, and board during their Royal Academy attendance.

"It is such an honor to be attending Phase 1 training, isn't it, Dan'L?" Kayla asked. "I promised my brother Olm I would do my best to make him proud, and to honor my late parents," Kayla shared.

"It is also a huge responsibility, and a great challenge, Kayla. Mother said probably half of the class can't tough it out, and will fall by the wayside. I sure don't want to embarrass my Mother and Father by having to enlist in the Space Cadre, or enroll in a regular university. Those who 'wash out' and cannot complete Phase 1 training can never be Space Cadre officers, and the Phase 2 wash-outs don't fare much better, from what I've been told. I want to qualify for Ranger training in Phase 2, don't you, Kayla?" Dan'L asked, and she quickly nodded her head. They talked about their upcoming challenge for quite some time, as did the other graduates. In a few hours, Dan'L fell asleep. Kayla stared out the porthole, looking at the stars, and the ever-shrinking planet of Home World.

Kayla wondered about her future, and what K'Halon Prime's moon named "Xau" would be like. It was a desert moon, she read, and not at all beautiful like Home World. Like all of the graduates, she had been well-schooled, clothed and fed very well. They had been forewarned prior to boarding to expect no pampering whatsoever from today forward. She determined to show no weakness. During the last night of their trip, Kayla meditated while the others around her slept, and mentally prepared herself to begin Phase 1 military training. Tomorrow morning, everything would change.

Royal Academy training included regular physical calisthenics, running, swimming, and swordsmanship. The new Phase 1 trainees considered themselves in good shape—that is, until the third morning of their training. They had run five kilometers, swam one hundred laps in the very long pool in frigid water, run the obstacle course, and ended their second day with another five-kilometer run back to their barracks. When the bell sounded to line up for breakfast, much moaning and groaning was heard. The Training Instructor loudly rousted the tired trainees out of bed, and into their clothing.

Breakfast never tasted so good to Kayla. She watched Dan'L sop his plate with his last bit of bread. Two hours of Imperial military history class was followed by their first martial arts training, where every trainee was pummeled by the woman instructor, Su'Sen. Lunch, and a fifteen-minute break; then the five-kilometer run, swimming, running the ever-changing obstacle course, and, finally, the exhausting five kilometers run back to the barracks. Showers revealed the many bruises from the obstacle course on their young bodies. And this was only their first week.

The fifty males and females trained together, but slept in separate barracks. As the training progressed, they were matched to fight against each other, to develop their skills. The first time Dan'L faced off against a female trainee, the gentleman in him held back. He didn't want to hit a girl. The martial arts instructor Su'Sen joined his female opponent against Dan'L, and he got over his chivalrous attitude right away. Kayla winced at him getting beaten, and realized she would eventually have to face off against Dan'L, as well as the other males in their class. Every trainee got soundly walloped in the first weeks of martial arts training.

The young men and women were pushed to the limits of their strength and endurance during the year of their Phase 1 Training. Their formerly smooth bodies were hardened, strengthened, and trained to become warriors. The trainees learned to march in many formations perfectly, and trained at all hours of the day, rain or shine. The natural human tendency to hesitate before firing a weapon or fighting was trained out of them. Weapons training was extensive, to prepare them to become fully competent with all the handheld field weapons of the Empire. They learned to field-strip and clean their laser rifles and pistols properly, even in the pitch black.

Trainees who showed reluctance to obey orders without question, or who demonstrated any persistent weakness of character were given the boot, and transported home the same day. Pain control and rudimentary survival skills were learned the hard way, to ingrain the lessons into their bodies, as well as their minds. They stood taller, and walked with confidence to the General Assembly on their last day.

The trainees were introduced to Commander Superior G'Rosk of the Borgund Rangers. G'Rosk was tall, with brown hair, and eyes of chestnut. He wore the daily uniform of the Rangers: black blouse and trousers, and black boots. His body armor, gloves, and arm bands were also black. The only color on his uniform was his Ranger belt buckle of solid gold, embellished with the Imperial seal, and his insignia on his collar. G'Rosk looked powerful in his full-length cloak. There was no question he was the man in charge.

He walked down the center aisle, intently staring at the remaining trainees, and announced, "You are the twenty-two survivors of Phase 1 Training. Your friends who fell by the wayside are now applying for entrance to university, or enlisted in the Space Cadre, the Navy, the Air Corps, or the Army; all honorable careers necessary for the continuance of the Empire."

A sly smile came over his face, and G'Rosk said, "But the Army, Air Corps, Navy, and the Space Cadre are not recruiting here tonight. You have proven yourselves 'over-qualified' for their enlisted ranks now." A few laughs came from the assembly. "You are at a crossroads today. The next decision you make will set your path for the rest of your lives. Several choices are yours to consider, and you must choose tonight. The first career choice available is to serve in the Space Cadre, Army, Air Corps, or Navy as a commissioned officer. Several openings are available for qualified officers in the Space Cadre." He turned and strolled back to the front of the room.

"Your second choice is to volunteer as an Imperial Guard at one of the Emperor's palaces, either on Home World, or K'Halon Prime. This is a highly visible assignment, one with opportunity to advance to higher court positions. A coveted commission, to be sure," G'Rosk said. "But only three openings are available at this time. Imperial Guardsmen have an immense responsibility."

C.S. G'Rosk continued, "The third choice is to continue on to Phase 2 and 3 Ranger Training, whereupon successful completion you qualify for Borgund or Shi'Lon Ranger. Please note: failure is not an honorable outcome for Phase 2 Ranger Training. You must commit to the path fully to complete the course. If you 'Wash Out,' or resign, you could still serve as a Palace Guard, or as a commissioned officer in the Space Cadre or the Imperial Army," C.S. G'Rosk cautioned, "but you will never qualify to be promoted to the senior officer ranks." He let his words sink in for a minute. "Consider your choice carefully. Ranger positions have several personal and private commitments required to be sworn to by the accepted trainee. Borgund Rangers are all-male, and Shi'Lon Rangers are all-female, as you know."

He looked intensely at each trainee and continued, "The choice for Ranger is the most exclusive opportunity. Not everyone who volunteers will be accepted into the Ranger path. It requires you to complete not only harsh Phase 2 Ranger training for another year, but also specialized training and study for an additional six months, in Phase 3. If your test scores are less than desirable, or if your senior officers feel you would potentially wash out, we will recommend you select a Space Cadre or Imperial Army officer commission. Better you serve the Empire in a career where you will succeed with honors. Becoming a Ranger is a serious commitment."

After assembly was dismissed, Kayla went outside and walked the desert in silence. She realized she was marked for the Ranger path at age five. Did she even have a choice? She climbed into the desert hills, sat on a large boulder atop a hill, and indulged in childhood memories of her fifth birthday: After the cake and ice cream treats, the children excitedly gathered for the treasure box hunt. The child who found the hidden treasure box got the first pick from its candy and toy surprises. Each child wanted the first pick. No one was satisfied with left-overs, especially little Kayla.

The children ran all over the Royal Palace grounds in search of her birthday treasure box hidden by Kayla's parents. Little Kayla knew Mama and Daddy wouldn't hide her treasure where an ordinary child would easily discover it. She came upon the old gazebo, run-down and badly in need of repairs and fresh paint. She walked around the old gazebo and saw a loose board on the top step. Little Kayla lifted off the board, peered under the steps, and found her treasure box. She cried, "I found it! It's here!" The other children ran over to see the treasure box.

Little Kayla opened the treasure box and found a red envelope inside with her name written in gold upon it. She let her friends help themselves to the candies and toys, and took the card to her Mama. The red card contained an invitation written on parchment. Her Mama proudly read the invitation aloud:

"My Kayla is invited to attend the Royal Academy of Home World, where she will train, study, and gain knowledge, and one day become the Beloved Daughter of the Most Benevolent Emperor P'Lau." Her parents and friends congratulated her on her appointment.

The Palace Guards soon landed an ornate shuttle on the lawn. A woman in a long purple cloak – an Imperial Guard - walked from the shuttle to Kayla and her parents, and formally announced, "The Benevolent Emperor P'Lau has chosen you above all others as his Beloved Daughter, Kayla. I am here to escort you to the Home World Palace of the Emperor, your new home." Her parents took her to the Royal shuttle and helped her inside. The lady in the purple cloak sat next to her, and they flew off, leaving behind Kayla's parents, her friends, and the Ranger Family Residences within the K'Halon Prime Royal Palace compound, where she grew up.

Beloved Daughter Kayla survived the shock of being taken from her home and loving parents. Her parents had told little Kayla many times of the generous gifts of Emperor P'Lau. Like the other children in her class of twenty, she was at first lonely, anxious and uncertain of what was expected of her, and her future. But Kayla never cried in front of anyone. The Emperor P'Lau greeted his young Royal Academy class of five-year-olds their first evening at dinner in the Palace, congratulated and welcomed each boy and girl, and comforted those who were afraid and cried. His face was painted white and his lips painted bright red. Emperor P'Lau knew them all by name, and handed wonderful gifts and toys to each child in red velvet bags.

After their feast, the Emperor presented each child their own trunk of school and court clothing and shoes, sized to fit them perfectly. They were allowed one live vid call home to speak with their proud parents before bedtime. Her parents were happy for her, and assured Kayla they would see her on school holidays and for her birthdays. She kept her composure during the entire day, but softly cried herself asleep with her pillow in her arms.

Now, she was sixteen years of age, and at the crossroads of her life, walking alone in the desert of Xau. The other two moons of K'Halon Prime were hiding behind the massive planet, and it was a very dark night. A night of decision. C.S. G'Rosk found Kayla, and walked with her towards the barracks. He waited several minutes, and then said, "Your performance has been extraordinary, Kayla. The 'Shi'Lon Ranger, Emissary and Beloved Daughter of Emperor P'Lau,' is a most respected and revered position, and one of great sacrifice," the Commander Superior said almost in a whisper to Kayla. She stopped and looked at the Commander Superior Borgund Ranger. "Both of your late parents were exemplary Rangers, serving Emperor P'Lau."

G'Rosk put his hand on her shoulder, stared into her eyes, and said,

"You must realize the commitment ahead of you is very great. As Beloved Daughter of Emperor P'Lau, you must obey as well as enforce his will. Many choices throughout your life will no longer be yours to decide, Kayla, once you choose the Ranger path. As his Emissary, you will represent the Emperor in any situation. You are to defend the honor and reputation of Emperor P'Lau. A Shi'Lon Ranger is granted license to kill anyone, or show the mercy of the Emperor. A very great power and responsibility, indeed." Kayla intently listened to his every word.

He softened his tone, and continued, "As I mentioned previously, the personal sacrifices a Ranger makes are significant. The bond of marriage is not available to any Ranger. Your allegiance is to Emperor P'Lau. But the Emperor is not heartless. You can have a life partner, and be permitted to bear a child; but that child belongs to the Emperor, and must be given to him at age five, as were you and your brother Olm. Upon graduation of Phase 3, you must kneel and swear a blood oath to Emperor P'Lau for your service, your will, and your life. Do you accept?"

She knew it would be the greatest opportunity and challenge of her life. The teenage warrior embraced her destiny in the cold, very dark night on Xau. Trainee Kayla stood tall and straight, and answered, "I will serve the Great and Benevolent Emperor P'Lau, with my will and my life, as he wishes."

C.S. G'Rosk smiled and saluted her. He personally escorted Kayla, Dan'L, and ten other Ranger trainees to their new training facility farther away in the barren desert, for Phase 2 Training the next morning. G'Rosk was her mentor and Commanding Officer for eighteen months of brutal, highly specialized, intense training. The Rangers-in-training would become masters of specialty hand weapons, the new plasma pulser pistols, T'Ly martial arts, and the trademark weapon of the Rangers, the plasma sword. No one survived Phase 2 Training without a few plasma burns permanently scarring their hide, but they were badges of honor for them. Kayla became good friends with a few of the men there, especially Dan'L and Sham'S, and earned their respect by her hard work and fighting skills.

III

"The two primary weapons of a Ranger are your mind and your body. This year you will learn to master the secondary weapons a Ranger will carry, the weapons of our Imperial Army, and T'Ly martial arts, the highest of the martial arts disciplines. There will be no military history classes this year. But there will be advanced survival training, advanced mathematics, astrophysics, computer programming, and physical training designed by the greatest sadists of the Empire," the new instructor declared loudly to the twelve Phase 2 Trainees in front of him. "You have one last chance to decline Phase 2 Training with honor, and leave. You have five minutes to get on the shuttle." He turned and stepped over to the door of the waiting shuttle, closely watching his timepiece.

After five really long minutes of waiting, the twelve trainees were told to pick up their bags and find their bunks. The camaraderie was high, and so were the expectations of the trainees. Three days later, a few were wondering why they did not get on the shuttle and go home when they had the chance do to so honorably. Now, to walk away meant disgrace for their families, and "FAILED" being stamped in red on their service records. They had to succeed now.

The third moon of big K'Halon Prime, Xau was primarily a large desert moon. It had its own atmosphere and large ice caps at its poles. The southern hemisphere of the moon featured an oasis of fresh water surrounding a large mountain where a splendid "Temple of the Creator" was built. The Temple Complex, as it was known, was beautiful. The trainees ran through the desert for two hours and saw the first shimmering images of the Temple Complex, and it appeared as a mirage; a vision of the Afterlife itself. But they were not allowed to take the long, winding path into the Temple of the Creator until after their Phase 3 Training. Pilgrims from K'Halon Prime journeyed to the Temple to pray and be purified, and sometimes, seeking healing. It would have been sacrilegious if the curious trainees interfered with their pilgrimage.

Because of the diverse climates on Xau, it was perfect for survival training. The trainees suffered through desert survival training near the moon's stifling equator. Frozen sheets of ice and snow provided the environment for winter survival training at the moon's ice caps. There was no natural jungle environment in which to train the twelve hardy trainees; but the holographic computer recreations provided very accurate simulations for them.

Next came the "Erasing of Fear" exercises. Each trainee was placed inside a holographic environment wearing brain scanners strapped around their heads. Seemingly innocent pictures of beautiful landscapes; people of all colors, shapes, and sizes; and hundreds of animals in their natural environments played within the holograph while the trainee watched. But the brain scanners isolated their worst fear. Special tests were designed for them by their instructors to rid the trainees of their fears, by immersion techniques. The tests were administered at all hours of the day and night, to enhance the experience.

Each trainee was placed in a situation to face and defeat their biggest known fear. Dan'L was awakened at 3a.m., and taken blindfolded to the holographic chamber. He had to deal with his fear of confinement when they removed his blindfold, and shut him inside a pitch-black locker, with moveable walls. He initially panicked when the walls began closing in on him. Dan'L was sweating profusely, and began screaming for help. He pounded on the walls for several minutes to be let out. But he gathered his wits about him and braced his legs against the walls, pushing his back and legs against them, until they stopped short of crushing him. With all his strength, he pushed back hard enough to make them stop closing in on him, and reverse. Only then did the instructor let him out.

Kayla finally got over her fear of snakes inside the holographic simulation room, when her instructor suddenly "dropped" her into a viper pit. The drop was a computerized holographic simulation, but the snakes in the pit were real; slithering, cold, and disgusting, and crawling all over her. She screamed for less time than they expected. After a time of freaking out, she braced her arms and legs against the side of the pit, and climbed out by inching upwards, out of the pit. She only got snake-bit twice, but she could feel the poison stiffening her muscles. The instructor gave her an anti-venom injection when Kayla reached the top rim of the pit. She used all her self-control not to pummel his smiling face.

Poor Sham'S had a well-known fear of heights, complicated by high anxiety. He awoke one morning on the edge of a real cliff, high above the desert floor. When Sham'S looked over the cliff, he got dizzy, and felt as if he were falling endlessly. He threw himself on the ground, panting, sweating, and stifling tears. But he was forced to climb down the cliff. The instructors established a fire ring around him, preventing him from walking down the cliff using paths. It took him nearly the entire day, choking in the smoke, and suffering in the blinding hot sunlight without water or food to brave the unassisted climb down, but he did it. Kayla and Dan'L met him at the bottom with cold water, and she stopped him from attacking the laughing instructor. He was grateful to her for stopping his aggressions—the next day.

The primary weapons training for them in Phase 2 was learning to master not only their hand weapons of various knives, spears, and swords, but also the weapons of the Imperial Army Special Forces troops. Hand-to-hand combat skills were developed day-in, day-out, by their own instructors, and instructors from the Army.

"A Ranger must be ready to fight at a split-second's notice, with any weapon, in any situation. Anything physical can be utilized as a weapon," the Army instructor said, drinking tea from a porcelain cup and saucer. Two trainees were chosen to attack him, and the Army man defended himself with the teacup and saucer, inflicting three flesh wounds on the trainees before Su'Sen stopped the demonstration. He held up an expense card, and bragged, "I used my plastic Imperial Expense Card when I was jumped in a club once, and lacerated the attacker's neck. Anything in your hands must be viewed as a potential weapon."

By the end of their Phase 2 Training, each trainee had completed T'Ly martial arts training with ninth-degree ranking, and all their weapons training. They all knew their natural specialty now, and concentrated on those areas which needed perfecting. Each trainee was now capable of defending or attacking with either hand, with any weapon, or bare-handed. Everyone passed their final exams in advanced math, astrophysics, and computer programming. Their graduation was celebrated with only a dinner, and orders to pack up and move to another location on Xau. After the graduation dinner, C.S. G'Rosk announced to the class, "Congratulations on passing Phase 2 Training. The easy part of your Ranger Training is completed. Now the hard training begins," and a few of the trainees groaned. Kayla and Dan'L looked at each other, wondering what the Ranger Training instructors could possibly come up with to make the last year of Phase 2 Training be called "easy." They would soon find out.

Phase 3 Training for Kayla and L'Mun, the only other female, involved daily lessons in Contract Law, contract bargaining, mediation, arbitration and negotiations; etiquette; court and military protocol; and body language interpretation. The males learned the tools and tricks of deadly, personal assassination, and how to kill and escape without a trace. But all trainees performed their specialized physical training together. They trained on their own time in smaller pairs, preparing for their final tests. Failure was not an honorable option, after all. They had come this far. They had to pass.

Their bodies were now hard, with good definition of their muscles. Kayla looked at her backside in the full-length mirror, and was amazed at the muscles in her back. She now had a warrior's body. Her friend L'Mun held up her long blond hair and looked at her own back, and cried, "I'll never get a date now! He'll be afraid of me!" She laughed with Kayla, comparing their hard bodies.

There were several weapons practice ranges for the trainees: long-range target practice for laser rifles; medium range target practice areas for laser pistols, pulser spears, and the new pulser pistols; and the body armor range. The ten males and the two female trainees used the long and medium ranges for target practice together. But the body armor differed enough for them to separately practice in the body armor range, once their Phase 3 Training began.

Shi'Lon dark red breastplates held concealed stun gas pellets, tiny smoke bomb pellets, and various knives hidden inside the edges, as did the Borgund breastplates. But also concealed within the beautiful pattern of the Shi'Lon breastplates were small darts capable of stunning or killing the intended target; more subtle weapons for the Emperor's Beloved Daughters and Emissaries. Merely touching the correct spot with the right amount of pressure quickly shot a dart. Longer darts capable of farther range were concealed in their arm bands.

The practice breastplates did not contain poison darts, but their real breastplates would. Already achieving "Master Marksman" with the laser rifle, pulser spear, and both pistol types, Kayla concentrated on her darts. She spent many extra hours firing the small and long darts, learning how to use her body position to target the darts properly. She trained frequently with L'Mun, and they challenged each other to shoot their darts perfectly.

Their final armor test consisted of white table tennis-size balls fired in a scatter pattern; one ball for each tiny breastplate dart. She had to pierce the white ball in mid-air before it dropped to the ground. Then, human-shaped targets popped up from all angles, one target for every two long darts. L'Mun tested first. She passed her final exam, but had difficulty with the long darts in her arm bands.

Commander Superior G'Rosk arrived to observe Kayla's "Personal Weapons Final Test" in the protected booth with the instructor. "Did you tell your trainee Kayla she only needs to hit 75% of her dart targets to pass, Commander Superior?" The instructor asked. G'Rosk slowly shook his head. The instructor chuckled, and then hit the yellow "Ready" light.

Standing calmly with her hands at her sides as ordered, Kayla saw the yellow light come on. In three seconds, the green light flashed, and the little white balls were fired in a scatter pattern inside the range. Her fingers touched the many darts on the breastplate, firing the small darts at the little white balls. She turned, twisted, and shifted her torso in quick movements to target her darts, and successfully shot every ball.

Then, the large human-shaped targets began to pop out from various places: behind partial walls, up from the floor, and from the ceiling. Kayla held both arms out straight, and fired the longer darts with sharp movements of her wrists. Each human-shaped target received one dart in the heart, and one in the center of its neck. The entire test took one minute.

"Good job, Trainee Kayla. We'll have your final score in a few minutes," the instructor announced. He walked through the armor range with his scanner, looked at the read-out, and scanned the white balls and body targets again. He returned to the booth, and showed C.S. G'Rosk her results. The instructor tossed his scanner on the table and shook his head, laughing with G'Rosk.

Anxiously waiting for her final weapons test results, Kayla looked at the white balls and targets, trying to estimate her score. After the instructor returned to his booth, another human-shaped target popped out from behind a partial wall in front of one of her original targets. Instinctively, Kayla drew two knives from her breastplate edge and hurled them at the target, and both knives hit the target's heart.

The instructor looked at G'Rosk with his mouth open in amazement. The last target was a malfunction; not part of the test. He turned on his comm link and announced, "Trainee Kayla Personal Weapons Final Test score: 100%, plus extra credit for killing the mischievous rogue target."

Word quickly circulated through the training camp about Kayla's "more than perfect" score. Her fellow trainees congratulated her, and razzed her without mercy at dinner. Kayla blushed, and took her friends' verbal jabs with class and grace.

"I thought I did well to get 92% on my personal armor test," Dan'L said, amazed at his best friend Kayla's score. The Shi'Lon test was far more difficult than the Borgund. The Borgund breastplates primarily featured small weapons for assassination, like the piano wire garrote, poison injection pens, small tubes of concentrated oxygen to be inserted into the mouth of the Ranger after discharging poison gas pellets, martial arts blades for throwing, poison thumb needles, and so on. Borgund arm bands held concealed, powered assassin's knives, which would spring forward upon jerking their wrist upward.

Kayla remarked, "We still have the final obstacle course test to run tomorrow, and then the smelly sulphur springs swimming test in three days. You and Sham'S will leave the rest of us in your dust!"

"I'm going to try and beat him," Sham'S said, backhanding Dan'L's arm. Dan'L was without equal in his running ability. No one in their class could catch him.

The trainees waited at the starting line for their last obstacle course run.

"Course record is five minutes, forty-two seconds. Try to beat it, you sorry-assed excuses for Rangers," the course instructor yelled, then flipped the switch for the green light.

They ran a quarter kilometer up into the hills; leapt from boulder to boulder along the dry creek bed; climbed a sheer vertical wall of rock out of the canyon; swung on ropes over a wide crevasse; and crawled on their bellies while live laser fire blasted above their heads. The trainees climbed tall poles, and carefully walked the wire strung between the poles above boiling mineral pools. The hand-pulley zip line down the mountain was actually fun. The final leg was the quarter-kilometer sprint to cross the finish line.

The average time for the trainees was six minutes, twenty-seven seconds. Dan'L beat the course record of five minutes forty-two seconds by one second, with Sham'S right on his heels. Kayla crossed the line next, with six minutes one second, followed by L'Mun and three other trainees. They all passed the course.

One day of rest before the sulphur springs swimming finals. Each trainee received a special "Onesie" swimsuit, specially designed to protect their bodies' sensitive areas from the hot springs. They also were issued insulated goggles to protect their eyes, ear protective caps, and fitted, sealed face shields. Still, it would be a test of speed, and burning hot spring water on their skin.

"I don't even like real hot showers," Sham'S confessed to Kayla. She could tell he was nervous about this final test, and tried to calm him. No one liked the idea of jumping into the hot sulphur springs, six interconnected pools of bubbling water and stinking gases. But it was mandatory to complete.

Kayla suggested, "Look at the pools, Sham'S. No more than six swim strokes each. One pool on your belly, one on your back, and so on. Why, you're so tall, you'll probably cross each pool in four strokes. Just chant, 'Belly, 1, 2, 3, 4; Back, 1, 2, 3, 4;' and repeat. You'll be through in less than a minute!"

Dan'L listened to her, and added, "I'm looking at those pools as the last enemies to vanquish. Then I'll be a Ranger!" They both bolstered their friend's determination to succeed, as the three of them had done with each other the last year.

One by one, the trainees jumped into the hot sulphur springs pools, and swam as fast as they could. Everyone had burns on their skin, especially those who did not alternate belly and back strokes, as recommended. When they reached the last pool, two instructors quickly pulled them out, and they were blasted by chilly water from a large hose to cool off their skin. Then, they were wrapped in large white towels, and given intra-nasal oxygen to clear their lungs. But they all passed. The remainder of the evening was spent spreading healing ointments on their burns, some vomiting from the burns, and most laughing about their experiences. But their class set a record: every trainee passed the entire year and a half of Phase 2 and Phase 3 Training without anyone "washing out."

The last two weeks of Phase 3 Training consisted of the trainees learning and practicing Royal Court Protocols, and learning to master their plasma swords. The powerful plasma swords were hand-held energy weapons, designed to be the trademark weapon of the Rangers. The plasma sword was sheathed in the Ranger's backplate, where the energy weapon was kept powered-up. The backplate utilized the Ranger's own body movements to keep the sword fully charged and ready for use at all times. The backplate and breastplate were mounted on special charging stands every night for maximum potency.

During the last day of plasma sword practice, Comm. Bok pulled Dan'L out of training and gave him grave news: Dan'L's Father, Master Commander K'Ser, was killed in action against attacking Rebels on abandoned Space Base 5, yesterday.

"Does my Mother know this? How is she, Commander Bok? I must go to her now," Dan'L said with urgency in his voice.

Comm. Bok replied, "Yes, Master Commander Javette has been informed of this tragedy. Commander Superior G'Rosk has authorized your immediate transport home to K'Halon Prime. I'll shuttle you to the transport station in one hour. Congratulations on graduating Phase 3 Training, Dan'L, Son of Master Commander K'Ser," Bok said, and saluted. Dan'L returned Bok's salute and ran to the dormitory to pack out.

The trainees were shocked and saddened when they were told why Dan'L had to leave training camp a few days early. The graduation ceremony for them was usually a formal affair; but this year, it was more solemn than normal. Death was always in the cards for any Ranger, and the young graduates were reminded of this fact acutely. The graduation ceremony for the Rangers-in-training was held one week after the funeral celebration for Master Commander K'Ser, at the Royal Palace on K'Halon Prime.

IV

M'Wati, Secret Rebel Base

Within a week of his escape and rescue by the Rebels, Major S'Loc was placed in charge of two search and rescue squads. Steph'N was relieved. When the men took him to the old destroyer's engineering deck, he praised the officers and crewmen profusely, saying, "How did you manage to bring this antique piece of crap back from mothballs? I'd have been hopelessly lost with these engines. I've never seen anything like them before," he remarked. The current Chief Engineer – a hard man over 70 years of age – was more than happy to get the cocky, former Space Cadre Major S'Loc off his engineering deck. The destroyer was of his era, and he knew every part of it well.

Emperor P'Lau ordered Steph'N to gain the confidence of the Rebel Leader Duma Wat while in deep immersion. For over a year, Major S'Loc was kept on the ground, searching and rescuing the Rebels who survived battles with the Space Cadre, or the Imperial Army. His Ranger survival training served him very well. He became an excellent tracker and map reader. The Rebels had their identification capsules removed the first day they joined, and wore no expensive comm links, ear buds, or other communications devices. Unless they were on high-profile missions, none of the modern comm links were used. It made the survivors very difficult to locate.

One of his primary worries was being ordered by the Rebels to attack Space Cadre or Imperial Army personnel. So far, Steph'N was not involved in any battles or outright conflict situations. The Rebel senior officers were all former Space Cadre, Army, Air Corps, or Navy senior officers. They made the new Rebel volunteers prove themselves, and did not assume the new volunteers were trustworthy enough to place in command, or in battle, and be well-armed.

Steph'N listened night after night to the crystal recordings of the files for Major S'Loc, trying his best to assume the man's life beyond suspicion. The mission—and his life—depended on it. Because the original S'Loc was such an unholy terror as a team leader, no one who worked for him socialized with him. The few Rebels who'd met Major S'Loc before he turned traitor tried to avoid any association with the brutal taskmaster.

He saw the Rebel numbers growing. The High Command of the Space Cadre was nervous about losing an increasing number of officers and crewmen to the Rebellion—and rightly so. But Steph'N recognized the Rebellion's primary weakness was their lack of superior vessels and weaponry. On an outer planet or inhabited moon, the Rebels could invade and quickly establish a base, maybe even fortify a stronghold. But their equipment was sub-standard. Their laser rifles were at least ten years old or more. Land craft lined up for maintenance was easy to steal during lightning-fast raids by the Rebels against an Imperial Army base of sleepy security teams. But they had few replacement parts with which to work, and effect repairs.

Duma Wat had tried and failed repeatedly to commandeer any modern Space Cadre attack vessels in service today. He had a rag-tag fleet of mercenaries, pirates, and former Space Cadre Rebels flying the poorest and oldest vessels still in service. His men were excellent at refurbishing old, "Mothballed" vessels waiting salvage. They stole the vessels, or bought them from salvage dealers at dirt-cheap prices. Their technicians brought them back to operational efficiency, and retrofitted them for newer weaponry. Most of their technicians were retired Space Cadre or Imperial Army men, collecting retirement pension checks from the Empire, and being paid by Duma Wat.

Thank the Creator Duma Wat never got his hands on a new Space Cadre destroyer. The Rebel Leader had railed against Emperor P'Lau for twenty years, and promised his followers independent, democratic, separate planetary rule. But Steph'N was not one of Duma Wat's brainwashed Rebels; he knew the Rebel Leader wanted Emperor P'Lau's throne for himself, democracy be damned. In their camps at night, the Rebels talked about Duma Wat as if he were a demi god. He was called the "Savior of the People." Steph'N nearly choked the first time he heard their tales of Duma Wat's victories in battle, and recordings of his speeches. The legend was greater than the man.

After tracking a retreating Rebel attack force into the hidden and abandoned mining tunnels on M'Wati, Major S'Loc and his Rebel search and rescue squads rescued one hundred nineteen Rebel troops from starvation and infected wounds. The Rebel troops were over-run by M'Wati Imperial Army commandos and their attack vehicles, and retreated into abandoned mines for protection.

The old, unfortified tunnels at first looked like the perfect place to hide and await Rebel reinforcements. But the air inside the old tunnel was fouled with poisonous gases. The unused tunnel dead-ended into heaps of rubble and discarded ancient mining equipment, blocking further advancement through the tunnels. When the Rebels lit fires to warm themselves and cook what little food they had, the gases in the tunnels exploded, collapsing the only exit. They had many injured men, and were trapped.

Major S'Loc and his men tracked the retreating Rebels to the old abandoned mines, but they had no access to the tunnel where they were trapped after the gas explosions. The Major studied mining and geological maps from half a century ago, when those mines were working. Major S'Loc discovered the old air shafts for the mines. His men used robotic borers to reopen the air shafts, bringing fresh air to the trapped Rebels. Then he lowered comm links through them, and used their signal to pinpoint their exact location.

After three days of tunneling a perpendicular cross shaft from a parallel tunnel, S'Loc's men broke through and rescued the trapped Rebels. Major S'Loc was brought before Duma Wat, at last. He was given a bronze star for rescuing the one hundred-nineteen Rebel troops in the mines. From that day forward, Major S'Loc was assigned to Colonel Vas, the second-in-command Rebel leader. It was during the second year of Steph'N's deep immersion mission.

Major S'Loc was now a hero of the Rebellion. Colonel Vas held a feast on the M'Wati Rebel base in his honor, attended by over two hundred Rebels. Major S'Loc maintained his hard face throughout the feast, and drank only water. After he entered his quarters, a knock on his door was heard. Steph'N opened his unlocked door, and was greeted by two young teenage boys, "presents" from Colonel Vas. This was the moment he had dreaded from Day One of his mission. If he did not have sex with them, would Colonel Vas and Duma Wat suspect Steph'N's duplicity as the traitor Major S'Loc?

He let the boys inside. As he closed the door, he said, "A man of my distinct and particular needs chooses carefully those with whom he finds his pleasure." He invited them to sit on the sofa. The dark-haired, younger boy produced a bag of white pleasure-powder, and offered it to S'Loc. Thank the Creator; it was his "out."

"Our leader, Lord Duma Wat, does not permit any drugs to be used by his men, and neither do I. You both need to leave me, right now," he said forcefully. He stood and held his door open for them to leave. Both boys left and he closed and locked his door. Steph'N was grateful he avoided a potentially revealing situation. He got into bed alone, and rolled over. How much longer would this mission last? Steph'N wanted the mission over. But he wanted to gain the trust of Duma Wat even more. If he could just get closer to the Rebel Leader, perhaps he could discover his plans and tell the

Emperor. If he could save just one Space Cadre or Imperial Army trooper's life—all this would be worth his sacrifice.

What an incessantly boring flight. Steph'N rose from his seat, walked up and down the narrow aisle, and used all his self-control to not pull the pilot out of his chair, and take over the flight. The Rebel pilot flew the old fighter like an illegal taxi shuttle driver in Capital City, too slowly. Steph'N could fly this bird in his sleep. But his cover, Major S'Loc, was not a pilot.

Steph'N missed piloting so much. He flew the Emperor's newest "ES" class warbirds; well, he used to fly them. They were small, highly maneuverable, and flew twice as fast as standard fighters. And, some ES warbirds even had the new stealth mechanisms installed, rendering them virtually invisible to scanners.

Would he ever get to go home? The other Rebel officers on this flight chalked up his frustrations to Major S'Loc's being such a control freak, and an obsessed taskmaster. He walked to the aft section and did two hundred push-ups. Month after month of being the homosexual Major. Bloody hell. It was really wearing on him.

They finally landed on Space Base 5; what was left of it, anyway. Major S'Loc and the officers stepped into their space suits and prepared to disembark. Steph'N realized he was in a thirty-year-old space suit, about to step onto a decommissioned space base deemed "Uninhabitable" by the Space Cadre forty years ago. Nearly a third of the base was missing, having been decimated by the humongous, errant "bomber" asteroid way back then. The direct hit on SB5's engineering and central power core forced emergency evacuations of all personnel who survived the attack from Mother Nature's bomber asteroid. The space base lost its ability to maintain orbit. It now floated in the White Belt with all the other "Space Junk," broken planetary matter, and asteroids. The former Empress Tan reasoned the White Belt was too dangerous to send in Space Cadre salvage ships, forty years ago.

Duma Wat ordered SB5 restored to support human life. No one could repair SB5 to the point of controlled orbit outside the White Belt; no one without the resources of the Empire, that is. But Emperor P'Lau chose to leave the abandoned space base to natural forces, as did his predecessor, not willing to lose one more life trying to save the old base. Duma Wat believed SB5 could be partially restored, and used as a potent Rebel base.

Major S'Loc was now a trusted senior member of the Rebellion. He was assigned the task of restoring SB5 to minimum functionality. They assigned sixteen engineers and tech specialists to him for their task, all experienced former Space Cadre officers. Steph'N was a highly trained Borgund Ranger, and a certified pilot. But the former Space Cadre officer he was impersonating was a Chief Engineer, and a university graduate in Astro-

Engineering. Steph'N knew he was outside his knowledge and experience level, and was not competent in a Chief Engineering capacity.

This deep immersion assignment became far more challenging than he ever considered. But he was determined to succeed for the Emperor. Being schooled and experienced with space fighters and their highly sophisticated computer control systems helped him a great deal. But knowing massive ship engines, and now, Space Base engines, life support systems, and operations systems, was another matter entirely. He studied the technical specifications manuals, engine computer control schematics, and everything he could find in the ship's library on space vessel engines and their control systems. He quickly became familiar with the terminology. Hopefully, his assigned engineers and technical specialists would overlook any perceived flaws in his knowledge as unfamiliarity with old, arcane engines and previous-generation technology. Steph'N spoke very cautiously to his men and made copious notes of their conversations, to reference at night when he studied privately.

He implemented duty rosters for the officers, and asked for his men's recommendations to proceed with repairs to the space base. Steph'N decided to implement those repairs for life support first, then engineering, and bridge control a distant third objective. It made sense to him. His men worked diligently to fulfill the Major's priorities. S'Loc drove them hard; Steph'N had to keep up the reputation of the Major and be a tough taskmaster.

The Rebels sealed off the destroyed sections of the space base and insulated the adjoining areas completely. Once life support was achieved in the living quarters and engineering decks, the remainder of their tasks flew towards completion. Steph'N read the status reports for the third time: half of the space base was completely sealed off, and was now fully functional. When the cargo ships delivered the replacement parts in a few weeks, the weapons systems would also be operative. Why did the Empire turn its back on the base so soon? Duma Wat did not.

With SB5 restored, Duma Wat reinforced its personnel with troops and attack fighters. The landing sites and docking bays filled with his old fighters, pirate and mercenary ships, and his rusty old cargo ships docked alongside the restored base. Talking in code language, Steph'N let the Emperor know the status of the base as the weeks passed, calling the private comm link every week and reporting, as ordered.

But his contact, "Nephew D'Wayn," never transmitted any coded orders. All the comm links he sent were strategic on Steph'N's part, and their responses mundane. Were they afraid the communications were monitored? Of course, they were monitored.

He looked at his face in the mirror after inserting his fresh brown-eyed contacts. *I am Steph'N, a Borgund Ranger,* he said internally. No way would he say it out loud. His quarters were most likely bugged. Everyone else's was; he and his men installed the recording microphone chips. It was so long since he'd seen his family, or his real face in the mirror. His former life seemed so far away, getting further out of reach every day.

Colonel Vas was arriving on SB5 today for an inspection. What if Vas brought him another "Present?" More boy-toys? He paced in his room most of the night, and worried about being discovered as a spy. Steph'N was not a very religious man, but he did believe in the Creator; so, he prayed, asking for Divine help in his mission. He left his quarters and walked quickly down the corridor. He took a brown food paste ration tube out of his pocket and sucked it down. What did real food taste like? He'd been on this base for months now, all of them living on food paste tubes and hard algae chip rations. They needed fresh food. Over twenty-three months of deep immersion. His own family wouldn't even recognize him now, let alone Va'Pal. His face was now thin, drawn, and gaunt, and his uniforms loose.

After the formalities of the inspection and base tours were complete, Colonel Vas was shown his quarters, and wanted to rest for the night. Good. Vas brought a few cases of canned food for the men on SB5. Slimy canned beef stew beat out brown food paste rations, hands down. He tried hard not to think about fresh food, and yelled at any man who talked about it.

Steph'N checked his schedule for the remainder of the evening. One more machine component fine tuning, and then he was off for a few hours. After being on this base for months, he knew the technical specs and schematics of the engines well. He could tear them apart by himself now, and rebuild any engine component unaided. He was fully immersed as the Chief Engineer of SB5, and did not have to fake it. His men no longer looked at him sideways in their meetings, wondering if he was qualified to run the department. It was his to command.

Major S'Loc walked back to his quarters alone, not joining in the celebration of the base passing inspection, and being re-commissioned by the Rebellion. Let them party. He went inside his quarters and slammed the door shut, and locked it. He put his hands behind his neck and rubbed his tight muscles. No wonder some men never came back from deep immersion. It was easier. All he had to do was to let go of his inner self, his true identity. He could forget about Commander Steph'N; his family; his Warrior Class; his hopes and dreams. It would be so much easier now. It was very difficult to recall his old life, his family and friends; when he did, it was painful. He had trouble remembering their faces sometimes. Were they even curious what happened to him, after nearly two years? Did anyone care about him? He felt so lost, so alone.

It would be so easy to let go and continue to be Major S'Loc. He was a hero of the Rebellion now. The Rebels treated him with respect. He was now the SB5 Base Commanding Officer, and Colonel Vas promised him another promotion and pay raise tonight. Within the next few months, Vas would promote him to Captain. The voice of "D'Wayn" on the secret comm link weekly transmissions only said "Yes," and "No," never offering recommendations, a few instructions, some encouragement, or any suggestions to him.

Steph'N poured himself a Brandywine drink from the bottle Colonel Vas gave him, and belted it down. Strong and sweet, it burned his throat a bit, but it tasted good. He could, perhaps, let Major S'Loc have a change of heart and find a woman, in a few months. Stranger things have happened. There were several nurses and female officers serving on Duma Wat's destroyer, and many more working on the M'Wati Rebel Base. Duma Wat treated the women well, and paid them equally to the men of equal rank. The women liked the "bad boys" of the rebellion.

All he had to do was let go, and forget about his old life. What was left of it, anyway? Nothing left of his Ranger life; nothing left of his family memories; and nothing left for Va'Pal to feel for him. He never felt so empty and forlorn. It would be so easy now; just forget, and let go. Be the Rebel Major S'Loc, the newest Hero of the Rebellion. Far easier than to force himself to hold onto his old self, hoping he had someone still caring about him. Far easier… just let go.

No wonder Emperor P'Lau painted his face white. It helped hide his true feelings. The history books said the Emperors and Empresses painted their faces white for hundreds of years, and their lips red. Now Steph'N understood why. The slightest facial twitch, or movement of his eyes could give him away. He looked at himself in the mirror, at his tough face, furrowed brows, and scowling mouth: Major S'Loc. His mask. He didn't remember how he used to look with his long hair, wearing his Ranger black cloak, with the special smile only Va'Pal could give him. Can't remember what they looked like. Mother. Sister. Va'Pal…

Steph'N drifted away into the shadows of his mind. The faces of his Mother and Sister were blurred and distant. They were so far away. Did they think he was dead? He felt dead to them. Another Brandywine was downed. He felt emotionally hollow. Alone. A vagabond in empty space, surrounded by traitors. Abandoned by the Emperor. He floated in the netherworld. All seemed without purpose, devoid of hope.

Then Steph'N snapped out of the dark abyss of his mind, and slapped his own face as hard as he could several times. He began his T'Ly martial arts workout, punching and kicking as hard as he could, slapping his face, and hitting his own abdomen, to come back. Come back, Steph'N. Believe again. Keep on the path, Borgund Ranger.

V

Major S'Loc inserted his 20-credit gold coin into the live vid comm booth, and keyed in the secret call numbers. In thirty seconds, he was connected to his "Nephew D'Wayn," on Home World. "Hello, Uncle S'Loc. Is all well with you?" D'Wayn asked, in an effeminate voice.

"Quite well, nephew. I am still one step ahead of Imperial oppressors targeting my hide. How goes the business without me?" He asked, his usual opening. This is where the conversation usually got shortened, and became insignificant.

D'Wayn blinked twice quickly, and then replied, "The customer traffic is steady, but not increasing in its growth rate. I'm afraid I do not have your social and marketing skills, Uncle S'Loc." This was a new path for his weekly calls. D'Wayn shook his head twice.

Major S'Loc rubbed his chin, and said, "Just keep it going. Our family needs more income. Treat the best customers the best, but give good service to everyone, D'Wayn."

D'Wayn smoothed his hair, pursed his lips and said coyly, "I give excellent service, as you know very well. If you were here…"

"If I was there, I wouldn't have to spend so much on a bloody intra-system vid call," S'Loc interrupted. "I have important work here to do, and cannot be with you. Just do the best you can, until victory reunites us. S'Loc, out." The Major impatiently hit the "End" button, pulled out the recording chip, left the private booth, and walked to his room.

Major S'Loc slammed his door loudly, on purpose. He wanted whoever was observing and listening to his call to think he was pissed off at his "Nephew D'Wayn." Everyone would stay out of his way for a couple of days when word got around the Major was ticked off at his Home World boy-toy.

Steph'N opened a drawer in his desk and took out the bottle of

Brandywine, and poured a stiff drink. He unbuttoned his shirt, kicked off his over-worn boots, and plopped down in his chair. He put his personal feelings aside and concentrated on his call to "D'Wayn." He slipped the recorded chip in his ear buds, listened to the call again, and carefully decoded the message.

The comm link number belonged to C.S. Vu'Duc. "D'Wayn" was a young Shi'Lon Ranger assigned to Vu'Duc, and given a script to read for each call, complete with facial and vocal "tells" for him to decipher. She cut her hair short, and wore a fake moustache for their calls. He chuckled; she had all the Rebel leaders and observers convinced she was the young homosexual man the Rebel Major had to leave behind on Home World. She perfectly used an exaggerated effeminate voice.

The hidden messages in his call today were the first in many moons. "The customer traffic is steady," meant Space Cadre ships were now in position around SB5, but still out of scanner range. "Not increasing its growth rate" meant no one else was sent to help him. He had another "asset" in place, a Rebel pilot, but they rarely interacted in their daily routines.

Nephew D'Wayn's comment, "I do not have your social and marketing skills," meant the Empire had not gained any further information on Duma Wat's financial activities; and D'Wayn shook his head twice to ask Steph'N if he had any information on the financial state of the Rebels. When Steph'N rubbed his chin and said, "Keep it going. The family needs more income," he told C.S. Vu'Duc the Rebels had just received another huge donation from an unknown sympathizer for the Rebellion. The big donations kept pouring in for Duma Wat, and no one loyal to the Emperor knew who was making the donations, or exactly how the funds got into his coffers.

Steph'N finished his drink, showered, and got ready for bed, excited there was factual information for the first time in many months. The power, life support, water purifiers, and oxygen suppliers on board abandoned SB5 had all been restored to full functionality within the last year, thanks to him. He was the Space Base 5 Commanding Officer, in full command there now, and given credit for restoring the old abandoned base. The next phase of SB5 refurbishment was to add more docking stations. It was the newest Rebel stronghold in the Central Core. When the base's weapons systems were fully functional, it could pose a real threat to the Space Cadre ships, and the Empire. Hopefully, they listened closely to his coded messages over the last few months, and were aware of the danger SB5 now posed.

SB5 was established more than one hundred years ago to provide protection for Ban'Ti and M'Wati. Little Ban'Ti was just on the inner side of the White Belt, and M'Wati just outside the White Belt. They were inhabited, productive, and important planets to the Empire. But the Empire left SB5 adrift after its damage from the bomber asteroid for more than forty years. Ban'Ti and M'Wati were protected only by their Imperial Army troops assigned to the planets now, and regularly-scheduled Space Cadre ships patrolling their sector. Easy pickings for Duma Wat. Now that SB5 was restored, he could potentially exert control over the two smaller planets of the solar system. When SB5 came into closer position to the Central Core planets, Duma Wat could eventually use SB5 as the point of origination to attack Home World and K'Halon Prime.

Steph'N had secretly shorted out circuitry and the power crystals of the base's weapons systems for months, and his deception had not been detected. Even the weapons control programming was corrupted as much as he could manage. But Steph'N was a Ranger, and not a computer programmer. They would correct his subterfuge soon. He realized every man had his own set of skills, and capacity for knowledge. But every man also had his limitations of competency. There was only so much time to devote to learning. He could only do so much.

Just after 3a.m., the "Intruder Alert" sounded. Steph'N jumped up and quickly dressed. As he was running down the corridor to the bridge, SB5 was hit, and the entire base rocked from the impact. Alarms and sirens shrieked loudly all over the base. A large explosion was felt.

"Status reports now!" Major S'Loc demanded, taking the Captain's chair on the bridge. The reports came in quickly, and were not good news. An unknown ship had crash-landed on SB5. It had attempted to land on the main deck, but crashed into the engineering section. With so much of SB5 cut off from its original design, there was precious little room for a crash landing. The base's main power generators were failing. Major S'Loc sounded the "Abandon Ship" alarm, and activated the emergency beacon. He ordered all personnel to evacuate SB5.

"A ship of unknown origin has crash-landed on SB5, taking out engineering. Power generators are down. Life support systems are failing, and temperature is dropping. Water and air purifiers down to 30% and falling. We have to completely shut down and abandon this station now," Major S'Loc reported to Colonel Vas. "Respectfully request you abandon the station immediately, sir. The ship that crashed into SB5 is not Space Cadre, or any recorded design. No life forms registering, but there are large androids aboard, according to our scanner reports. We have to assume we are under attack, sir, armed with only a few laser rifles."

Vas replied, "Then evacuate the station. Try to seal off a control area and lock it down. If possible, remain with a squad and investigate the aliens and their ship, Major S'Loc. We must gather as much intel as possible before the Space Cadre ships get here. My ship is leaving in two minutes. A rescue ship will be sent for you. Vas out."

Steph'N's deep immersion mission just changed radically. He used the chaos of the Rebels abandoning the base to cover up a call directly to "Father," the Emperor P'Lau. Steph'N quickly relayed the emergency information, and his new orders from the #2 Rebel Leader, Colonel Vas, to stay and reconnoiter intel on the alien ship and its androids.

Father replied, "Reconnoiter and report. Stay alive, and succeed."

The Major directed traffic leaving SB5, and asked for volunteers to remain with him. After getting everyone else off the wounded base, Major S'Loc and fifteen volunteers donned space suits, and proceeded to seal off all entryways to the auxiliary bridge and engineering. He shut down all systems except auxiliary life support, and the men made their way to the auxiliary bridge quickly.

In storage was one week's supply of oxygen, onboard water for four days, and precious little ammo for their laser rifles. They carried all the bread, brown ration pouches, crackers, and bottled drinks the galley had available to the auxiliary bridge. Major S'Loc broke out emergency water, food pouch rations, and first-aid kits. He ordered his men to locate every available space suit, and bring them to the auxiliary bridge, with extra blankets. They were set to observe, reconnoiter intel, and survive.

It was only a few hours before an ES-class warbird landed on the main hangar deck. The volunteers reminded Major S'Loc about their big cache of laser rifles and ammo stored in the cargo bins. From the auxiliary bridge, Major S'Loc and his men watched the Borgund Ranger step out of the warbird and scan the entire deck. He found the cache of weapons and scanned the cargo hold. Soon, the Space Cadre would know of their stored weapons. The Ranger, in his black spacesuit and jetpack, slowly and cautiously flew into the section where the alien ship rested. Several lights were either lit or blinking within the alien craft, but no signs of life were apparent.

"Are the vid cams still working? We've got to record the Ranger's every word and movement," Major S'Loc said softly, as if the Ranger could hear him. But the cameras worked intermittently, and did not provide the full scope of the damaged alien ship. The Ranger returned, and moved his warbird closer to the damaged alien ship. He attempted to communicate by calling out to anyone who might be aboard the alien vessel. No response came forth. Then, the head of an android raised up and looked out of their ship windows at the Ranger. The Ranger held up his arms to show he was unarmed, and the hatch of the alien ship opened. The Ranger cautiously walked up the hatch, into the alien ship.

For several days, Major S'Loc and his men monitored the Ranger's attempts to communicate with the alien androids, speaking through the computer translator; holding up hand-made signs with words and letters: math formulas; sign language with his hands; cuneiform lettering; ancient script; and pictographs. Apparently, nothing worked. The Ranger bowed to the androids, and left their ship. He walked aboard his ES warbird.

S'Loc was called to listen to the sound bite half an hour later, when the Rebel vid cams detected music and drumming coming from the ES warbird. The androids entered the ES, and various forms of music and drumming were picked up by their vid cams for hours on end. They could not see exactly what was taking place on the ES warbird, but the androids were eventually seen leaving the ship. In a few minutes, the Ranger approached the alien ship again, and the androids came out, held up red memory crystals, and then handed them to the Ranger. The Rebel vid cams recorded the androids showing the Ranger how to use the red crystals with some kind of encoder, and talked with the Ranger for a long time, now speaking in his language.

Then one android handed a longer, green crystal to the Ranger, saying, "Caution. Very powerful. Careful." Major S'Loc watched the exchange in total fascination, as did his crew. The alien androids were exchanging technology with the Ranger. S'Loc tried secretly to erase or corrupt the recordings, knowing his men were actively transmitting them to Duma Wat, but could not do so without being detected. The Ranger returned to his ES and flew off, presumably to the nearest Space Cadre ship.

Having watched the recordings showing the alien androids give red and green crystals to the Borgund Ranger, Duma Wat ordered a Rebel squadron of four fighters to SB5. His intention was to persuade the aliens to share their crystals with his Rebels. But the Ranger returned before the Rebel squadron arrived, landed his ES warbird near the alien ship again, and continued his communications with the androids. When the Rebel squadron identified the ES warbird, they attacked, firing at both ships on the hangar deck, and the alien spacecraft flew off. The Rebel fighters landed their men on the hangar deck, and a fierce fight between them and the Borgund Ranger began.

It was difficult to suppress his smile and feeling of pride as Steph'N watched the seasoned Borgund Ranger expertly kill more than twenty Rebel fighting men. The Ranger had to know he would be killed in a fight against four fully-armed fighters, full of armed Rebels. The Ranger in his black space suit took out as many Rebels as he could in his last stand. The Rebels retreated to their ships after several of their men were killed in action, and flew out of the hangar bay.

Rebel Squadron Leader Petrov ordered the ES to be destroyed, and they fired a plasma disrupter arc cannon shot at the ES warbird. Everything in the hangar deck and adjoining bay was obliterated, and the old base was jolted from the huge explosion. Two of the Rebels who volunteered to wait with Major S'Loc were also killed, hiding too near the cargo bay doorway. The main hangar bay now contained only dust and body shadows.

Petrov ordered his men to land two fighters on the deck they had just blasted to rescue any SB5 survivors. When the fighters landed, Major S'Loc and his men rushed aboard the Rebel fighters, sat on the hard floor, and were flown to the Rebel command destroyer. The rescued men were weak from hunger and thirst, and lack of oxygen. Major S'Loc and his rescued men were treated for malnutrition and dehydration for one week. Then, the Major resumed his duty as Chief Engineer of the Rebel destroyer.

Duma Wat was very angry the Rebel Squadron leader Petrov used a plasma disrupter arc cannon on his recently-restored SB5. One unwise decision too many had been made by the hot-headed Petrov. Duma Wat only ordered the Borgund Ranger killed. He did not order the very costly ES warbird destroyed. The ES was a prize Duma Wat could have used against Imperial ships successfully. But not now.

Months of arduous work and over one million credits had been spent restoring SB5 as a full-service base. Any chance of using SB5 as a potent threat against Home World was now gone. Duma Wat shouted at Petrov and demoted him, and ordered him transported back to K'Halon Prime the same day.

A former Imperial Army Captain, the Rebel Petrov had succeeded only in incurring the wrath of his leader. Petrov was a brutal, domineering leader who trusted no one, not even the "Savior of the People," Duma Wat. Petrov was assigned an untrained group of miscreant traitors and escaped felons, to carry out small incursions against Imperial Army bases and installations on K'Halon Prime, going forward. Saddled by demotion and humiliation, Petrov drank his beloved vodka even more frequently than before. No one respected Petrov now, but they feared him.

Petrov grew to resent his reassignment on K'Halon Prime, making small raids in the long, freezing winter, up to his belt in snow. He loathed Duma Wat for demoting him. But he hated Emperor P'Lau the most, for being such a spineless, soft-hearted Emperor, who could not bring himself to order his half-brother executed.

VI

Starlight pierced the blackness of the moonless night, forming the canopy of twinkling lights above him. Adventure and glory awaited the young man who walked the road towards the celebration in the city. His future and life's calling beckoned him to cross over into the unknown.

Few things demonstrate life's major events as markedly as graduation. This morning Dan'L graduated Phase 3 Training in a private, yet uplifting ceremony, and was now an official Borgund Ranger Novice, a Faithful Son of the Emperor P'Lau. A Ranger was the top level of the Warrior Class he was born into, and it was a significant achievement. He was a tall, dark-haired young man, the good-looking son of a beautiful Mother and a handsome Father. Dan'L felt like the luckiest man on K'Halon Prime.

Next week he would be fitted for his breastplate and backplate armor, coded to his DNA, and full of hidden weapons. He would also receive his plasma sword that fit inside his backplate, its handle also coded to his DNA. The powerful, fiery white plasma sword was the trademark weapon of the Rangers for over 200 years. It could cut through solid steel, and slice human tissue easily. The Rangers were the only ones trusted with the powerful energy weapon.

In his entire life, Dan'L saw his Mother cry three times: when his sister K'Rissa was born; last week, when the ceremony for his Father's death ended, and the guests left; and today, at his Ranger graduation. Dan'L now joined his family as top-tier members of the Warrior Class. His Mother Javette was a Master Commander Shi'Lon Ranger, the "Beloved Daughter and Emissary of Emperor P'Lau." Today would have been perfect if his late Father, Master Commander K'Ser, could have been there.

"The last thing your Father would have wanted is for his Son to let a past event drag you down. We cannot change what happened in the past. We must continue forward; ever forward, Dan'L. I want you to celebrate your achievement with your friends tonight, and enjoy yourself," Javette said. She handed him two gift boxes with a big smile. "For my Ranger son," she said proudly.

Mother gave him a new jacket and boots for his graduation gifts. Both were coded to his DNA, and only Dan'L could wear them without a severe series of electric shocks. *I'll never have to worry about my pockets being picked in this dark green jacket,* Dan'L mused. Inside each front pocket was a 100-credit gold coin. The boots contained power cells inside the soles, enabling him to run even faster than he normally ran. But tonight, he wanted to walk, and savor every minute of his celebration.

Dan'L hopped onto the moving sidewalk on the edge of Centralia and strolled along, heading for the downtown entertainment district. His friends were having a graduation party for him at a local club called "The Rogue Wave." He saw the club marquee flashing from a block away. Music with heavy drum beats and bass poured from the club, adding to his excitement.

The hard cider flowed all night. Dan'L wisely skipped the neon-colored, smoking shots of hard liquor offered to him, not wanting to pay too dearly tomorrow for his party tonight. He danced with several girls and met even more at the bar. Tonight, the world was his. Dan'L had a well-deserved blast. His friends made sure the Emperor's newest Ranger partied his brains out.

When the Rogue Wave closed, everyone said 'Good-night,' and meandered towards home, a happy crowd of good friends. Dan'L walked down the main street for a couple of blocks, and then turned to take the moving sidewalk back home, to the Royal Palace compound.

"Hey, Ranger!" A man shouted. Dan'L turned in response, and received a face full of stun gas sprayed by a stranger at him. He struggled to fight the stranger for a few seconds, then collapsed, unconscious.

The stench of his own vomit greeted Dan'L when he began to regain consciousness. He had thrown up all over his new jacket, and more than once, it looked like. Where was he? His eyes could not yet focus. The place smelled musty and oily, like an old motor. The ropes around his torso and feet kept him from moving his cramped body. How long had he been out? A strange vibration on his back and butt indicated he was on a craft of some kind, probably a shuttle. He felt sick to his stomach, and rolled over.

"Boss, he's waking up. Aw, shit! He's puking again!" A dark bearded man with a deep scar on his cheek said. The scarred man jumped back to avoid the hurling vomit, but got some on his pants and shoes, anyway. He back-handed Dan'L's face and cursed at him.

"You had fun, eh, Ranger? Lots of hard cider. It's all over your nice, new jacket and boots," the Boss said, laughing at Dan'L. "Clean him up. Our Client won't like it if he is brought before him covered in his own puke." The scarred man complained, and got hit on the back of his head by the Boss for it.

Another man came over to Dan'L and stabbed his leg with a hypo pen. "For your stomach," he said, and wiped Dan'L down with a big, dirty towel. The scarred man wiped off his new boots too well, Dan'L noted. When he was sort of cleaned up, the men started taunting him.

"He's paying a lot of credits for you, boy. Who are you anyway?" The third man asked. Dan'L tried to focus on his face, but couldn't. "You won't need this nice green jacket. It will look better on me." The man reached for his zipper pull.

"Don't touch it," a weak Dan'L warned, but the man slapped his face. He grabbed the zipper pull and received an electronic shock, knocking him back against the side of the shuttle.

"Leave it alone, dumb ass. He's coded it, you stupid jerk. Only he can wear it," the Boss calmly said. Watching the scarred man reach for Dan'L's boots, the Boss warned, "I said leave him alone. Our Client doesn't want him harmed. It's in the contract, moron." He walked forward to his seat, shaking his head.

Within a few minutes, Dan'L could focus better, and he assessed his surroundings. He was strapped in the cargo hold of an old shuttle. There was no light outside the small porthole; it was still night. "Where are you taking me? Who is your Client? And what does he want? I don't know anything about anybody," Dan'L said weakly.

"Shut up, boy. You'll find out soon enough," the scarred man said, and backhanded his face again. The men all laughed at him. Dan'L looked around the cargo hold, and saw seats with slashed cushions, filthy portholes, and the emergency exit hatch. Two moldy parachutes were hanging near the exit hatch, next to a first aid kit.

Dan'L knew he had to escape. Whoever their Client was, and why he was kidnapped, it was not for anything good. Slowly gathering his wits about him, Dan'L moved his fingers inside the cuffs of his new, green leather jacket. Mother wouldn't give her only Son a plain jacket, he reminded himself. Dan'L felt inside a little farther and his fingers touched a metal edge; a small knife was concealed inside the seam.

The shuttle flew on through the night, while Dan'L worked the small, thin knife blade quickly and methodically through his plastic cuff ties, and then his torso ropes. Taking care not to cut the ropes completely and have them fall off him, Dan'L sliced his bindings. When the men began talking among themselves about their reward, Dan'L pretended to dose off. Then he quickly cut the ropes around his legs.

Dan'L had no idea where they were or how long they'd been flying, or the shuttle's speed. All he knew was he had to get out of there. When he felt the shuttle slow and start its descent, he bolted for the cargo door, grabbed an emergency chute next to the first aid kit, pulled open the emergency exit hatch lock, and jumped out of the shuttle in the darkness.

He stuffed the knife into his trouser pocket and fumbled with the emergency chute during his free fall. How high up was he? All was blackness below him. No city lights. No lights anywhere at all. He managed to put the chute on and pulled the ripcord, and held on tightly. The shuttle doubled back and shined its landing lights looking for him. Dan'L could not tell where the ground was, and could not steer or land properly, as he had been trained in Phase 2.

He fell into the trees, and got scratched repeatedly by branches. The ground soon stopped his fall, but Dan'L turned his ankle when he landed. He cursed loudly and grabbed his ankle in pain. Then he gathered the chute fabric from the lower branches of a fir tree, and hobbled off into the darkness. Trees. Lots of fir trees. He could smell them ahead, but couldn't see a thing. He stuffed the torn chute under some bushes and continued.

K'Halon Prime had millions of square kilometers of dense forests. One entire side of the large planet was forested, and the other side was barren desert. He could be anywhere on the forested side. Dan'L felt a pain in his neck. It was a bleeding gash where his identification chip was cut from his neck. No one could track him. In the total darkness, Dan'L controlled his instinct to panic, and relied instead upon his excellent survival training. He was a Ranger. He would succeed at any cost.

Dan'L focused on the North Star. Travel straightaway, he told himself. He heard the shuttle's engines sounding farther away. Wherever he was, the kidnappers expected him to be traveling south or southwest, not north. Good. He made his way through the thick forest, tree to tree, hobbling best as he could on his sprained – or broken – ankle. He tripped on a broken branch. He decided to use it as a crutch to help him move. The power cells in his boots helped his hobbling and made it somewhat easier, but he could not run at all. All night he hopped from tree to tree.

After a seemingly endless, hobbled hike, the dawn began to break. Forest; the boundless forest surrounded him. No sign of a city or town anywhere, just millions of trees. Dan'L hopped ahead, realizing he needed water, rest, and a splint for his ankle. As if in a dream, the outline of a cabin came into view. It stimulated his adrenaline, and he hobbled there quickly. The forest cleared for a small cabin, and an adjacent dirt landing pad. There were no vehicles in sight, no lights, and no signs of people. Perfect.

Dan'L hopped to the cabin door and knocked, but no one answered. He pulled the latch and the door opened to a small, two-roomed cabin, sparsely furnished. There was no food printer; no canned food on the open shelves; no toilet; not even a working faucet. He called out, "Hello? Hello? I need some help," and then collapsed on the floor, unconscious.

The young girl approached the body on the floor cautiously, holding her small laser rifle defensively. "Are you okay, Mister? Are you hurt?" She softly asked, and stood near his body. She knew not to come too close to a stranger. He moved his foot a little, and she stepped back.

Dan'L opened his eyes, and saw a tall, blonde teen-age girl standing a prudent distance from him. "I'm sorry. I'm lost. I stumbled here, trying to find someone to help me, or let me use their comm link," he said hoarsely. "I need some water, please," he whispered, and began to cough. His throat was so dry.

The girl got a bottle of water out of her backpack and handed it to him. She said, "This is a dry cabin. Off the grid. No facilities or power, Mister. Are you a fugitive, or a murderer? Nobody comes here. Nobody but me."

"My name is Dan'L. I just graduated Ranger training. I'm no criminal. But I am running from some men who kidnapped me," he said, taking the offered bottle of water from her. He downed it in seconds, and then wiped his mouth. "Thank you. I'll leave and get out of your hair. I don't want to cause trouble for you." He tried to stand, and fell.

"Let me help you, Dan'L," she offered, and helped him stand. He hopped to a chair, holding onto her arm. "My name is D 'Anna. This is my cabin. It's my refuge," she admitted. She watched him take off his boot and sock. His ankle was swollen and purple. She went to her pack and took a scanner out, and then scanned his lower leg. "A bad sprain, but no broken bones. You'll be okay in a few days, Dan'L."

She went to a shelf and located a first-aid kit, and said, "If you can break a plank off that chair, we can make a splint for you. I'll tape it." Together, they fashioned a splint for his ankle. They chatted for a few minutes while he put his sock and boot on, and left the boot unfastened for the splint. Then the sound of a shuttle was heard as it approached the cabin.

D 'Anna quickly walked to the cold fireplace and moved a stone, and the wall parted a bit. "In here, Dan'L. Behind the fireplace. Go down the steps and don't move or make any sound," she cautioned. "Hopefully, I'll get rid of them."

Dan'L trusted D'Anna and did as she said, hopping down the dark stairs. "Light sticks are on the left, but wait until they leave to strike one," she whispered. D'Anna quickly lit a small tinder fire in the fireplace after closing the secret opening, and sat on the now-broken chair backwards.

"Hey! Anybody home?" A rough male voice asked.

"What do you want? Go away!" D'Anna shouted back at him. Three men opened her cabin door and saw the girl sitting there, a laser rifle pointed at them.

"Easy now, girlie. We're looking for a fugitive. A man in a green jacket and black pants. Seen him?" The scarred man demanded, eyeing the young girl.

"Nobody lives here but my brothers and me. Anybody else comes around and they'll shoot him. Or you, if they find you. Now get out!" D'Anna yelled, raising her rifle at them.

"Okay, okay. No need to shoot. We're gone," the Boss said, and they left. D'Anna went to the narrow window and watched three men board the shuttle, and fly off.

She pulled out her scanner and swept the area. The men were gone, but she knew the bastards would be back. They'd come for her next time. She stomped out the tinder fire and touched the stone. Gathering her pack and rifle, D'Anna walked down the steps to Dan'L. She touched another stone and the opening closed tightly again.

"Nice friends you got, Dan'L. We'd better go now," D'Anna said. She led him through the underground dirt tunnel, helping him hop for nearly a half kilometer, until they reached stairs leading up. She helped him up the stairs, and then raised the hatch above their head. Several people were inside the room, watching her come up the stairs. Pistols were pointing at them.

"This is Dan'L, the man who found the cabin," D'Anna explained. "He says he's a Ranger, and was kidnapped. The men who were after him found the cabin." They lowered their pistols and cautiously watched Dan'L sit in the offered chair. They watched D'Anna tend to his injured ankle, and try to make him comfortable.

Dan'L was weak, dirty, and injured, but he patiently told his story to them, and asked for a comm link to call his Mother to come get him. "I can honestly tell you I have no idea why I was captured. But I've done nothing wrong. I graduated Ranger Phase 3 Training on Friday. My Commander Superior G'Rosk will vouch for me, or my Mother. She's a Shi'Lon Ranger, Master Commander Javette," he explained. "Please. Can you help me?" He looked so innocent.

The oldest man walked over to Dan'L, watching him suspiciously. He downed a shot of liquor in his hand, and grilled D'Anna about her discovery of Dan'L several times. The poor girl was verbally reprimanded repeatedly for bringing an unknown, injured man to their apartment, and potentially exposing their whereabouts. "But Petrov, we always help the innocents, you said," D'Anna said, trying to justify her decision to help the young Ranger Novice.

Dan'L was just out of training, and without any real field experience. But, as he looked at the faces of the people in the apartment, it suddenly dawned on him: these people were Rebels, the very people against whom he would be sent to fight. The look on his face betrayed him.

Petrov noticed his countenance change immediately, and said to Dan'L, "So. The curtain lifts now, eh, young man? You are not a full Ranger yet, but a Novice. You have no plasma sword, black armor, or cloak to conceal your moves," he said, watching Dan'L. "If we help you, we alert the Empire to our whereabouts, our safe house, and tunnels. I should kill you now." The man quickly belted another shot glass of liquor, and slammed the empty glass on the table.

The people in the apartment started openly discussing their dilemma, and then Petrov told them to be quiet. "He is a spy, Petrov. He knows our cabin location," another man said. "And he knows about this apartment. What can we do?"

"This is your doing, D'Anna. Perhaps you should have given him to those men," a woman suggested bitterly. "They will keep looking for him."

"It is not our way to harm innocents! He is young; he is naive; and he never fought against us!" D'Anna cried. "The Creator showed him to our cabin. How else could he have found it, injured as he is, not knowing anything about us? We were meant to help him, Petrov," she protested. "He is an innocent. We help innocents!"

Dan'L listened to the Rebels argue his fate. Petrov watched Dan'L with a deep scowl on his face. It was obvious Dan'L was not an innocent to him. He finally announced, "We will find these men and check out your story. If you are telling the truth, the Emperor's Rangers will be out in droves, searching for their youngest. Your Mother will never stop searching for you. You will stay here tonight, young Ranger, and enjoy our meager hospitality, such as it is," Petrov said. He pulled Dan'L out of his chair, contorted his hard face, and scowled at the young Novice.

"Wait, sir. I am no freeloader. I can pay for my stay," Dan'L said. He took out a 100-credit gold coin from his pocket and handed it to D'Anna. "From Mother, her gift for my graduation. Buy us all some food with it," Dan'L instructed. D'Anna hesitated, but then took the 100-credit gold coin, and left. The older woman led Dan'L to a closet in the back room with a narrow air mattress. He thanked her and took off his boots, laid down, and slept for two days.

VII

Dan'L opened his eyes late in the afternoon and shook his head, trying to awaken fully. He carefully stood; his ankle felt better than it did when he laid down. There was a proper splint and bandage on it, not the chair plank splint, as before. The swelling had gone down a lot. But he still had to hop and not put pressure on his ankle. He hobbled into the kitchen. D'Anna was sitting at the table, watching him enter the room.

"Thank you, D'Anna. I am in your debt," Dan'L said, and a little smile found its way onto his face. "What time is it? Or, should I ask: what day is it?"

She quietly answered, "It is Wednesday, Dan'L. You slept nearly two days. Are you hungry or thirsty?"

"Famished, D'Anna," he answered. She served him a big bowl of beef stew with bread and butter, and gave him a pitcher of water. He tried to eat slowly, to not upset his distraught stomach. The food was delicious. She watched him in silence.

"I brought you clean clothes, and put new toiletries in the shower for you, Dan'L, if you want to clean up. You smell awful," she said. "Sorry, but it's true."

Dan'L asked her forgiveness for his present state. He hobbled to the bathroom, showered twice, shaved with the new razor, and brushed his teeth with the new toothbrush. He emerged from the bathroom fresh and clean, feeling and looking like a new man.

Using lots of paper towels and water, Dan'L cleaned the smelly gunk off his green leather jacket while she watched, and talked with him about Centralia, the capital of K'Halon Prime. She'd never been there. D'Anna told him about being an orphan, and how Petrov rescued her, and raised her as his own daughter. They spent hours together, and enjoyed being with each other. She had no one her own age to talk with in the apartment. It was evident D'Anna felt like a servant for the others.

"You can come back with me, D'Anna. My Mother would love to meet the girl who rescued me, I'm sure," Dan'L offered. "There are several guest quarters available. I have lots of friends, and we could show you around Centralia. It'd be a fun visit for you."

"She's not going to Centralia, Ranger," Petrov said gruffly, walking into the room. "But you're leaving today. We'll take you to a way station near the northern shuttle field. You can make your own way from there. Your Mother has promised not to pursue us—today, at least," he added sarcastically. "She gave me her word."

"The word of a Shi'Lon Ranger is always true, sir." Dan'L struck his left breast with his right fist to salute him.

Petrov scowled and said, "Save your salutes for your Emperor P'Lau, young Novice Ranger. Pray we never meet again. Take him now, D'Anna," he ordered. "And make certain he wears suede boots, not his own. He should look like a Northern forest man, not a Centralia boy," he cautioned. "Those mercenaries are still looking for him." He tossed a ratty old backpack to Dan'L and said, "Put your fancy jacket and boots in here. Go now, before your Mother comes here looking for you," he smirked. "I have no desire to meet her in person."

D'Anna and Dan'L left the apartment in ten minutes, and kept to the back streets. After a few kilometers, they approached a brightly-lit shuttle field. They entered the busy "Nord" way station, crowded with travelers awaiting the next shuttle. Dan'L went to the vid comm link and called his Mother, Javette. She kept the call short, staying on just long enough to lock in his position. Dan'L bought meals for D'Anna and him with some wine. He remarked, "Your cooking is much better, D'Anna." They had just finished eating when the sound of a shuttle landing close to the way station was heard.

The way station main door opened and a tall woman in a long, hooded black cloak entered. Dan'L stood and tapped his knuckles on the table to get her attention. "It's my Mother," he told D'Anna quietly. D'Anna cautiously watched the woman approach.

The Shi'Lon Ranger came to their table and held her smiling Son's hand against her cheek with both hands, and returned his smile. She touched the red wound on his neck where his ID chip was cut out, and then they sat. No wonder she lost track of him. She pushed her hood back and looked at the young, blonde girl with her Son. "So, you're D'Anna. I am Javette. Thank you for helping my Son. Was he much trouble for you, D'Anna? Dan'L can be a handful, at times," she remarked with a smile.

"No, Ma'am. He was no trouble at all," D'Anna shyly answered. "Dan'L was hurt, but very polite and gentlemanly. Nothing like the Northern men," she added. Javette had dark hair, and looked beautiful, but intense. She gently smiled at D'Anna, and studied the girl's face.

Dan'L said in a whisper, "D'Anna and her family were kind to me, a complete stranger, Mother. I was filthy, lost, and injured, and D'Anna rescued me. She helped me heal."

M.C. Javette stood and said they had to leave now. She knew Petrov's Rebel spies were somewhere inside the way station, watching them. They walked out together to her Imperial shuttle, and D'Anna said, "I've never seen a shuttle like this. So new! Not a scratch on it!" Javette offered to give her a ride home, but D'Anna refused. "Petrov will think I'm complicit. Not a good idea, Ma'am, but thank you anyway."

Javette held her gloved hand out to D'Anna and placed two 5000-credit gold bars in her hand. Javette said, "Give one to Petrov, with my regards. He asked for 5000 credits for the safe return of my Son. The other gold bar is for you, D'Anna. You may need to get away someday," the Shi'Lon Ranger advised. "A woman should always have her own money in case of an emergency. Thank you again, and good luck." She stepped into the shuttle. Dan'L hugged D'Anna, and then boarded. They flew off quickly, and he sighed heavily, from relief.

"She's a very pretty girl, Dan'L. Did you sleep with her?" His Mother asked pointedly.

"No, Mother. She was kind to help me, and very brave. Her friends were angry she took me in and brought me to their apartment. She took a significant risk to help me," Dan'L said, and told his Mother what happened to him. He told every detail he could recall, and described his kidnappers. He said, "They would not tell me why I was kidnapped, or who their Client was. All I heard was they had a large contract to kidnap me, and deliver me to their Client. Why would anyone want me? I don't know anything about anyone, Mother."

Javette shook her head and answered, "We will find out, eventually. Rest tonight, and tomorrow we'll meet with your Commander Superior G'Rosk, to update him about this situation, Dan'L. It is most unusual for anything like this to happen to a Novice," she said.

Bright and early at 6:30a.m., Novice Ranger Dan'L and M.C. Javette met with C.S. G'Rosk. Dan'L articulated the whole story of his graduation party and his kidnapping. In as much detail as possible, Dan'L shared his getaway, injuries, and rescue by D'Anna. When he spoke of her family and said the name "Petrov," his Commander Superior's face changed.

"Are you certain his name was Petrov?" G'Rosk asked.

"Yes, sir. His name was Petrov. Everyone called him by that name. D'Anna said she was an orphan, and Petrov rescued her, raising her as his own daughter. Her family was angry she brought me through the underground tunnel, and into their apartment. But we had to get away from those mercenaries," Dan'L explained.

"How did Petrov know you were a Ranger?" G'Rosk asked, now staring intently at his Novice.

"I told D'Anna, and them, sir. I told her the truth about being kidnapped, and escaping when she found me. She helped me heal, sir," Dan'L said innocently.

Javette said, "My Son has no idea who Petrov is, Commander Superior G'Rosk. Petrov called me and offered to give my Son back to me, if I promised not to attack them to rescue Dan'L," she explained.

"What bounty did Petrov demand?"

"5000 credits. I gave the girl D'Anna another 5000 credits and told her to keep it, in case she ever needed to escape. She seemed young and innocent, Commander Superior. And she helped my Son. My Commander Superior Bette approved it, in advance," Javette said.

"Sir, if I may ask: why would mercenaries want to kidnap me? I don't know anyone important or any aristocrat. I have no information they could use," Dan'L said. "Why me, sir?"

G'Rosk answered, "The answer to your question is presently unknown, but it will be discovered in due time. Could you find that cabin again, Dan'L?"

He thought for a moment and replied, "It's a dry cabin in a clearing in the Northern forest of K'Halon Prime, somewhere near Nord, sir. I honestly could not pinpoint its location."

G'Rosk tapped off his com tablet recorder, and said, "Pity. The Rebels probably smuggle men and weapons through there. You say the tunnel led into Petrov's apartment?"

"Yes, sir. Several family members lived there. It was a large flat," the Novice answered.

"They are Rebels, Novice Dan'L. They are criminals, thieves, murderers, and traitors. They are not your friends. I doubt they are living there now," G'Rosk said flatly. "Nevertheless; you will report here in two days for fitting of your breastplate and backplate. Be sure to wear the special garment we gave you, as regular clothing will melt and burn your skin when the nano-titanium armor is fitted to your torso and chest. Report after our meeting to the Royal Physician for a complete physical. You cannot begin full duty and transport to Home World until he clears you." Dan'L acknowledged his orders.

G'Rosk took a new com tablet out of a storage cabinet and handed it to Dan'L, saying, "Write a full report in as much detail as possible and send it to me by end of today. Upon receipt, I will download some of our files on the Rebel Petrov. It is important you know who this Rebel is, what he is capable of, and some of the things he did. Petrov killed your Father, Dan'L," G'Rosk revealed. "Petrov led the Rebel attack against Master Commander K'Ser on SB5."

Dan'L's eyes instantly grew as big as a deer in headlights. "Petrov knew who I was?"

Javette answered, "He did when you told him my name, Dan'L. I swore a blood oath to find and kill Petrov. And my Son was delivered to the bastard hurt and weakened, by an innocent girl! The Creator has intervened directly with your life, my Son," she said decidedly. Dan'L saluted his Mother and C.S. G'Rosk, and limped to the Palace hospital. The past three days' events took on new meaning for him, consuming him in thought.

G'Rosk asked Javette, "Will you still carry out your threat to skin Petrov alive before slicing him to death with your plasma sword, then?"

She laughed with him, and replied, "He spared my Son because of his innocence. Maybe I will only skin one side of Petrov before carving him into pieces." Javette saluted him and left.

G'Rosk went to his window and watched Dan'L limping across the walkway to the Palace hospital. K'Ser had been his best friend for many years, even before Dan'L was born. He silently swore to find out who ordered the kidnapping of K'Ser and Javette's son. Novices had little exposure to the Rebellion. They were only seventeen or eighteen years of age, without any field experience, and knew little of the real world. G'Rosk walked to his desk, took out his personal tablet, and began contacting his private informants. He had to discover who did this. Javette had suffered enough.

VIII

The final Confirmation Ceremony for the newly-graduated Borgund and Shi'Lon Ranger Novices was in two hours. Dan'L looked at himself in the full-length mirror, dressed in his formal uniform for the first time. He lightly touched his new armor, the breastplate and backplate, fitted to his body and encoded to his DNA. Only he could touch it, or wear it. The armor was filled with concealed, deadly weapons front and back: gas pellets, several knives, piano wire garrote, and more. Two plasma pulser pistols were hidden in the backplate. His new plasma sword rested in his backplate, its handle also coded to his DNA. His armor kept him cool or warm, whatever his torso required. It was black, with a bold pattern on the front.

"Don't fry your hair when you draw your plasma sword to salute the Emperor, Dan'L," another Novice teased. Every Novice had a few scars from the fiery, deadly plasma sword. Dan'L had a scar on the back of his head from practicing returning his sword to its sheath inside the backplate. The Novices' hair was short now; but a Ranger could let his hair grow any length, unlike the military officers. Most of the Rangers had long hair, tied with leather ties, hanging in loose ponytails. Having long hair was a statement, a rite of passage, really. It meant they were genuine Rangers, and could draw and sheathe their plasma swords without setting their hair on fire—beware.

The young Novices would live together in the Royal Palace basement dormitories for their first year, Borgunds separate from the Shi'Lon Rangers. Three bells sounded, and the Novices removed their full-length black cloaks from their lockers and put them on. Then they donned their shiny black helmets with the short black feathers. They wore knee-high boots, and long gloves with a DNA recognition chip in the center, designed to transmit their DNA code to the handle of their plasma sword. The young men spent a few minutes admiring themselves.

"Rank and file. Fall in!" Commander Bok ordered. "Fall in love with yourselves on your own time. Any Novice who embarrasses me today will be scrubbing latrines for six months!" He threatened, a stern look on his face. Bok marched the ten Borgund Novices to the Palace Courtyard, positioning them in parade formation next to the two Shi'Lon Ranger Novices Kayla and L'Mun.

Dan'L chanced a wink at his friend Kayla, and they checked each other out in their formal uniforms. The Shi'Lon formal uniform was a long red dress, split front and back for ease of movement. It featured a beautiful black, gold, and white-patterned, red panel from their waist down the front length of their skirt, for modesty. Their long cloak was red, and so were the feathers in their gleaming gold helmets. High-heeled boots up to their knees in red leather completed their uniform. They certainly looked like the Emperor's Emissaries, now. Their breastplate and backplate were dark red. It was a dramatic change from their daily uniforms of black trousers and blouse, and black boots, worn by both the Borgund and Shi'Lon Rangers.

Courtiers, military officers, and VIPs were lined up on the sides of the Main Court, watching the Borgund and Shi'Lon Novices march in. The Novices were all sons and daughters of proud Warrior Class parents, most of them Rangers themselves, watching the Novices take their Confirmation. Every military officer and Ranger wore their formal uniform for this occasion. This was a solemn, very important day for the Warrior Class and the new Novices.

Emperor P'Lau wore fine robes and his crown today for the Confirmation Ceremony. He was escorted in by his Imperial Guards, and took his throne. Shi'Lon C.S. Bette announced: "The Great Emperor P'Lau, Ruler over all Known Worlds and Conqueror over the Unknown Domain. Your Novice Shi'Lon and Borgund Rangers appear before you, to confirm their lives and service to you." Every Ranger Novice knelt on their right knee, and bowed their head.

C.S. G'Rosk and Bette stood at either side of the Novice Rangers. A loud bell chimed, and the Novices put their right hand over their heart, and said in unison: "I swear my service, my loyalty, my will, and my life to the Great Emperor P'Lau, and to our Creator." Each Novice removed their left-hand glove, took a knife from their backplate, cut their left palm, and held their bleeding left palm high for all to see; their blood oath. Then they put their gloves on again.

"Draw swords!" Bette commanded. Each Novice drew their plasma sword, and the fiery white-hot swords gleamed and crackled pure energy, as they held them high above their heads with both hands. "Salute!" She cried. They sharply pulled their swords down to their left breastplate with both hands, in the Royal Salute.

"Sheathe swords!" G'Rosk ordered, and they returned their swords to their backplates properly. No one set their hair or helmet feathers on fire, to the satisfaction of Commanders Superior G'Rosk and Bette. The Novices stood, and the large audience in the Main Court applauded and cheered for them. It was done. They officially belonged to Emperor P'Lau, now.

When the crowd quieted, Emperor P'Lau said, "My newest Faithful Sons and Beloved Daughters: you have made your Emperor very proud today. You represent the highest tier of your Warrior Class, and follow in the footsteps of the great Borgund and Shi'Lon Rangers who came before you, serving the Empire for over 2,500 years. Be proud of your calling and Confirmation today, and know this: We all serve the Empire, and the Creator of us all."

The High Priest stepped up and blessed the Novices, in the ancient language. Emperor P'Lau walked up and personally handed the Borgund Novices a solid gold belt buckle on a black leather belt, resting in the finest black silk, set inside a black box. The heavy buckle bore the Imperial seal, with an onyx stone prominently set in the center.

Emperor P'Lau then ordered the new Shi'Lon Rangers to remove their left-hand gloves. He held the left hand of each Shi'Lon Novice, and placed their long gold and jewel-laden Confirmation Ring on their third finger, as a husband would do for his bride. Emperor P'Lau returned to his throne, levitated up two meters above them, and declared, "Our young Shi'Lon Novices are now our Beloved Daughters, and our Borgund Novices are our Faithful Sons. Congratulations to our brave protectors!" Everyone in the Main Court applauded and cheered again, and the ceremony was complete.

The remainder of the day was spent with their proud families and friends in celebration. A lavish banquet was served to all the guests, with many treats from all four worlds of the Empire. Entertainment by professional dancers, musicians, and magicians made the evening very festive. The celebration was a wonderful gesture from the Emperor for his Novice Rangers, and their families.

Novice Kayla was surprised by the appearance of her brother, First Commander Olm, when he came up to her and offered his congratulations. He said, "My Captain Mur sends his regards to his friend, the new Novice Kayla. My wife Tara and I are so proud of you, little Sister!" He started to hug her, and Kayla quickly put up her hand to stop him.

"You came halfway across the solar system to honor me today, Olm. Let's not have to call the medics to resuscitate you, dear Brother!" Kayla said, and they both laughed until tears came to their eyes. Olm kissed her cheek, and remarked how impressive she looked in her formal red uniform and cloak, and red high-heeled boots. Kayla called Dan'L and M.C. Javette over, and introduced them to her only living relatives, Olm, and his Space Cadre Commander wife, Tara. They all had a wonderful, memorable day.

The next day, Novice Dan'L was called into a meeting with Commanders Superior G'Rosk, Vu'Duc, Bette, and his Mother, M.C. Javette. "We now have information about your kidnapping, Novice. We located the three mercenaries who abducted you outside the Rogue Wave Club. We also have their shuttle pilot. Their Client is the Traitor Duma Wat, half-brother of Emperor P'Lau, who has led the Rebellion for over two decades. But why he wanted you remains a mystery, Dan'L. A contract is still out for your live capture for 500,000 credits. The Emperor was shocked to hear of the bounty for your capture, Novice," G'Rosk stated.

C.S. Bette ordered, "Tell us everything you know about Master Commander K'Ser's death, Novice Dan'L." She tapped on her com tablet to record his answer. "What were you doing at the time?"

Dan'L looked at his Mother, and she nodded ever so slightly. He recalled, "I was in the last month of Phase 3 training. Those of us who were left were anxious and determined to succeed. We were training even after dark, in secret with each other, and sleeping very little."

"That's what's supposed to happen," Bette said dryly. "Continue."

"When Commander Bok pulled me out of Phase 3 Training to tell me of my Father's death, I was in shock. I didn't ask him how, or why, or even where Master Commander K'Ser was when he was killed. I asked if my Mother Javette was all right, and if I could go to her," Dan'L said quietly. "Mother told me he was killed by Rebels and mercenaries on SB5, near the White Belt. She said K'Ser killed many Rebels before he was killed, and was honored by Emperor P'Lau as a Hero of the Empire." Dan'L sat back and looked at his Mother.

"Yes, it is all true, Novice. You will soon see Master Commander K'Ser's picture enshrined in the Hall of Honor in the Royal Palace," G'Rosk said. "K'Ser called you before he died. Did he send you anything? Did you receive anything from his final will?"

"Everything was sent to Mother. He left me his Great-Grandfather's ring, his Ranger belt buckle, and his bone-handled belt knife. Those were in his will. Oh – and the ES technical manual he sent me on the red memory crystals a week earlier. He wanted me to know my fighter before I entered Flight School," Dan'L added.

Javette leaned forward and said, "There were no red memory crystals mentioned in K'Ser's will, or any sent to me in his last remains, Dan'L. When did your Father send the crystals to you?" She looked closely at her Son.

"It was right before our sulphur springs swimming final, Mother. I received them on Friday or Saturday by express delivery. He called me every other Friday after 10p.m., usually with you in the vid, too, Mother," Dan'L said defensively.

C.S. Vu'Duc demanded, "We need you to hand over those red memory crystals for testing, Novice Dan'L. There may be more to them than technical specs. Where are they now?"

He reached into his pocket for his wallet, and took out the two red memory crystals. The Novice handed them to his Mother, placing them in her outstretched hand. She asked, "Have you played these crystals, Son?"

"Yes, of course, Mother. I studied the schematics again last night. It's just a tech manual," he said. "I want to pass fighter training this year."

C.S. G'Rosk smiled at his Novice, and said, "I'm sure you will pass, if you work as hard in Flight School as you did in Phase 1, 2, and 3 Training. We will have these memory crystals analyzed, and then return them to you shortly, Dan'L. Thank you for your cooperation," he closed, and dismissed his Novice.

The small red memory crystals were analyzed and copied, with nothing out of the ordinary discovered on them. G'Rosk was ready to return them when he got a call from M.C. Javette, asking, "Did your techs analyze Dan'L's crystals, Commander Superior G'Rosk?"

"Yes, Javette, and nothing unusual was found. I was going to return them to Dan'L today," he replied, "before we depart for K'Halon Prime."

"May we meet again before we leave Home World, with you and my Commander Superior Bette? I need to show you something, sir," she asked. He agreed, and invited her to his office that afternoon. Shi'Lon Commander Superior Bette joined them.

Javette entered G'Rosk's office with Dan'L, carrying a small box with her. "These are the things I was sent from K'Ser." She gently placed each article on G'Rosk's large desk: a plain, gold partnership commitment band; a holographic photo of Javette, Dan'L, and daughter K'Rissa; and his wallet. Javette opened K'Ser's wallet, showing them his Borgund Ranger chip card for expenses, several gold credit coins of various denominations, and a beautiful portrait of Javette, out of uniform, with her long black hair down. G'Rosk picked up the picture and looked at it closely.

Dan'L unwrapped a bone-handled knife; a Borgund Ranger belt buckle with the Imperial seal; and a large, gold ring with a ruby gem set in it, and laid them down. He put the ring on, made a fist, and pointed the ring at the belt buckle. Instantly a fifth dimensional pattern emerged, half a meter wide and high.

"What is that? How did you do that?" Bette demanded. "What does it mean?"

Dan'L shook his head, and asked, "I do not know, Commander Superior Bette. May I see my crystals, Commander Superior G'Rosk?" Dan'L took the crystals and carefully stood them side by side. He pointed the ring at the crystals, and another fifth dimensional pattern emerged, much larger than the first one. Then he pointed the ring at his Father's commitment band, and a holographic picture was projected, like a type of blueprint.

"These are the remains of my Partner, K'Ser. After our meeting yesterday, I went through his things again. Then, I remembered: K'Ser's ring from his Great-Grandfather had a bloodstone set in it, not this large ruby, or whatever the stone really is. I called Dan'L to come over, and – well, you see the results for yourselves. He thought the crystals would reveal something when the ring was pointed at them. We cannot decipher the fifth dimensional information, but I recognized part of the blueprints. They are from the Imperial Command Battle Cruiser Emperor P'Lau uses to travel throughout the Empire. I believe it is his stateroom, Commander Superior Bette," Javette said, with urgency in her voice. "There appears to be some sort of anomaly inside the bedroom."

Bette sent an emergency signal to the Emperor. Within minutes, Emperor P'Lau entered the Borgund Ranger High Command office and was shown Javette's new revelation. P'Lau stared at Novice Dan'L and his Mother Javette. He said, "Our scientists have only developed fifth dimensional storage pattern functionality very recently. Top-secret. We have no idea what properties these 5D storage crystals possess, besides their obvious data storage capabilities. Master Commander K'Ser sent one red crystal to us the first week he arrived on SB5, prior to the battle that took his life there. We are testing the 5D crystal for many purposes, including weaponry. Highly destructive weaponry," P'Lau revealed.

G'Rosk asked, "Sire, where are the red crystals from? They look like regular colored memory crystals. K'Ser never reported to me his discovery of these red crystals."

Emperor P'Lau picked up one of the red memory crystals and answered, "I can only say that they are not found within our solar system. And the ruby stone in this ring, you see? It is a dodecahedron, twelve-faceted. Twelve is the universal number, very important in astrology, celestial calculations, religious teachings; those sorts of things." He stared at the ring, turning it so that the daylight reflected from it. "Amazing."

Javette and Dan'L showed the holographic blueprints to the Emperor, and he was astonished. He ordered them to bring everything and come with him at once. C.S. G'Rosk ordered Novice Dan'L's personal effects moved out of the K'Halon Prime Novice dormitory immediately, and sent to an executive suite in the top-security area of the Royal Palace, usually reserved for Commander Borgund Rangers. His Novice had been swept into a web of intrigue far deeper and darker than anyone imagined. C.S. Bette assigned apartments to Javette in the First Echelon wings of the Home World and K'Halon Prime Royal Palaces, also top-security areas, and placed her on "Special Assignment" for an indefinite time, all per Emperor P'Lau's orders.

"K'Ser must have uncovered this information from the androids he encountered. There are many more questions now, G'Rosk. First and foremost is, why did your Ranger not report these discoveries to us, and send them to his family, jeopardizing his son's life? Who is on K'Halon Prime that K'Ser did not trust with this ground-breaking science? Why did the Emperor not inform us of this red crystal discovery? And, what on the red memory crystals was worth K'Ser's life, and a 500,000-credit bounty from Duma Wat for K'Ser's son, Novice Dan'L?" Bette asked G'Rosk. She studied his face intensely.

"We must find out, and soon," G'Rosk answered, then stopped and looked at Bette. "Master Commander K'Ser was killed by a plasma disrupter arc in a battle against Rebels, on SB5. How did his wallet, ring, Ranger belt buckle, and a damned holographic picture survive a plasma disrupter arc? Nothing should have survived, not even ash!"

The eldest Commander Superior offered, "Obviously, his remains were planted. But by whom? What if they were not truly the remains of Master Commander K'Ser at all? What if he is still alive? Could it be possible?"

IX

Scientists inside the top-secret research lab were understandably nervous with Emperor P'Lau, two Rangers, and twelve Imperial Guards in their lab. It was a hidden facility deep underground, several floors below the Capital City Space Base. When Dan'L and Javette laid out the remains of K'Ser and demonstrated their newly-discovered secrets, each scientist was thrilled, and afraid.

They looked intensely at the fifth dimensional holograph emanating between the two red crystals and Dan'L's ruby ring. The lead scientist, Dr. D'Vre, moved the red crystals farther apart, then turned them in towards each other. He asked Dan'L for his ruby ring, and set it in between the two red crystals. Suddenly, an immense, fifth dimensional red holograph projected up to the ceiling, spreading out the full length of the very large lab.

Seven scientists walked within the holograph, excitedly talking with each other in highly technical terms Dan'L did not understand. He watched them move within the hologram, talking and pointing. Then he saw an object appear; a long box appeared near the top. The box top lifted off and stacked box upon box atop itself.

"Mother, look!" He cried. When he pointed his arm out to show her, Dan'L's body flew up to the top. The young man was surprised, but elated to fly within the hologram. All talking stopped in the room. Dan'L touched one of the long boxes in the stack, and his Father's voice spoke, "Highly advanced android technology here. Cannot send to K'Halon Prime without the Rebels discovering it, too. A blank red crystal was sent to the Emperor on Home World. The fifth dimension is the space between matter; the world in between worlds. It is time, within time. Endless space and time. The green crystal could have ultimate power. Use extreme caution. Total control. All time, all here and now."

Dan'L touched each box one by one, and listened to the messages within them. Then, he flew around the hologram seeking more messages and boxes from his Father, but found no others. Then Emperor P'Lau ordered Dan'L to come down. P'Lau said, "We have unlocked a power and realm unknown to us. Its wonders boggle the mind, amaze us, and fill us with awe. But K'Ser's message also contains a warning for us. Let us take care. Maximum care."

"Who is on the other side of this new realm watching us make this discovery?" Dan'L asked aloud, looking inside the hologram again. "Dr. D'Vre, could my Father be trapped inside the fifth dimension? How can we find out? And, who are the androids he talked about? Where are they from?"

The doctor answered, "We do not know, young Ranger. I'm sorry. But we will endeavor to find out, if we may keep these things for study."

M.C. Javette said, "You have my permission to study my property, but do not break or destroy anything. They are all that remains of Master Commander K'Ser, my Partner, and Dan'L's Father."

Dan'L agreed to the same arrangement for his red crystals and ruby ring. He handed his Father's knife to Dr. D'Vre and asked, "Is this knife just a knife?" After several minutes of testing and many various scans, D'Vre smiled and gave the knife back to him.

"It is just a knife, or so it appears on our equipment," he said. "The metal in the blade has been folded over three hundred times, however. Highly tempered, very strong, and worth thousands of credits, to be sure." Dan'L put the knife back in its sheath, and gave it to his Mother. Only when he was promoted to full Ranger could he wear a knife on his belt. They followed Emperor P'Lau and the Imperial Guards out of the research lab, and then shuttled to the Royal Palace in silence.

In a few days, Emperor P'Lau flew in the Imperial Command Battle Cruiser to K'Halon Prime, in secret. Accompanying him were Commanders Superior G'Rosk and Bette, M.C. Javette, Novices Dan'L and Kayla, and many Imperial Guards. Conversation was kept to routine and mundane topics. Something was happening on K'Halon Prime which caused the late K'Ser to be very suspicious – and his Emperor, as well. Emperor P'Lau ordered a General Inspection of his Imperial Battle Cruiser, now in position above K'Halon Prime.

There was a feeling of foreboding and distrust in the air aboard the Imperial Command Battle Cruiser. Emperor P'Lau was consumed with worry over potential traitors within his midst, especially within the walls of the Royal Palace of K'Halon Prime. Throughout the twenty years of the Rebellion, several attacks had taken place in various locations within the solar system, but none in the last nineteen years had even come close to the Emperor. Many of his trusted courtiers both in Home World and K'Halon Prime Palaces thought the Emperor was becoming paranoid, and his worries were without merit.

Com tablets from unknown sources were unpacked from sealed crates, and delivered into the master bedroom of the Emperor. He ordered the Cruiser to fly at half standard speed, instead of its usual full standard speed, extending the trip intentionally. Home World was very close in its orbit to K'Halon Prime this time of year. The trip should have taken only two days, eighteen hours. The Emperor spent the entire trip alone in his private suite, ate his meals in private, and refused to see any visitors, even the concubines traveling with him. He was continuously surrounded by Imperial Guards, and slept with them protecting his bedroom doors. The Cruiser was escorted by two full squadrons of Space Cadre fighters for the duration of the trip. The senior Rangers were unsettled, knowing this was not at all the typical excursion for Emperor P'Lau.

K'Halon Prime

The small Royal Court was the private court for Emperor P'Lau. It was his favorite court. The Royal Palace on K'Halon Prime was only two hundred years old and, although it was roughly the same size as the main Royal Palace on Home World, it was much nicer. It was decorated with light, brighter colors, with many trim touches the Home World Royal Palace designers never considered 800 years ago. It was beautiful as well as functional inside, and featured technologically superior controls for the Emperor. The small Royal Court was also very ornamental, with lapis lazuli trim around the high columns, bordered in gold, and with gold-trimmed dark blue drapery covering its many windows. The deep blue colors were a harmonious compliment to the green forest planet of K'Halon Prime.

No courtiers or aristocrats milled about in this Royal Court; it was private, only for the Emperor and his invited guests. Novice Dan'L and M.C. Javette were summoned to appear before the Emperor that afternoon in his Royal Court. Several senior Borgund and Shi'Lon Rangers were already inside, waiting for them to arrive. Javette and Dan'L quickly walked up to the gold line between the two marble pillars in front of the steps leading to the throne, knelt before Emperor P'Lau, and saluted him.

P'Lau said, "Rise, Javette, my Beloved Daughter, and Dan'L, my new Faithful Son. Your Emperor has a special assignment for each of you, assignments we do not want to give, but must." He rose up in his flying throne a meter and hovered in front of them.

"The Empire has many undercover assets engaged in various assignments, some for many years. Within five days' time, certain assets will be repositioned to assist you with your assignments, at elevated risk for all of you," he said mysteriously.

Emperor P'Lau lowered his throne to the floor, and ordered, "Master

Commander Javette: your will fly your ES warbird to Ban'Ti for top secret negotiations of the highest importance. You will mediate those negotiations as your Emperor's Emissary. Be prepared to enforce my will, and succeed at any cost. Depart at first light tomorrow, my Beloved Daughter." She saluted him and turned to leave, but C.S. Bette motioned for her to stand next to her, and listen.

"Novice Dan'L, my newest Faithful Son: circumstances have placed you within a dark web of intrigue, the likes of which we have never seen, especially for one of your Novice rank. After many discussions with our undercover assets, as well as those present today, we have reached a decision. Your Emperor asks you to volunteer to once again become a captive, and be delivered to the Traitor Duma Wat."

The Emperor moved around on his throne, as if he was suddenly uncomfortable sitting there. He continued, "You will be assisted by assets in place whom you have never met, and cannot recognize. They will not reveal themselves to you. You will be accompanied by Commander Bok to the place where we will leave you to the mercenaries. They will capture, confine, and deliver you to Duma Wat. You will discover what Duma Wat wants from you, and why he is offering a planet's ransom for my Novice. The risk is great, but it is not more than you can bear, according to your superiors. Do you volunteer, Novice Dan'L?"

Dan'L bowed his head and answered, "Yes, your Majesty. I volunteer for this assignment to serve my Emperor. May your Novice make one request of your Majesty?" Dan'L boldly asked. "May I request Novice Kayla to accompany me, instead of Commander Bok?" C.S. G'Rosk was at Dan'L's side in a flash, absolutely glaring at the young man for being so impertinent. Novices were only to speak when spoken to, in the presence of the Emperor.

But the Emperor was intrigued by his request, and asked Dan'L, "Another Novice? Why my Beloved Daughter Kayla? This is most unusual."

"Sire, Kayla has superior skills of negotiation and interpreting body language, my Emperor. She is my best friend, and I trust her implicitly," Dan'L said with his head fully bowed.

Emperor P'Lau studied him for a moment, and then said, "Then know you are now trusting my Kayla with your life, Novice Dan'L. You will depart at midnight. May the Creator bless you both!" P'Lau hurriedly left the Royal Court.

Here came the expected backlash from Commanders Superior Bette and G'Rosk. They verbally blasted Dan'L for having the audacity to speak directly to Emperor P'Lau, and ask for a change to their well-thought-out plans. Dan'L stood stiffly at attention while they ripped him up one side and down the other. Javette stood at the side and listened to them lambast her Son. He had to learn.

Nearly apoplectic, C.S. Bette demanded, "Why my Novice Kayla? Neither of you have any field experience. It is proper for one Borgund Ranger to accompany another!"

G'Rosk stated, "Commander Bok is your Company Commander, in charge of your safety and development. He has many years' field experience, and is an excellent Ranger."

Dan'L waited until their verbal attacks tired out, then requested permission to speak. "Commander Bok is a Borgund Ranger of the highest order, and I respect and admire him. But his eyes are those of a trained assassin; that 'do-or-die' look of a ruthless, uncompromising warrior, Commander Superior G'Rosk. The mercenaries will know it is an attempted set-up. Novice Kayla is a trained Emissary and Ambassador of Emperor P'Lau. She can withdraw from her emotions and reveal nothing in return. I am much safer with Kayla than Bok, Commanders Superior Bette and G'Rosk."

No one had rebuttal to Dan'L's logic. He was ordered to report to G'Rosk at 10p.m. to receive mission-specific information. They gave him copies of his red crystals to carry on his person, knowing the Rebels would also be curious about them.

C.S. Bette walked to her office quickly with Javette, and commented, "Your Son has your stubbornness. What Novice was ever so bold?"

Javette tried to suppress a smile, and said, "He has his Father's logic, and bravado. I would fight any battle with Commander Bok at my side. But he couldn't talk his way out of a paper bag, Commander Superior Bette." Both women chuckled. "How have you planned for Dan'L to escape from Duma Wat? Alive, I trust," Javette asked.

"Most certainly alive. The entire assignment is futile if we do not discover the answers to our questions. We will continually track his whereabouts, 24/7, and rescue him, Javette," Bette assured her.

"The mercenaries will scan and remove his ID chip capsule, as before. Any tracking device will also be found and removed," Javette commented.

Bette smiled and revealed, "We will track his DNA signature; our newest technology. Our Emperor does not want to lose a valuable Novice, Javette," she assured her. Javette saluted her Commander Superior and left to pack for her new assignment.

Dan'L shared his "last meal" with Sham'S and his fellow Novices, as if nothing special was happening at midnight tonight. Then he met his Mother at 9:30p.m., and they talked quietly in the Palace garden. "Do you think Father may still be alive, Mother?" He asked.

She replied, "I honestly don't know, Son. K'Ser was a very resourceful Borgund Ranger. But it's been months since he was reported killed in combat. I cannot have my hopes too high for his miraculous survival, and neither can you, Dan'L. You must focus your awareness and thoughts as never before during your meeting with the Traitor, Duma Wat. He was a graduate of the Royal Academy and Phase 1 Training, same as we were, and a favorite of the Court. He is wise, and wily, and not some common criminal," Javette cautioned. "He is also charismatic, so I've heard."

Dan'L nodded after listening to his Mother. He stood and gently touched a rose on the vine as she continued, "Duma Wat has successfully gained financial and political backing from some of the most influential aristocrats, Guild and Union leaders, and, some say, even top military officers. He is powerful. Be very careful, my Son. Very careful," she warned.

"And you take care, as well, Mother. I hear the little jungle planet Ban'Ti has more snakes and rats than the other planets combined. Keep your boots on!" Dan'L said, and they laughed together, walking through the garden to the Ranger residences.

Javette kissed her Son's cheek and said, "It's the two-legged snakes in the grass you must beware of Dan'L. Be safe, and return to me."

X

An outdoor entertainment mall at midnight is a perfect place for a date—or a kidnapping, Dan'L realized. He'd played games at this holographic arcade years ago. But now he looked at the mall stores, restaurants and arcades differently, with Ranger eyes.

Kayla and Dan'L strolled along, dressed in casual clothes, and held hands, as if they were on a date. They stopped in a café for a light meal. Dan'L ate little, remembering his prior experience being stunned with a belly full of hard cider. The arrangement was for the mercenaries to kidnap Dan'L and not harm the one who handed him over to them. Kayla was fun and looked very pretty, with her long black hair loose around her shoulders. *Maybe too pretty*, he suddenly thought, now wondering if asking for Kayla to help him was the safest idea for her.

They left the café and walked slowly along. Kayla asked him with a little more volume in her voice, "They have the newest games in here, Dan'L. Want to try your luck?" That was the signal. He agreed, and entered the open arcade with Kayla. The holographic machines in the front were powered down, tagged "Out of Service." A brightly-lit machine at the end caught his eye and they walked towards the back.

Dan'L slipped in a 5-credit coin to play. When he put his finger on the button to launch a holographic fighter, he was hit on his shoulder from behind. He turned to fight, and received a face full of stun gas. Dan'L collapsed on the floor. He awoke in a stifling darkness, and realized they had him restrained, and covered his head with a dark hood, tied around his neck. He coughed and gagged, but did not vomit, this time. Another attacker, a really ugly man, raised his hood and sprayed his face again, and Dan'L passed out.

After the three men tied up Dan'L, they attacked Kayla, attempting to gang rape the very pretty accomplice. They got more than they expected from Kayla. The attackers tried to spray her in the face to subdue her with stun gas, but she quickly fought them off, and eluded them. A bruised

Kayla made her report to C.S. Bette, and described the three men who hit and stunned Dan'L in detail. "After they knocked Dan'L out, the assailants tried to drag me in the back," she reported. "I batted the vial of stun gas out of the ugly man's hand, and fought the three men, just enough to get away from them. Then, I fled the scene, as ordered. Dan'L was unconscious."

Bette furrowed her brow and stated emphatically, "You're lucky you escaped, Kayla. We should have sent Commander Bok with Novice Dan'L. It was our original plan."

"Begging your pardon, Commander Superior, but those men were armed with laser guns. Commander Bok would have been shot," Kayla said matter-of-factly. "After I got away from them, I hid inside the alley and watched them load Novice Dan'L into a shuttle. Here are its tail numbers. They flew off at 12:46a.m., in a south-westerly direction." She handed a small note paper to Bette.

Bette said with conviction, "You are young and innocent, Kayla. Straight from the Royal Academy, into Phase 1, 2, and 3 Training. The world is more than you have experienced. All people are not respectable, loyal citizens of the Empire. You are not used to the type of men sent to capture Dan'L. If they had successfully subdued and raped you, they may have killed you afterwards, in order to eliminate the victim and only witness. These are not honorable men. But you did well, Novice Kayla."

Kayla thanked C.S. Bette for her concern, and Bette dismissed her. The eldest Shi'Lon Ranger watched the young Novice walk down the hall. The girl had confidence and carried herself well. Her skill with T'Ly martial arts in Phase 2 and 3 was well documented. But Kayla still had the veil of innocence about her. She was lucky tonight. Bette entered a recommendation in Kayla's file to have her serve in the Main Court, where she could meet and become familiar with many types of people. It was time for the girl to get acquainted with more of the world.

Bette called G'Rosk and updated him with the latest information. Kayla had described each man down to the color of their eyes and hair, clothing type, size and colors, and each wrinkle, scar, and mark on their faces. The men were located in the police database, and warrants for their arrests broadcast. "Where is Dan'L now, G'Rosk?" Bette asked.

"Off K'Halon Prime, on trajectory towards M'Wati. No other info on him is available at this time," he answered, and they clicked off. G'Rosk watched the DNA tracker for Dan'L very closely. He kept his trained eyes on the son of his late best friend K'Ser, and Javette.

Dan'L was fully restrained on a gurney, and being unloaded from the shuttle. The morons nearly dropped him coming down the hatch. They left his gurney near the shuttle to greet more men joining their party. Still hooded and restrained, he heard men arguing over credits, demanding their bounty. Then Dan'L heard laser blasts—their real reward for kidnapping him.

"Pick up the gurney and let's go," a man shouted. Where were they taking him now? Dan'L's thigh was stabbed by a hypo needle pen. He was knocked out again, for much longer, this time.

M'Wati, five days later

The nurse checked her patient's IV lines after changing his drip solution. She had never seen someone so young in such a dehydrated, heavily sedated state. "You poor boy," she said, and checked his vitals. A crewman walked in, demanding information on her patient. "He is recovering slowly, but remains unconscious. He needs a lot of work, and complete rest," she said, looking intently at the messenger, who took her information and quickly left.

The mercenaries kept Dan'L sedated the entire trip from K'Halon Prime to M'Wati. It was a long five-day flight, with M'Wati at its farthest orbital point from massive K'Halon Prime. The mercenaries slept, took drugs, and generally ignored their heavily sedated captive. They neglected him completely, never letting him awaken, never giving him water or nutrition. If Dan'L stirred, they sedated him again with the sedation drugs mixed with heroin. They were so drugged up they didn't realize they nearly overdosed their captive fatally.

In another two days, Dan'L awoke. He was suffering from hallucinations and delirium tremens due to severe dehydration, early heroin addiction, and overdosing on sedation drugs. His body was restrained with padded belts head to feet to keep him from harming himself. It took seven days to withdraw from the heavy sedation drugs and the heroin. Dan'L was so malnourished his ribs and cheekbones protruded; he looked gray and ghastly. When he could stand by himself, he was bathed and shaved, and brought to Duma Wat.

Dan'L was escorted to an empty room with amber lighting and told to sit in a chair at the long conference table. Several men walked into the room and stood behind their leader, Duma Wat. "Welcome, young Dan'L, son of K'Ser. I am Duma Wat, your host." Duma Wat watched silently while water was served to Dan'L. The young man drained every drop from the glass. He looked at his host with glazed-over eyes, trying desperately to focus.

"Let me first apologize to you, Dan'L. It was never my intent to drug you to the point of overdose, I assure you. I detest narcotics and all drugs, and do not permit their use among our personnel. Those who neglected and over-sedated you have been severely punished for the disregard of your wellbeing," Duma Wat said convincingly. "Are you now in control of your faculties?"

Dan'L answered hoarsely, "I cannot yet focus, sir. I am parched with thirst." More water was served to him, and again he drank the entire glassful.

Duma Wat said, "I am truly sorry, Dan'L. In a few days, your withdrawal symptoms will subside, and the drugs will be gone from your system. I will return you to your hospital bed in a few minutes. But, let me ask you this: Do you know why you are here in front of me now?"

Dan'L shook his head several times, and replied, "I do not know why. I have done nothing wrong, or done anything against you. I don't know anyone important. I'm only a Novice, newly confirmed, sir. I know noth…'" Dan'L suddenly passed out again, his head falling on the table with a loud "thud."

"Take him back to hospital now. Notify me when he is stronger," an angry Duma Wat ordered, and walked out.

"Withdrawal from the red poppy is difficult. Add a synthetic sedative to the mix, and the physical symptoms are brutal," the Doctor stated, shaking his head. "His kidneys nearly shut down. I hope whoever did this to the boy is punished. If he had been under sedation and injected with heroin much longer, he would be brain dead." The physician wrote orders for Dan'L's continued treatment and dietary requirements, checked him out thoroughly once more, and left his room. Nurses inserted feeding tubes into his stomach through his esophagus and delivered liquid protein into his system. But the fluid was immediately rejected by his stomach.

In three days, some color was returning to his sunken cheeks from being able to eat soft foods, and keep them down. Dan'L chewed fruit-flavored syrupy ices all day long, and drank pitcher after pitcher of cold water. Vanilla pudding became his favorite food, and he ate bowls of it. They added protein supplements to it in a day or so. He was given red ginseng powder fruit smoothies, and ice cream shakes mixed with fruit and soy protein powder. But the smell of cooked food made him nauseous. Nutritional supplements were given to him four times a day.

Once more in front of Duma Wat, Dan'L proclaimed ignorance as to why he was there. "If you tell me what you're looking for, I will try to help you, sir. I don't know why I'm here. You brought me here for some reason. But I don't know what it is. I know nothing. I have no fortune. I am a Novice Borgund Ranger, and I belong to Emperor P'Lau. I live where I am told, wear my uniforms, and do my assigned work. How can I help you, sir?"

Duma Wat was losing patience with him. He said, "You are the son of K'Ser, a Master Commander Borgund Ranger. He called you the night before he was killed. We have the comm link recordings. He sent you something a few days beforehand by common carrier. What did he say to you, and what did he send to you, Novice Dan'L?"

"My Father called me every other week when I was in Ranger Training, Fridays after 10p.m. We last talked about Phase 3 Training, and the sulphur springs swimming finals. The springs are near-boiling, and you must swim through the many interconnected springs very fast, or burn. All he sent me was the ES tech manual, to give me a head start on the technical specs for flight training. I swear, Duma Wat; I swear!" Dan'L stood, emphatically pleading his case. He vomited on the floor violently, and then collapsed.

Dan'L was taken to his hospital room again. He had lost several pounds of muscle mass in the last two weeks. Liquid protein was again infused directly into his small intestine to build up his strength. But his weakness and failure to recall recent events surrounding his Father, and his failure to remember the remains sent to his Mother, worked to his advantage, although unbeknown to Dan'L. Duma Wat had to keep him alive longer.

XI

Ban'Ti

Negotiations between two warring, hostile Rebel leaders were not her usual assignment. But Imperial Planetary Governor Lem had personally requested emergency Imperial assistance. The Governor managed to postpone the Rebel negotiations for several days, in anticipation of the Imperial Negotiator's arrival. Javette received her full briefing regarding the dangerous situation on Ban'Ti the day before she landed her ES warbird on its space port, one of the few areas cleared from the planet's thick jungle. Her track record of successful negotiations for the Emperor during the last twenty years was without equal. Javette was the top Imperial Negotiator.

A Space Cadre destroyer group nearest Ban'Ti was ordered in immediately after her departure from K'Halon Prime, but the Imperial ships needed two and a half more hours to get into firing range of the orbiting Rebel ships. Javette had to negotiate for Governor Lem's release, and stall the quarreling Rebels at least three hours. An Army security shuttle picked her up and flew her to the Ban'Ti Governor's mansion in H'Lel, the little planet's capital.

The Imperial Army had surrounded the mansion with every type of land assault craft in its arsenal. Rebels had the mansion wired to blow top to bottom. Their old, dilapidated vehicles were parked right next to the mansion. The Rebels held the Planetary Governor hostage, with his family and staff—the reason the experienced Shi'Lon Ranger was sent in to negotiate.

"Sure you want to me land, Master Commander, ma'am?" The Army pilot asked Javette, looking at the beautiful woman in her black cloak. "Not a very nice place for a lady like you," he observed quietly. She smiled and touched his hand, and thanked him as she stepped out of the shuttle. Javette walked through the open front door, knowing fifty or more Rebel laser rifles were pointing at her.

She stopped inside the mansion foyer, looked at the armed Rebels pointing their laser rifles at her, and raised her hands, showing she carried no rifle. She announced, "I am Master Commander Javette, Shi'Lon Ranger and Emissary of the Great Emperor P'Lau. I have come in peace, and you will let me pass." The Rebels were ordered to show Javette to her room by Colonel Vas, where she could freshen up and wait to be called.

The Rebel Colonel Vas knocked on Javette's door in ten minutes, and escorted her to the large dining room, where "negotiations" were taking place. Laser rifles and pistols were piled in a corner. Imperial Planetary Governor Lem sat in a chair, bound and gagged, and shaking. The Rebels were not going to let him get another emergency message off to the Emperor. At one end of the long table was a Rebel General. His face was hard and rough, with a scar running from his scalp through his now-blind left eye, down his cheek. Javette could smell him even from the doorway.

At the other end of the table, Colonel Vas politely signaled for her to sit in the middle, between the men. Vas was a former Imperial Army officer, defector to the Rebellion, and loyal to Duma Wat. He was the second-in-command for the Rebellion, and Duma Wat's right-hand man. Opposing factions within the Rebel forces both claimed the upcoming Ban'Ti harvest profits. The only real trades Ban'Ti had going for the entire planet were fresh vegetables, sweet, highly prized delectable fruits, and natural gas. Snakeskin for making shoes and fashion accessories was also important. *Plenty of snakes here*, Javette thought to herself.

Colonel Vas spoke first: "We landed here as one force, to take food and harvest profits for our comrades. We took Governor Lem hostage without incident, and all was going according to plan. No one was threatened, or hurt. Then, this animal arrived with his criminals, and began killing off the field workers, demanding credits, and women for his men to ravage!"

Other officers at the table began shouting, making threats, and starting to fight. General Int stood and bellowed, "Shut the hell up!" He fired one shot of his laser pistol into the ceiling, and the men quieted down. The ceiling was full of holes. Javette held out her gloved hand and quietly took his pistol from him.

"Duma Wat has not shared his spoils of war and good fortune with us for sixteen months. My men are hungry as wolves, for both food and comfort," General Int said, licking his lips at Javette. "Duma Wat owes us. We are not leaving without the harvest and its credits, and the women of Ban'Ti!" The General yelled, pounding his dirty fist on the table, and his men agreed. The arguing and shouting then continued.

Javette arbitrated the "Negotiations" for more than three hours, asking strategic questions of each man, to keep the conversation alive. Vas was asking for only the harvest profits; Int wanted to rape, pillage and plunder everything on Ban'Ti, including taking the harvest profits. Emperor P'Lau sent her there to convince both groups of Rebels to surrender Governor Lem to her, and leave Ban'Ti peacefully. The Governor was terrified, full of fear for his wife and four daughters, and his female staff members. He had good reason to be afraid for them. The women were locked in the basement by Colonel Vas for their protection when General Int and his Rebels arrived, and kept under constant guard—a wise move in his favor. The man still had honor, Javette noted.

It was a true test of Javette's skills to set aside her disgust of General Int and his filthy men, all of them murderers, thieves, and rapists. Not one of them displayed any shred of decency. Duma Wat had cut these despicable men free, hoping they would break off from the main Rebellion, dry up and blow away. But they followed Duma Wat's Rebel fleet to little Ban'Ti, with its harvest at hand. Shrewd move.

The negotiations reached a lull. Neither side would budge an inch, or allow Governor Lem and his family to be released. The men appeared tired from screaming at each other, and answering Javette's endless questions. They took a short break and returned to the dining table. Sandwiches made from undisclosed meat were served. There were no large mammals on Ban'Ti. No deer, hogs, sheep, or cows were raised there, so the meat in the sandwiches was probably snake or rat meat. Javette politely declined any food. General Int and his men gobbled up the food with their filthy hands. Colonel Vas grimaced in disgust of the men's total lack of manners.

Javette checked her incoming comm link text from C.S. Bette, and it confirmed the Space Cadre destroyer attack group was in position. Her stalling techniques worked. Imperial Negotiator Javette opened the final session: "We have reached a stalemate, gentlemen. Unless either Colonel Vas or General Int have any other pertinent information to be considered, it is time for a resolution to this matter." She waited patiently, but no one else spoke.

"The Great Emperor P'Lau has sworn protection for each Imperial Governor and his or her family, including Governor Lem. Any hostile action taken by either of you against Imperial Planetary Governor Lem or any of his family members will result in the swift retaliation from Imperial forces." Javette swept her arm and said, "This entire compound is surrounded by the Imperial Army, its well-trained troops and their weapons."

"We have them in our sights!" General Int bragged, and his officers at the table laughed.

She looked at the greasy villain intensely, and said, "That is true, General Int. But, consider this, if you would: for each 'lean wolf' with a laser rifle, there are a hundred Imperial troops with him in their sights. Your vehicles will be demolished in seconds by Imperial Army missiles. A Space Cadre destroyer attack group is now in orbit around Ban'Ti, waiting for my signal, or lack thereof. They will obliterate your orbiting vessels. But the two of you, Colonel Vas and General Int: you will be captured alive, to stand trial before the High Court Tribunal, after many months in solitary confinement in the prison under ground, with only porridge to eat." She let that image sink in for a few seconds.

"There is nothing to be gained here now. No harvest profits will be given to either of you. You have reached an impasse. Your forces are completely surrounded, both here in this mansion, and in Ban'Ti's orbit. This has become a suicide mission for your men. It is too late. If even one of your Rebels takes it upon himself to fire his weapon, all will die—except you, General Int, and Colonel Vas," Javette calmly assessed, staring each man in his eyes.

Realizing he had been expertly played by Javette, Colonel Vas asked, "Then, what is to be done? You did not come here empty handed, I'm certain of it, Shi'Lon Ranger. What does your Emperor offer us?"

"He offers us only death!" Int yelled, and pounded the table again. His men were silent, looking at Javette.

Javette stood and said, "The Great Emperor P'Lau is offering to let all Rebels retreat from Ban'Ti without threat of Space Cadre pursuit for twenty-four hours. This is your only chance. Shoulder your arms, and withdraw. Board your ships and leave now, and live. The word of the Emperor is true. Leave now, and live." She subtly crossed her arms, targeting Colonel Vas and General Int with the hidden stun darts in her arm bands.

Several moments of silence passed. "The loyal followers of Duma Wat accept your offer. We leave in peace. We leave now, Ranger," Colonel Vas said. He stood and said to his officers, "Order our men to shoulder arms, withdraw without fire, and shuttle to our ships in orbit. Full retreat. Everyone. Right now!"

M.C. Javette reported the information to C.S. Bette. The Imperial Army was ordered to let the Rebels retreat, and leave in peace. General Int's officers peered out of the windows. "It's true, sir. The Army is letting them board their shuttles. Colonel Vas's men are lifting off now. We can go," an officer said.

"You should all leave in peace now," Javette calmly advised. "Leave now, and live."

"I'm not leaving until Ban'Ti is mine; her credits, and her women! And you will be my personal pet, Ranger!" The General shouted. But his officers ran outside, ordering their men to shoulder their weapons and run to the shuttles. More Rebels boarded their beat-up shuttles and lifted off. Javette was alone with the General, and the terrified, bound Governor Lem.

"Cowards!" General Int yelled through the open window, watching his Rebels run to their shuttles. He ordered his men to fire, screaming at his retreating Rebels. Not one shot was fired. The furious General reached for a hidden laser pistol from his boot and pointed it at Governor Lem. Javette drew her plasma sword and cut off his hand holding the pistol in one quick move. The General screamed in agony, and bellowed a stream of profanities.

"Your pain is just beginning, Rebel," Javette said. She touched a particular place on her breastplate, and a sedative dart was shot into the General's chest. He collapsed on the floor. She removed the governor's gag and bindings, and he was reunited with his grateful wife and family. Javette reported the situation to C.S. Bette. Then, the Imperial Army Captain and his security squad secured the Governor's mansion, and successfully removed all the Rebel-installed incendiaries. Army troops and drones patrolled the compound, the surrounding buildings in H'Lel, and the jungle perimeter of H'Lel for hours, and found not one Rebel.

M.C. Javette watched the Imperial troops take the sedated body of the criminal General Int to their transport. Thank the Creator she didn't have to haul his disgusting, smelly body back in her ship for five days. Now— where was her Son, Dan'L?

XII

Home World

The Great Emperor P'Lau was secretly flown back to Home World by Commander Bok, and escorted by another three ES-class fighters flown by other Borgund Rangers. Only highly-qualified Shi'Lon and Borgund Rangers had the super-fast ES-class fighters. The Emperor left his Imperial Command Battle Cruiser hovering above K'Halon Prime, still undergoing General Inspection.

"The blueprint plainly showed the interior of our Imperial Command Battle Cruiser. If your scanners cannot reveal any anomaly within the ship, then dismantle the craft, and examine every section individually with teams of inspectors. Something is amiss, Fleet Admiral U'Ret, and you must discover what it is!" Emperor P'Lau ordered. How could that man not discover the unidentified mass so clearly shown in the 5D holographic blueprint? It was inside his personal chambers in the Royal Suite, in the very center of the senior officers' deck.

"Recent scans showed nothing in your quarters, Sire. And my men have searched every millimeter of your Royal Suite, my Emperor," Admiral U'Ret stated. It was obvious the Admiral expected the Emperor to accept his explanation; but the Emperor later order the search to be resumed by his Imperial Guardsmen. Still, nothing was found. Commander Nat'N, the commanding officer of the Imperial Guards recently assigned to the Battle Cruiser, suggested whatever was showing on the holographic blueprint had been secretly moved prior to their search. Unfortunately, no one could tell what the anomaly was; it was in a large insulated crate or box.

The Emperor cancelled the next few days of K'Halon Palace Court activities, to not draw attention to his absence. He visited K'Halon Prime three times yearly; M'Wati twice a year; and little Ban'Ti once every other year. He kept an "open court" policy, so he was usually available five days a week in person or by live vid comm. But it was now imperative to be unpredictable. P'Lau called an emergency Ranger High Command meeting in his private, small Royal Court at the Home World Palace. C.S. Vu'Duc was with Commander Bok. From K'Halon Prime, Commanders Superior G'Rosk and Bette, and Novice Kayla was vid conferenced in with them.

P'Lau was noticeably anxious. He asked, "Do we know where my newest Faithful Son Dan'L is today? What about his signal strength; has it improved?"

Vu'Duc answered, "Yes, Sire. Dan'L is still on M'Wati. His signal is weak, but positively identified. He appears to be gaining strength, as his signal is registering sharper than a few days ago." Kayla looked at C.S. Bette anxiously; this was the first she heard anything about her best friend Dan'L in many days.

The Emperor paced in his Royal Court, while they waited for him to speak. "And where is Master Commander Javette? She concluded that nasty business on Ban'Ti quite handily. The Mother is most likely consumed with worry over her Son. Where is she?"

Bette answered quickly, "She is within range of K'Halon Prime, my Emperor, due to arrive tonight, as ordered." *Emperor P'Lau appears very disconcerted*, Bette thought to herself.

Emperor P'Lau sat at his table and said, "We have sent our youngest, finest, and most brave Faithful Son into the jaws of the dragon; directly into the hands of Duma Wat. No words of his visit, communications, or demands from his Rebels are forthcoming. If nothing is heard in five days, we must assume the worst. So, prepare for retaliation, but take no actions without my direct command. We must give our Novice Dan'L every chance. But he must not be abandoned," P'Lau stated firmly. "Novice Dan'L must be returned to us unharmed."

Novice Kayla whispered into Bette's ear, then Bette asked, "Are there any other messages from within the red crystal holograph, Sire?"

He shook his head and replied, "No, nothing new has been found."

"What about the reference to the advanced androids and the powerful green crystal, my Emperor?" Novice Kayla asked him directly, and received a glare from Bette.

Emperor P'Lau looked at Kayla and replied, "Nothing, yet. But we are highly concerned about the reference, Kayla. A research vessel has been dispatched to the White Belt and SB5, where K'Ser was killed in battle. The circumstances are a bit...sketchy," the Emperor revealed. "Follow this line, my Beloved Daughter. There may be more than a mere reference to them," P'Lau said, and smiled at his newest Beloved Daughter, pleased with her contribution. But the Emperor's smile would not save Kayla from receiving a comeuppance from C.S. Bette later.

Dan'L was regaining his health and strength. When he completed his first martial arts routine since being on M'Wati, he was brought before Duma Wat again. He asked Dan'L, "Why did your Father K'Ser call you the day before he died? What did he leave you? What was contained on the red crystals? And do you know why I have brought you here, Novice Dan'L?"

A frustrated Dan'L answered, "Duma Wat, sir, I have told you all I know. My Father called me every other week after 10p.m. He called after the burning sulphur springs swimming finals. My only inheritance from my Father was a beat-up Borgund Ranger belt buckle, a bone-handled knife, and two red crystals containing the tech manual for the ES warbirds. My Commander Superior G'Rosk analyzed the red crystals and they checked out, sir." He took his wallet out of his pocket, removed the two red memory crystal copies, and handed them to Duma Wat. He asked, "Are you building an ES warbird, sir?"

The men guarding Duma Wat laughed with him at Dan'L's question. "No, young Ranger. I could buy an entire squadron of fighters for the cost of one ES," Duma Wat said. "We checked those crystals out while you were unconscious. You may keep them, Novice."

"Thank you, sir. They were my Father's and are important to me. May I ask again: Why am I here, sir? Am I a hostage?" Dan'L asked. He was thinking much more clearly than when Duma Wat questioned him earlier, when he was recovering from being overdosed, and dehydrated. He had to pose his questions carefully, now.

Duma Wat replied, "You are my guest, Novice Dan'L. Now; will you willingly submit to a truth analyzer? Or will I have to give you truth gas?"

The young man quickly replied, "I'd prefer no more drugs enter my body, sir. I volunteer for the truth analyzer." Maybe then he'd discover what Duma Wat was probing for, depending on what questions they asked.

An old truth analyzer was set up on a side table. Dan'L had clamps clipped onto his index fingers. Wide sensor bands were strapped onto his forehead, chest and forearms. Then he was asked his name, rank, address, and so on, to establish a base line for questioning. After minor calibration adjustments to the analyzer, the real questions began from the Rebel interrogator: "Why did K'Ser call you before he died?"

"He called me to make certain I'd passed the sulphur springs swimming finals," Dan'L replied calmly. The same questions were posed to him over and over about his Father's calls to him the night before he died; what was on the red crystals; and why was he brought before Duma Wat. Dan'L answered each question the same way he had before. When Duma Wat looked at the analyzer's read-out, he became angry, and ordered Dan'L to be sprayed with truth gas.

When his eyes dilated, the same three questions were once again asked of Dan'L. He answered each question identically, as he had done so before.

Then Duma Wat stooped down, nose to nose with the seated Dan'L, and asked a new question, "Do you know how and where your Father, Master Commander K'Ser, was killed?"

Dan'L answered with red eyes, "By plasma disrupter arc fire, I was told, sir, in the White Belt, on the ruins of SB5." A few tears silently rolled down his cheeks.

Duma Wat eased up, and casually asked, "Have you ever personally witnessed plasma disrupter arc fire, Novice Dan'L?"

He replied while shaking his head, "Oh no, sir. It's too dangerous. But I've seen vids of them in training. We don't get those guns issued to us until our second year."

The Rebels chuckled at his answer. "Would you expect to find in-tact remains of a human body killed by such a weapon, young Ranger?" Duma Wat asked, strolling in front of him.

"No, not very much. The vids showed much damage," Dan'L answered. Then he looked directly at Duma Wat and asked, "Are you going to kill me this way? Or are we going to SB5, to investigate the scene of my Father's death?"

"Perhaps we will go to SB5. I have not decided yet," Duma Wat answered.

Dan'L asked, "We have to travel near the White Belt to go home to K'Halon Prime, don't we? An investigation would take us how far off course, sir?"

Duma Wat smiled at his question, and answered, "A day and a half. But why do you want to go to K'Halon Prime, Dan'L? M'Wati is beautiful with a warm climate, and not as cold as K'Halon Prime."

"It's my duty station, and my home. Mother will be very angry I missed roll call this morning. I should be going now," Dan'L responded, and tried to get up. He was forced to sit again by a Rebel.

"Spray him again," Duma Wat ordered. He kept the temper of his questioning light, keeping the young man conversing freely without fear. For over an hour the interrogation continued. But the information Duma Wat was searching for did not surface. "Either you're hopelessly honest with nothing to reveal, or you've been trained in deep submersion techniques. Which is it, Novice Dan'L?"

The young man's eyes lit up, and he excitedly sat bolt upright. "Submersion? I'm a certified diver, sir! Are we going diving today?"

That was too much for the Rebels. They burst out laughing, even Duma Wat. "Oh, Dan'L, Dan'L. I think I paid too much for you, Novice. One last question: do you know why I brought you here?"

"To go diving on M'Wati!" Dan'L quickly replied, and they all laughed.

Duma Wat threw his hands in the air in frustration. He had used every ounce of patience with the young man. "Prepare our command destroyer.

We will leave as soon as it is fueled and provisioned. Everyone prepare to depart in three hours."

The Rebel destroyer and its support vessels departed in three hours, on course for the floating, abandoned wreckage of SB5 in the White Belt. Duma Wat reconsidered his options regarding the young Ranger. He had initially decided to interrogate him and get the answers to his questions, then demand a large ransom from the Emperor for him. Duma Wat was prepared to torture the boy to get answers, but perhaps another path had opened for him. After the last interview, he determined silently to turn Dan'L to his side. The Novice was open and honest with him, and seemed to have nothing to hide. They had a good repartee going.

No one was sent to rescue the boy, either, highly unusual. Rangers were the top tier of their warrior class, and their training was worth more than a million credits. He would use that fact to convince Dan'L his Emperor had given up on him, and left him for dead. The Emperor P'Lau would be furious to lose one of his treasured, young Faithful Sons to the Rebellion. Converting a Ranger would be a victory for Duma Wat, and a direct hit to the gut of his half-brother, the Emperor P'Lau.

XIII

Home World

A full Imperial Battleship group and several support vessels were deployed to M'Wati, escorted by two squadrons of fighters. Comm. Bok and M.C. T'Anh traveled with the battleship, on direct orders of Emperor P'Lau. Novice Kayla was sent with T'Anh, for reasons never fully disclosed to the senior Shi'Lon Ranger.

"You are to negotiate for the release of Novice Dan'L, Master Commander T'Anh. I want my Faithful Son returned to me unharmed," Emperor P'Lau ordered. "We are sending Novice Kayla to assist you in this endeavor. She is showing great promise. Her talents may blossom even more while under your expert guidance. It is my will," he stated, noticing T'Anh's disposition change when he mentioned Kayla's assignment to her. T'Anh bowed and quickly left the Main Court for her mission.

T'Anh stood on the observation deck of the battleship, contemplating her upcoming task with the Rebel Leader, Duma Wat. She met Duma Wat twenty years ago, when he was a favorite of the Court, prior to Emperor P'Lau being crowned. This was a dangerous assignment, made even more so by having to babysit a Novice. The girl talked every hour she was awake, or so it seemed. T'Anh was not the talkative type of woman, and "friendly chatter" annoyed her. She socialized infrequently, had only a few close friends, and kept to herself most of the time. The senior Ranger felt put-upon by the Emperor's decision to have Novice Kayla accompany her. The Emperor obviously favored the young, raven-haired Novice.

"Is that the White Belt ahead, Master Commander T'Anh? It is beautiful!" Novice Kayla exclaimed, suddenly next to her. This was her first flight beyond K'Halon Prime and its moons. The young Novice was fascinated.

T'Anh answered, "Yes, it is the White Belt, full of asteroids, broken planetary matter, many sizes of ice rock crystals, and mercenaries. From

75

here, it is beautiful. But travel inside the White Belt is very dangerous. Even experienced pilots lose their way; have their ships damaged by wayward asteroids; or fall prey to ruthless mercenaries. A course we fortunately do not have to take for this mission, Novice Kayla."

Kayla listened to her senior Shi'Lon Ranger describing the While Belt intently. She turned her gaze from T'Anh, to not make T'Anh feel compelled to correct or chastise her for some reason. Kayla could feel the woman's constant irritation with her, like a pebble in her boot. T'Anh could not hide her resentment towards Kayla, for her being assigned to tag along during this important mission. But fortunately, the battleship was very big with many places to explore, and many people to converse with besides T'Anh. Kayla thanked T'Anh and left the observation lounge.

The next day, the comm link on T'Anh's breastplate beeped from C.S. Bette, who said, "The DNA tracking now shows our package is on a trajectory towards old SB5, near the White Belt. The battleship group will change course soon. Be prepared to launch in three hours for SB5, in stealth mode. You and your Novice and Commander Bok will hold in orbit near SB5 and await further orders, Master Commander T'Anh. Bette out."

"My Novice," she mumbled to herself. Novices were usually assigned to Commanders or First Commanders, not Master Commanders. T'Anh notified "Her Novice Kayla," and packed out of her room on the battleship. The ES warbirds were super-fast, but small. The chatty Novice asked about everything. You can't understand everything on your first mission, T'Anh knew. Novice Kayla walked quickly to the hangar deck, where M.C. T'Anh was already at the controls, readying her ES warbird.

While performing her pre-flight systems check, T'Anh looked at Novice Kayla, busy documenting the test results. Kayla was young and strong, with smooth, porcelain-white skin, bright green eyes, and a very pretty face. No wonder the Novice was the new favorite of the Emperor. Looking at her own reflection, T'Anh saw the hard face of a mature woman. Many freckles helped hide the lines at her eyes and mouth, but the wrinkles showed when she smiled, or frowned. Her red hair was in its usual long braid. *Once upon a time, I was P'Lau's favorite,* she mused. T'Anh felt suddenly tired; she was now a babysitter to his newest pet.

By the time Duma Wat's Rebel command destroyer was in range of abandoned SB5, Commander Bok and M.C. T'Anh were hovering around the station, concealed in stealth mode. Only the ES warbirds had the new stealth defense system. A shuttle launched from the Rebel destroyer towards SB5. Bok and T'Anh were ordered to follow the shuttle, and land on the same deck with it, still in stealth. Their ships' stealth mode kept them undetected, but it would have to be disengaged before they could open the hatch and leave their ES warbirds.

The Rebel shuttle landed on the damaged main hangar bay of SB5 carefully. Dust and debris from the earlier plasma disrupter arc explosion swirled around the landing shuttle, keeping the Rebel occupants from seeing much of anything until the dust clouds settled. The swirling dust gave the ES fighters perfect cover, and they landed on the opposite end of the hangar deck. Their ships also stirred up dust and debris, but the Rebels did not notice. After ten minutes, the Rebels opened their shuttle hatch and descended, wearing their old space suits. They roughly pushed Novice Dan'L down the hatch. His DNA tracker onboard T'Anh's ES warbird flashed brightly, and pointed at Dan'L as he walked slowly. *He is clumsy in a full space suit*, T'Anh noted. *Another inexperienced Novice.*

T'Anh selected her full space suit from the three types stored onboard her ES warbird, and stepped into it. She watched Kayla put on her own space suit and check the seals. They attached each other's heavy jet pack to the suits, and tightened their helmets' seals. With all suit seals tight and breathing apparatus unobstructed, T'Anh signaled Commander Bok they were ready. In precisely three minutes, both ES warbirds disengaged stealth mode, and the Rangers quickly left their ships.

"Close and lock hatch. Shields on half power," T'Anh said to her warbird. The three Rangers walked carefully well behind the Rebel landing party, aware their presence on SB5 was now known to Duma Wat and his Rebels. They kept some distance from the Rebel landing party. Only Bok was armed, his laser rifle slung over his left shoulder.

SB5 was over one hundred years old. It had been the victim of far too many errant asteroid impacts. The largest, most destructive asteroid knocked SB5 out of orbit, into the edge of the White Belt, and into the paths of many asteroids. The crew and civilians aboard were evacuated after another errant asteroid "bomber" tore off half its main docking bay, and caused many explosions from ruptured fuel and oxygen storage tanks. SB5 now floated along the edge of the White Belt with all the planetary fragments and other space junk. The Rangers were told SB5 had been restored to partial functionality several months ago, but the previous plasma disrupter arc explosion and crash landing of an alien ship on the main hangar deck sealed SB5's fate, once and for all. No one could live there now, at least not full time.

The Rebels took Dan'L with them into the adjacent cargo storage bays, where M.C. K'Ser died in battle. K'Ser traced Rebel spies there and uncovered their hidden lair of stolen fuel cells, and a large cache of field weapons and ammunition. K'Ser also reported discovery of several autonomous androids in the crash of their alien ship. The androids were highly advanced, non-violent towards him, and definitely not of Imperial origin. They were alien androids, over two meters tall, and looked very futuristic in design.

The Rebel Captain told Dan'L, "This scorched bay is where K'Ser met his fate. Our plasma disrupter arc fire destroyed nearly everything, including the ES, and one of our own Rebel fighters. A few of our men beyond the security door were able to evade the battle, and stayed hidden until they could be rescued. But everything in this cargo bay was annihilated."

"By Petrov," Dan'L stated. He walked about carefully. The destruction was in a clear arc pattern: emanating from a tight, narrow point of origin, then spreading out to cover a very wide angle. Cargo boxes and storage locker doors were deformed from the intense blast. Well-defined body shadows out from the point of origin still lie undisturbed on the floor. One of those body shadows belonged to his Father, Dan'L realized. He stared at the body shadows, and his emotions swelled inside him.

Now Dan'L realized why C.S. G'Rosk and Duma Wat questioned the authenticity of his Father's remains. K'Ser—or someone else—must have put his belt, knife, and his wallet in some type of container, planting them safely before the battle. Or, K'Ser survived the battle and destruction, and left the artifacts behind for the Space Cadre troops to find. But why? And, if he was still alive, where was his Father? Was he hiding on board SB5, still alive? Dan'L looked around the cargo bay, and wondered how anyone could have survived the battle, or still be alive in this wrecked heap of metal.

The Rebels watched their "guest" walk slowly through the burned-out bay, recording his every move for Duma Wat. Dan'L suddenly looked up, and used his space suit thrusters to fly to the top of the bay. Watching silently from the opposite entrance of the storage bay, the three Rangers notified C.S. G'Rosk when Dan'L flew to the upper area of the bay. G'Rosk ordered the Shi'Lon Rangers to follow, and for Bok to hide and give them cover, if necessary.

Dan'L caught the twisted rail of the upper catwalk, and guided himself to the top corner. It was completely scorched and black, except for a small, blinking green light. He slowed his forward movement significantly, and then stopped. "It's an android head! His eyes are blinking! Look!" Dan'L exclaimed. "He's blinking at us!"

The Rebels used their space suit thrusters and flew to the catwalk where Novice Dan'L was holding on to the damaged support rail. The remnants of a large android head and partial shoulder lie on the catwalk, and the android's eyes were blinking green light. M.C. T'Anh flew in front of the Rebels and Dan'L, cautioning, "Stand back! Do not approach it! I am Master Commander T'Anh, Shi'Lon Ranger, sent to observe. For your own safety, do not go any closer to the android. It is of alien origin, and its capabilities are unknown." The Rebels were briefly taken aback to see the two Shi'Lon Rangers in their black space suits, but they quickly raised their laser rifles at them when T'Anh began speaking. T'Anh and Kayla raised both their arms, showing they were unarmed, and the Rebels did not fire at them.

"The android is signaling, sending some sort of communications, Master Commander T'Anh. His blinking pattern is repetitive," Novice Kayla noted. "He is calling for help." She touched her helmet vid cam to zoom in and record the android and his blinking green eyes in greater detail. The Rebels motioned with their laser rifles, indicating the group was to return to their shuttle.

The only armed Ranger, Commander Bok, watched the scene from his hidden position. Bok saw the Rebels point their laser rifles at T'Anh and Kayla. When they motioned for the Shi'Lon Rangers and Dan'L to move to the Rebel shuttle, Bok silently disappeared into the wreckage. He waited for the Rebel shuttle to depart SB5, then quickly flew to his ES warbird, and called the situation in to his Commander Superior. G'Rosk ordered Bok to engage the stealth mode, remain on SB5, and monitor the Shi'Lon Rangers' movements through their suit vid cams. He did so, and connected the Shi'Lon Rangers suit vid cams to his comm link, enabling them to be monitored both on his ship and at the Ranger High Command on Home World and K'Halon Prime.

The Rebels delivered the Shi'Lon Rangers to Duma Wat immediately, and removed their helmets while the two women stood with their hands in the air. "We have been sent to observe your expedition to SB5, and to ascertain the health and well-being of the Borgund Ranger Novice Dan'L," T'Anh explained to Duma Wat. "We carry no laser rifles. We made no aggressive moves against your men, although we surprised them with our appearance in the cargo bay of SB5. We come in peace."

Duma Wat stared at the senior Shi'Lon Ranger cautiously, with his brows deeply furrowed. He said, "I am fully aware of a Shi'Lon Ranger's hidden weaponry. You are never unarmed." He looked at Kayla, noticing her calm demeanor, and made a mental note of the young woman's face, and her lack of fear of him. "Your presence here is an unwelcome surprise. We claimed the right of salvage for the abandoned Space Base 5 several years ago, and do so, again. This property is ours. You are trespassing on our property."

T'Anh buried her emotions, and calmly said, "I am Master Commander T'Anh, the Emissary of the Great Emperor P'Lau. You and I met many years ago in the Royal Palace, Duma Wat. Our Emperor authorized me to negotiate the peaceful return of his Novice Dan'L. I come in peace." She looked at Dan'L, standing beside Kayla, watching and listening.

Duma Wat looked directly at Kayla and asked, "And why are you here, young Shi'Lon? What is your duty?"

Kayla replied, "I am Novice Kayla, sir. I am to assist Master Commander T'Anh, in whatever way she deems necessary. We want Dan'L to return with us, sir." She bowed her head a little to him.

Duma Wat motioned towards Dan'L, and said, "Novice Dan'L is my guest. He and I have business to discuss. You are both trespassers, and are now my prisoners. Enjoy the comforts of our brig," Duma Wat said firmly. "Be careful not to touch the Shi'Lon Rangers," he cautioned his men. "They are never unarmed, and their garments will shock you." He whispered something to one of the Rebel officers next to him. Kayla felt a sudden chill down her spine; she instinctively knew Duma Wat just ordered their execution.

Before his men came forward to take them down the corridor, Kayla boldly asked, "Sir, may this Novice ask one question of you, please?" Duma Wat nodded. "The alien android is signaling for help. What will you do when his rescue party arrives?"

Duma Wat jumped up from his seat and yelled, "Alien android? What alien android? Take them to the brig now!" He turned in anger to his men as the Shi'Lon Rangers were led down the hall to the brig. The women were ordered into an empty cell. They heard the adjacent cell door close loudly with a bang. Soon, they heard light tapping.

"Kayla? Is it you, Kayla? It's Dan'L, Kayla. Are you all right? How did you find me? We need to get out of here," he whispered. "I want to go home."

"Hi, Dan'L. Are you okay now? I heard you were sick for a long time," Kayla whispered to him. "We have to..."

"Both of you keep quiet. They are listening," T'Anh interjected. She removed her space suit and paced. *The damned Rebels confiscated their helmets so they couldn't escape without a ship. And now this Novice is talking again*, she thought to herself. The Rebels were smarter than she initially credited them. Would they give her a chance to negotiate, or would they just try to kill them? Both the Shi'Lon Rangers wore their breastplates and backplates and their arm bands under their space suits, as Duma Wat knew, and were not without some weapons. She touched the handle of her plasma sword behind her neck and smiled. The Rebels would not kill her without a fight. She looked at Kayla, who sat on the hard bed, watching her. The Novice was well known for her fighting skills among the new Novices. One thing in the young girl's favor, she realized, and almost smiled at Kayla.

Rebels came for Dan'L, and brought him before Duma Wat again. But this time, he was restrained and sprayed with a double dose of truth gas. An angry Duma Wat said, "I do not have the time for pleasant conversation any longer, Novice Dan'L. You have seen the battle site on SB5. Now, I ask you again: why have I brought you here?"

Dan'L tried to focus on the face of Duma Wat, but was too drugged to do so. He answered, "You brought me here as witness to my Father's last stand, and to see the body shadow left behind when your Rebel Petrov caused his death." Dan'L immediately realized his slip of the tongue was a grave mistake.

This was additional information coming from the young man. Duma Wat questioned further, demanding answers from Dan'L, and no longer treated the boy as his guest. "What about the power crystals? We recorded everything transpiring in the SB5 bay with K'Ser and the androids. We heard them tell him the crystals were very powerful. And you tell me they're only stored technical specs! Now, you will answer my questions, and cease this charade!" He signaled to his men to begin assaulting Dan'L, beating him and kicking his legs. "And how is it you know Petrov?" They beat Dan'L, and tasered him until he screamed. The next punch to his face broke Dan'L's nose, and his blood ran down his face and chin, onto his chest.

The Rebels punched his gut until Dan'L coughed up blood. Then they delivered several blows to his face. Dan'L finally revealed his encounter with Petrov. He told the entire story of his experience, from his kidnapping to his meeting the Rebel Petrov. He raised his bloody face and said, "My Mother negotiated my release with Petrov. I did not know he killed my Father until much later."

More hard hits landed on his body and face. Duma Wat stood and back-handed Dan'L's bloody face, and demanded the location of the green crystal. He slapped him hard until the boy cried out, "The reason you brought me here was to kill me where my Father died, is this not so, Duma Wat?" The men waited for instructions from their leader. Deathly silence in the room.

No answer was forthcoming from the visibly angry Duma Wat. He looked around at his men, showing his displeasure with them. The Emperor's precious Shi'Lon Rangers were on his ship. Alien androids were coming to rescue their own. And this boy still had no real answers to his important questions. Duma Wat overturned the table beside him and cursed loudly, and ordered Dan'L returned to his cell. He was furious. But there was no more time to waste.

Commander Bok updated C.S. G'Rosk on the Shi'Lon Rangers' situation, "They are still in their cell, sir. Novice Dan'L was taken away, presumably for questioning. Unable to monitor his situation. The alien android is still blinking his eyes. Novice Kayla was correct. My scanner identified a definitive pattern in his blinking, looped repeatedly. This situation could escalate dramatically, Commander Superior," Bok warned. He was ordered to remain onboard his ES warbird, continue to monitor the situation, and to prepare to engage the Rebels. Bok donned his battle armor suit, in case he had to defend himself against attacking Rebels, or alien androids.

XIV

Space Cadre ships within two days' range of SB5 were ordered to close in on the abandoned base, and the hovering Rebel ships surrounding SB5. Emperor P'Lau met with his Military Advisors and Ranger High Command regarding the android. Why were alien androids in their solar system? Were they scouts; a prelude to an invasion? They had to be prepared. Space Cadre craft solar system-wide were ordered to take defensive positions to protect the four inhabited planets and the Space Bases. The entire military of the Empire was placed on yellow alert.

The Rebel group surrounding SB5 consisted of an old destroyer, three support vessels, and several fighters, all old vessels incapable of outrunning the modern Space Cadre ships. But the Rebel ships were fully armed with deadly weaponry. It would take a full battleship group to successfully threaten Duma Wat, like the one currently en route to SB5—or alien android ships.

C.S. Bette was ordered to hail Duma Wat and demand release of all three Rangers. It took less time than expected to be connected to the Rebel Leader. Bette said, "Emperor P'Lau sent his Shi'Lon Rangers to negotiate the release of Novice Dan'L. They were sent in peace, as his Emissaries. The Emperor P'Lau demands the immediate release of his two innocent novices Dan'L and Kayla, and Master Commander T'Anh."

Duma Wat looked into the vid comm and answered, "Novice Dan'L is my guest. The Shi'Lon Rangers were not invited here. We claimed salvage rights to the abandoned property formerly called Space Base 5. It is now our property, in accordance with Imperial law. The Shi'Lon Rangers are trespassers and will be treated as such!" He clicked off. His intentions were now clear to Bette. She notified Emperor P'Lau immediately. There was precious little time.

"Contact our asset with Duma Wat. Send the emergency signal now," the Emperor commanded. A startled Major S'Loc felt the small chip concealed inside his right boot begin to vibrate for the first time since his deep immersion mission began. He casually left the engine room of the command destroyer and told his next in command he was taking a break for thirty minutes. He walked briskly to his quarters, took off in his boot in private, and removed the small chip. The chip fit inside the ear buds player he kept inside his locked drawer, and it activated upon insertion. The unmistakable voice of Emperor P'Lau himself then spoke, "Negotiations have broken down with my two Shi'Lon Rangers and Novice Dan'L, presently onboard your vessel. Arrange their escape at once. You are to escape immediately after their departure. Come home, my Faithful Son."

Steph'N knew only that a shuttle was sent down to SB5, and had returned a few hours ago. How did Shi'Lon Rangers get onboard the Rebel destroyer, or SB5, for that matter? No time to ponder his questions. He punched up his com tablet and located the Ranger prisoners in the brig, and read the notations regarding their disposition. They were tentatively scheduled for shuttling back to SB5, and termination. He had to act fast. He smiled as he ran down the corridor, thinking how pissed off Duma Wat would be after learning of his deception for over two years. Today was the last day he would impersonate Major S'Loc. He would free the Rangers, and get out. He was going home.

While he ran down the corridor, all senior officers were ordered to the bridge to deliver status reports to Duma Wat in person. Space Cadre ships were closing in on SB5. Duma Wat ordered his destroyer, support vessels, and fighters to enter the White Belt, to avoid a losing confrontation with Space Cadre ships. Then Duma Wat looked directly at Major S'Loc and ordered, "Dispose of the Rangers. Both Shi'Lons, and the Borgund Novice Dan'L, too. I'm through with him. I want all three of them taken to SB5, terminated, and left behind before we clear the SB5 docks. Only head shots will kill the Shi'Lons. Then, blow SB5. Do it!"

Major S'Loc walked casually to the brig, as if nothing was amiss. But Steph'N's mind was racing. He would not kill any Ranger, Borgund or Shi'Lon. He found the security locker next to the brig where the Rangers' space helmets were stored and took them with him. The prep room by the main airlock had old jet sleds in storage. Hopefully, the Rangers knew how to use the old sleds. They were no longer in service for the Space Cadre and outdated, but worked well for short flights. Steph'N took three jet sleds from their charging compartments and continued his casual walk. He hid the jet sleds in the airlock closest to the brig, used for prisoner and cargo transfers.

In their brig cell, Kayla watched T'Anh, and said, "Master Commander T'Anh, I respectfully request you sit and rest. You have been pacing the entire time we've been incarcerated here. Should we not conserve our strength?"

The Novice was correct. "Yes, you're right, Kayla. We should conserve our strength. I usually think best on my feet," T'Anh answered. "It may be some time before we are given food or water, or allowed to leave." She sat on the bed against the wall, folding her legs under her. The small cell had a toilet hole in the floor, but no running water. No window or porthole. Just a heavy cell door—which suddenly opened.

Rebel Major S'Loc opened the cell door and whispered, "I am Major S'Loc. Bring your space suits and come with me. Hurry!" When they stepped outside, the Major opened Dan'L's door, and collected the bloody Novice. The Major supported Dan'L, and he and Kayla helped him walk down the hall. He led them away from the ship's bridge and Duma Wat. Three Rebel officers rounded the corner and were surprised by them. Novice Kayla immediately spun and kicked two of the men unconscious, and M.C. T'Anh subdued the third man.

Major S'Loc said, "Better finish them off, Rangers. If they awaken before you escape, they will signal for help. We will all be killed, and all is for naught." T'Anh swiftly broke the necks of two of the men, and Kayla finished off the remaining Rebel. They continued down the corridor quickly. It was Kayla's first kill. *It was necessary*, Kayla told herself.

The Major stopped near the cargo bay, went to a locker, took out a space suit for Dan'L, and handed him a helmet. "Your Ranger on SB5 is watching you. Put your space suits on, and your helmets. Tether together and enter the air lock across the cargo bay. I'll open the outer hull access hatch when you're ready. May the Creator bless us all!" He struck his left chest with his right fist, saluting the three Rangers. They silently returned his salute, quickly crossed the cargo bay, and entered the airlock, with Dan'L being helped by T'Anh and Kayla.

Inside the large airlock in the cargo bay, the Shi'Lon Rangers quickly put on their space suits and helmets, and helped Dan'L into his suit. Then they tethered together, and checked their suit seals. Leaning against the wall were three old, neatly folded jet sleds, at least twenty years old. T'Anh signaled to the Major, and he opened the hatch of the airlock. Each Ranger took a jet sled and silently floated out of the airlock into space. The Novices had never seen a jet sled.

M.C. T'Anh held the jet sled by its top handle, and twisted the handle sharply. The sled unfolded to its two-meter length while she held it. T'Anh raised the wide arm handles on either side of the sled and put her arms through both handles. She watched the young Novices follow her movements perfectly, unfolding their jet sleds, and putting their arms through the wide side handles. When their jet sleds were ready, T'Anh showed them the sled controls at the top of the sled. Then she turned and slowly flew towards SB5. Dan'L and Kayla followed her, flanking the senior Ranger. They sped up, and made the SB5 hangar bay in minutes, landing in front of the ES warbird of Commander Bok, with his ES warbird now fully visible.

Duma Wat and the Rebels on his command destroyer were in a heated discussion about their situation. A full Space Cadre battleship group was less than one hour from firing range of their destroyer. They had neither the speed nor the firepower to engage the Space Cadre's superior ships. Duma Wat ordered the Rebel ships to move out, escaping into the White Belt, in hopes the larger Space Cadre ships would not pursue them. His bridge security officer suddenly turned to him and said, "Sir, the cargo bay outer access hatch has been opened without authorization, and three life forms have left the ship."

Duma Wat yelled out a string of obscenities, cursing at his bridge officers. He screamed, "Find their accomplice and bring him to me now! I will have his hide for this treason! Continue into the White Belt, full standard speed ahead. Don't let those Space Cadre ships find us!"

On SB5, Commander Bok took Novice Dan'L with him and launched quickly, followed by M.C. T'Anh and Novice Kayla. They flew in stealth mode towards the oncoming Space Cadre ships, and rendezvoused with them. After getting emergency medical treatment for Dan'L, their warbirds were refueled. In a full throttle launch, the four Rangers flew their two ES warbirds on course for Home World.

Three days later, the ES warbirds landed on Capital City Base on Home World, and were immediately escorted to the Royal Palace. In the office of C.S. Vu'Duc, the four Rangers were de-briefed together, with their K'Halon Prime Commanders Superior G'Rosk and Bette conferenced in via vid comm. Soon, Novice Kayla was dismissed and sent to temporary quarters to rest. M.C. T'Anh and Commander Bok were dismissed an hour later, and went to their quarters.

Novice Dan'L had many questions to answer. But first, he was given medical treatment, many scans, and tests. The hardy young warrior had several deep contusions, but no broken bones, other than his nose. No permanent organ damage was sustained. Then his de-briefing commenced, and continued until night fell. The young man answered all questions put to him truthfully, standing at attention during questioning, not moving a muscle for hours. His swollen face still showed bruises and scars from the beatings by the Rebels. His torso and legs were wrapped in tight, healing bandages under his uniform.

Vu'Duc said, "We will continue your de-briefing tomorrow at 9a.m., Novice Dan'L. You are dismissed. Please do something to quiet this boy's growling stomach, Javette!" Dan'L turned to see his Mother sitting at the back of the room, observing the de-briefing. Neither one could hide their joy seeing one another. She kissed his swollen cheek gently. His Mother took him to the Ranger dining room and watched him eat nearly three whole meals, down two glasses of milk, and a pitcher of cool water. Then they walked to the guest quarters to talk privately, strolling through the Palace gardens.

After several moments of silence, Dan'L shared, "Duma Wat used truth gas on me several times, and kept asking me to tell him why he brought me to him, Mother. I could not give him an answer, because I did not know. I still don't know why. When they showed me the blackened, destroyed cargo bay on SB5, I saw several body shadows," he said quietly. His eyes moistened with tears, but he did not let any fall. He continued, "I found the android with his blinking green eyes. The Shi'Lon Rangers appeared, and the Rebels took all of us back to the destroyer. Then Duma Wat asked me the same questions again," he said, and lowered his head.

All Shi'Lon Rangers were trained in interpreting body language, and Javette was as good as any of her sister Rangers. Her son had seen the last vestige of his Father, his body shadow. He was in real pain, both physically and emotionally. Dan'L slowly shook his head, and she saw the shame in her son's eyes and face. His Mother gently asked, "And what did you tell him, Dan'L? Did they torture you, Son?"

Dan'L stood and touched a white rose gently. "I told him he brought me to SB5 to kill me where Petrov killed my Father. Then, Duma Wat wanted to know about my experience with Petrov, and I eventually told him. He had his men punch me and hit me until I told him everything, but they didn't torture me. The truth gas made me tell him about my entire encounter, Mother. He kept slapping my face and asking about the green crystal. I was sure Duma Wat was going to kill me."

He sat next to her again and said, "If Kayla hadn't asked him about the blinking alien android, he would have killed all of us. I know it. I saw it in his eyes, and so did Kayla. She told me so, Mother. She knew just what to say to Duma Wat. Kayla saved our lives."

Javette stood and said assuredly, "Everyone talks, under enough truth gas and beatings, my Son. Not even our strongest warriors can resist the truth gas, if it is administered long enough, in strong doses, accompanied by beatings. That's why it is used. Sometimes the subjects are tortured, too, to get them to reveal what they know sooner. You did nothing wrong, my Son. The Emperor and your Ranger superiors know this. You have endured much more suffering than to which any Novice should ever be subjected. Discard your shame and hold your head high. The Son of K'Ser has done well," she said firmly, and smiled. Dan'L felt his shame lift and dissipate as if he threw off a heavy load from his back. He continued telling his experience to his Mother, and she listened closely to his every word.

They strolled through the gardens in the courtyard, and a more self-assured Dan'L reached the end of his saga. Javette walked with him in silence for a while through the many arched trellises of roses. Dan'L asked,

"Will they kill the Rebel Major who helped us escape, Mother?"

"He may indeed lose his life for helping you. But a good undercover asset covers his tracks, and always has an exit strategy, Dan'L. Someone else may take the blame for your escape, a crewman, or another Rebel. The Major knew the risk he took before he helped you, Son," she told him.

Javette led him to his guest room, bid him good night, and then went to her quarters. She knew why Duma Wat kidnapped Dan'L, and later brought him to SB5. The Rebels must have monitored the bay on SB5, and listened to K'Ser's attempts to communicate with the alien androids. They probably heard everything. The Rebel Leader thought K'Ser told his son valuable information concerning his discovery of the alien red and green memory crystals. Duma Wat ordered Petrov and the Rebels to attack the storage bay on SB5. Duma Wat wanted to own the green "power crystal" K'Ser referred to in his messages. Since the green crystal was not recovered by the Rebels after the scene of the battle on SB5, he assumed K'Ser sent it to Dan'L. Duma Wat was convinced K'Ser escaped the battle. Could her husband really be alive after three months, stowing away on damaged and abandoned SB5?

XV

Space Base 5

Steph'N ran down the narrow corridor to the storage bays off the main dock. He slapped his sweaty palm on the recognition pad and opened his private storage compartment door. He grabbed a packed backpack, and picked up the laser pistol and its holster. The holster was strapped low on his thigh, ready for quick action. The belt of extra ammo cartridges was the last thing he took. The compartment door was slammed shut, and Steph'N ran through the corridor, putting his arms through the backpack straps.

In his more than two years impersonating "Major S'Loc," Steph'N never did anything to give the Rebels the slightest suspicion he was a spy for the Emperor, or a Ranger. He had gained the trust of Colonel Vas and Duma Wat, and obeyed their orders to him. He did whatever they asked him to do to keep the ships functioning, but was never ordered to kill Imperial troops or Rangers, or attack Space Cadre vessels. But today was different.

The two Shi'Lon Rangers surprised Duma Wat on SB5 while the Rebel destroyer was docked there. They were sent to negotiate for Novice Dan'L's return, but Duma Wat was in no mood for negotiations. He supposedly paid half a million credits for Novice Dan'L, determined to discover the secrets and location of the green alien "Power crystals" the boy's Father, M.C. K'Ser, was given by alien androids. But K'Ser's Son Dan'L knew nothing about the green alien crystals. Duma Wat was uncharacteristically furious.

After making certain the three Rangers were safely off the Rebel destroyer, Steph'N put his escape plan in high gear. This was his last day working for the Rebels, and for their Leader, Duma Wat. He made it count. Steph'N ran down the corridor to the main hangar bay, jumped through the last hatch, and crouched low against the hangar wall. He reached inside his backpack for a small homing tracker and stuck the round device behind some crates, affixed to the wall. Duma Wat could not hide his destroyer from the Space Cadre any longer. Silently, he made his way to the fighter nearest the hangar bay doors. Up the open hatch of the fighter he ran, and punched the hatch lock.

It felt good to sit in the pilot's seat again. The old fighter's fuel cells showed 92% full. It had been more than two years since he had piloted a fighter, but he was trained on these older model warbirds, and knew them well. He took off his backpack and ammo belt, initiated the launch sequence, and strapped in.

In the fastest launch of his life, Steph'N rocketed off the main hangar bay of the Rebel destroyer full throttle, and flew straight towards the oncoming Space Cadre battle group. The Rebel destroyer didn't even fire at him, or send fighters in pursuit. Duma Wat was more interested in finding a good place to hide from the Space Cadre battleship.

Punching in the secret comm link numbers to C.S. Vu'Duc, Steph'N quickly relayed his information and current situation. Vu'Duc said, "Surrender to the Space Cadre Battleship, but maintain cover until you are delivered to me on Home World." The orders were expected. Better for Duma Wat to think Major S'Loc turned tail and ran away in the face of an approaching Space Cadre battleship group, than for word of a Ranger/agent's uncovering to potentially make it back to the Rebels.

He surrendered to the Space Cadre, and they sent two fighters to escort his old warbird to their landing deck. They confiscated his gear and laser pistol, and threw Major S'Loc in the brig. When the Battleship Captain reported his capture of the Rebel officer, he was ordered to leave him alone in the brig and return him to Space Cadre security on Home World. Steph'N was spared interrogation aboard the Battleship, and his gear was left untouched in the security lock-up. The battleship was ordered by Fleet Admiral U'Ret to not enter the dangerous White Belt. Major S'Loc was flown to Home World by a Space Cadre fighter. Duma Wat avoided capture again, and safely flew his Rebel destroyer group to the secret base near M'Wati.

One week later on Home World, Major S'Loc and his belongings were transferred to the Royal Palace prison. In the wee hours of his second day there, Steph'N was secretly smuggled out of his prison cell, and a dead man's body was left in his place, wearing Major S'Loc's uniform. The official report read Major S'Loc committed suicide by cyanide capsule.

Steph'N was sequestered in a private, secure suite in the Palace, and debriefed for several days. Inside his backpack were Rebel uniforms, with hidden micro data crystals containing all the information he could gather during more than two years of his deep immersion mission. Everything from the hierarchy of the Rebel leadership to the location and defensive capabilities of their bases and outposts was stored on those micro crystals. He even managed to download Duma Wat's accounting files from his command destroyer. Emperor P'Lau immediately ordered the Rebel account funds confiscated. Duma Wat would have to dip into his personal treasury to pay his men for the next few months. The Emperor was very pleased with Steph'N's results.

Steph'N was tired from being interrogated by his own Ranger superiors and High Command officers every day. He wanted a few weeks off to see his family, and have time to himself. When the debriefings were finally over, Steph'N stayed one more night in the Palace private suite to rest in peace. He was allowed to go back to his quarters in the Ranger section the next day. He finally tried the comm link number for Va'Pal, but the number was not working any more. She probably gave up on him two years ago, and found another man. She was a beautiful warrior woman, after all.

Palace psychiatrists and doctors cautioned Steph'N about the transition to his former life, and reminded him it would take a long time for him to adjust. They were right in saying his personality had been altered by his deep immersion and assumption of another man's persona. He would need time to get used to being a Ranger again. Major S'Loc was a hard, brutal taskmaster, intolerant of his men committing any errors; unforgiving, callous, and anti-social. These were not Steph'N's traits, and it would take time to discard them. Hopefully, he would become himself again.

C.S. Vu'Duc ordered stress counseling and mission de-programming for Steph'N to commence immediately. After the doctors and psychiatrists approved, he would be given a three-week vacation. He agreed to whatever treatments they recommended; he knew how close he came to surrendering to Major S'Loc's life and personality, and giving up hope of returning. He wanted to become Steph'N the Borgund Ranger again, and have his life back. But he made it out alive. And, he never compromised himself with another man. Steph'N looked at his face, and his own natural blue eyes in the mirror for the first time in two years, and silently thanked the Creator. He came back.

During his continued debriefing the following week in the Ranger High Command office, Novice Dan'L was asked by C.S. Vu'Duc if he would agree to be injected with hallucinogens, and be questioned in depth. Dan'L considered the request, and then answered, "Sir, I was sedated with strong synthetic drugs and heroin for five days and not given any food, nor water, or any fluids. I nearly died, and the Rebel doctors spent weeks helping me recover. I have been sprayed with truth gas for days on end while being questioned by the Traitor Duma Wat and his officers, and beaten, at the end. A truth analyzer was used on me while I answered his questions, too. May I be permitted to ask, sir: What do you possibly hope to discover that I have not been forced to reveal to Duma Wat, and you, already?"

Sitting at a table in the back, Javette listened to her Son's response.

Dan'L was every bit as logical as her late husband, K'Ser, yet respectful. He had been through a lot. She was anxious to hear the official response, too.

C.S. Vu'Duc took a deep breath and replied, "We acknowledge the facts of your delicate situation and your mistreatment while in captivity, Novice Dan'L. It is not my intent to make you the subject of more inquiries. But we're dealing with alien technology, and alien methods. The Royal Physician has recommended hallucinogenic injections be used, to discover whether or not you were given subconscious suggestions or information without your awareness. The best kept secret is one which is carried unknowingly, Dan'L," Vu'Duc said. "Will you agree to submit, Novice Dan'L?"

Dan'L sighed heavily and said, "Yes, I will submit. But I would like for my Mother to witness the session." Vu'Duc and the Royal Physician agreed.

The Royal Physician led them to a quiet room, and motioned for Javette to sit along the wall, not facing her Son. He lowered the lights, and explained to Dan'L what would happen to him, "I will inject you one time with a compound of hallucinogens and tranquilizers slowly, and attempt to induce a hypnotic trance to make the experience easier on you, Novice. No harsh interrogations or touching of your body will take place during our session. It may even be a pleasant experience for you. We will take a little trip through your memories, all right?"

Dan'L nodded apprehensively. The Royal Physician activated the vid recorder, and slowly injected him intravenously with a vile, orange serum. The Physician held up a large white crystal, and gently swung it back and forth on its gold chain while Dan'L watched. The Physician spoke softly and rhythmically, and Dan'L went into a hypnotic trance deeply. He began to move his head a little from side to side. He moaned a little, as if he was in pain.

The Physician asked, "Where are you now, Dan'L?"

"In the barracks with the guys. We all have skin burns from the hot sulphur springs. The ointment smells almost as bad as the spring water. I'm tired of throwing up. I'm burned, like they are," Dan'L said. "My belly is on fire! But I passed."

"The vid comm link is for you, Dan'L. Who's calling you so late?" The Physician enquired.

"It's Father! He says Mother is away on a mission tonight. Father seems anxious. Is someone listening, Father?" Dan'L asked in his trance, "Are you alone, Father? What's the matter?" He rolled his head, side to side.

"What did your Father say to you, Dan'L?"

"He asked me about the swimming finals in the sulphur springs, while the music plays. I told him I passed, but have some skin burns, like the other guys. They hurt," the boy answered, now moving his shoulders a bit. Dan'L's face relaxed, he smiled, and began humming.

The Royal Physician noticed his body movements, and asked, "Is the music pretty? What are the lyrics?" He watched Dan'L move his head and shoulders before answering.

"The music is strange. It's kind of like electronic dance music, but different. Rhythm without any drums. Mechanical. No bass. Sounds so unusual," he answered, moving his body to the beat in his trance.

This was information not divulged in any of Dan'L's admitted interrogation answers. The Physician pursued the line further. He asked in a gentle, punctuated voice, "Can you hear the lyrics, Dan'L? What do they say?" Not getting any response, the Doctor asked, "Are the lyrics fun to listen to?"

Dan'L was moving his shoulders, torso, and head to the music in his trance. He answered, "Backwards. It's all backwards. Father says I am almost through training now, and that he and Mother will be proud when I am confirmed, and take my blood oath to the Emperor. It's fun music, but backwards. Everything backwards, so strange." He began humming.

"Can you sing it for me, Dan'L?" The Physician asked.

Dan'L sang a tune for two minutes in an incomprehensible language, rocking his shoulders and singing. Then he said, "That's all." He fell into a deep sleep. The Physician let him sleep for thirty minutes, and then slowly awakened him. They brought him back into Vu'Duc's office again. "The Emperor P'Lau has ordered our meeting to be reconvened in his private Royal Court now, Dan'L. Please follow me," C.S. Vu'Duc said.

"Did I do something wrong, Mother?" Dan'L whispered. She shook her head "No," and continued walking with them. When they reached the Royal Court, they discovered several other Rangers were present, awaiting their arrival. All knelt before Emperor P'Lau. The Royal Physician stood off to one side.

Emperor P'Lau sat stoically during the official greetings while his Rangers knelt, saluted, and bowed their heads. Then he stated, "Rise, my Beloved Daughters and Faithful Sons. Your debriefings have all been elevated to an official inquiry. Due to the gravity of this situation, as well as the recently obtained information, formal charges may be brought against certain parties." The side vid screens activated, and C.S. G'Rosk and C.S. Bette were conferenced in from K'Halon Prime.

Dan'L and Kayla looked at each other, then Dan'L looked at Javette. Was he to be charged with some crime? Would he be kicked out of the Borgund Rangers, disgrace his Mother, and possibly be imprisoned? He controlled his initial panic and remained at attention, fully aware of the moment and those with him. M.C. T'Anh looked at Kayla and Dan'L for a moment, her brows deeply furrowed. Did they do something wrong?

C.S. G'Rosk received a hand signal from the Emperor, and read from his com tablet: "Three months ago, Master Commander K'Ser was sent to SB5 to investigate signals emanating from the dead, abandoned space base, on a top-secret mission. Upon arrival, K'Ser discovered a damaged ship of alien origin had crash landed on SB5 from some malfunction. On board were highly-advanced androids, one of which was still fully functioning. They were peaceful."

"Unable to communicate with the android verbally, K'Ser requested assistance from our High Command. Various means of communications were attempted over several days: all known languages, both in spoken and written form; hieroglyphs; pictographs; mathematics; hand signs; and so on. Then, feeling exasperated from all his futile attempts to communicate with the alien androids, he climbed back into his warbird," G'Rosk said. "Eventually, K'Ser realized the androids were repairing themselves and their ship while his communications attempts continued."

"K'Ser began humming a tune inside his cockpit, and sang a popular song aloud to himself while he drummed on his console in rhythm to the music. The androids stopped everything they were doing and walked up the hatch into K'Ser's warbird. They blinked their eyes, turned their heads back and forth a little, and began making drumming movements with their metallic fingers. K'Ser had a brainstorm: electrical signaling codes. They had been used for centuries in military drum signaling, telegraph and electrical communications, and were still in use for emergency signaling by maritime vessels. Could they understand the old 'dots and dashes?' He called our High Command and requested information and transcription help for the old maritime electrical codes. We found the old transcriptions and codes for the alphabet and sent the table of on-off tones, lights, or clicks. K'Ser showed the information to the androids, but they did not respond," G'Rosk read from the report.

"When K'Ser began to drum to them instead of talk, the androids drummed back exactly what K'Ser had drummed. Then, K'Ser drummed the elementary 'A, B, C' code transcription table to them while saying the letters, and flashed the light on his space suit on and off to correspond to the code. The androids repeated the information, and quickly learned our language. The androids flashed their eyes in electronic code while they drummed, and sang along with K'Ser. He then played dance music, popular songs, opera and symphonic music; and had them listen to talk shows on his ship's entertainment broadcast channel, and they were fascinated," G'Rosk stated.

Reading from his com tablet, C.S. Vu'Duc continued the report, "The androids continued singing and drumming with K'Ser for hours. Anything he sang or drummed, they repeated perfectly; but when they spoke directly to him, their vernacular was backwards. Then they asked him for more music and narrated stories. The recordings from inside his ES warbird show him taking memory crystals from his personal gear containing music and audiobooks to give them."

"When the alien androids saw K'Ser's red memory crystals, they went back to their ship for powerful, fifth dimension red crystals of their own, and gave them to him with an encoder. The androids taught K'Ser how to use the crystals; but his report did not specify exactly how to use the encoder, or what form it took. A larger, green crystal was also shown to K'Ser, and the android handed it to him with extreme care. They called it a 'Power Crystal.' We are not certain whether or not K'Ser was allowed to keep the green Power Crystal. He flew back to the nearest Space Cadre ship the next day to transmit his report to us, and arranged for the red crystals to be sent. One was sent to Emperor P'Lau by military top-secret document express, and the two others to his Son, Novice Dan'L, by common carrier," Vu'Duc finished.

G'Rosk concluded, "Master Commander K'Ser was ordered to return to SB5 and continue to communicate with the alien androids. He was there only two more days when Rebel ships reached SB5. The Rebels fired on the alien android ship, and it flew away in an instant. That's the information K'Ser's ship recorded. A battle ensued between the Rebel landing party and K'Ser. Our recorded file stops when the Rebel Petrov fired their plasma disrupter arc cannon at K'Ser's ship. Space Cadre ships arrived too late to capture the Rebels. Their forensics officers found the remains of K'Ser, and they were subsequently delivered to Master Commander Javette, his Partner."

Emperor P'Lau rose in his levitating throne and hovered above them. He said, "There are conflicting reports concerning the battle at SB5 and its aftermath, as some of you are aware. These reports are still under investigation. Our undercover assets reported the Traitor Duma Wat sent reconnaissance ships to SB5 periodically after the battle. We did not know what the Rebel Leader was after until our newest Borgund Ranger Novice Dan'L was kidnapped. Since then, Dan'L has endured more hardship, suffering, and personal injury than we ever envisioned, and it has sorrowed us greatly."

P'Lau lowered his throne to its place on the top of the golden steps, and said, "One hour ago, contact was made with an alien ship entering our solar system near Space Base Orioc. Our attempts at communication using the old electronic maritime codes have determined they are on search and rescue, to recover their property at SB5. Hopefully, we have translated their transmissions correctly. We gave permission to them to search and recover their property, the so-called "blinking android," as reported by Novices Dan'L and Kayla, and Master Commander T'Anh."

The Great Emperor P'Lau stood and said, "I command all of you to await final disposition of their search and recovery efforts. You will remain at the Palace here on Home World until then. We will allow the alien androids peaceful access to Space Base 5." He turned abruptly and left the

Royal Court, followed by his Imperial Guards.

XVI

The Space Cadre battleship and support vessels surrounded SB5. The security teams sent to investigate SB5 after the escape of the four Rangers found the alien android with his blinking green eyes, but were ordered not to touch it. No one was found anywhere on the ruins of SB5, dead or alive. The battleship group was ordered to pull back from SB5 and not to scan or target the incoming alien vessel on its search and rescue recovery mission.

Travel time from SB Orioc to the White Belt and SB5 was nine days at maximum speed in an ES warbird, plus several additional hours for refueling stops. The alien ship appeared next to SB5 in less than 45 minutes after the meeting with Emperor P'Lau. Their ship was a strange shape, and had a wide band of lights around the middle section. No weapons systems were apparent. Using an unknown tele-transport system, the blinking android head was beamed aboard the alien vessel, and it disappeared immediately.

Home World

In the Home World Ranger dining hall, Commander Bok asked, "The alien ship traversed our entire solar system radial length in 45 minutes. What type of propulsion system do they use, I wonder?"

"Crystalline power," Novice Dan'L replied quickly; then he realized the senior officers and Rangers having dinner with him were staring at him. He put another bite of chicken in his mouth and tried not to feel the weight of their stares. He had no idea how he knew the answer to Commander Bok's question; but he knew it, for certain. The uncomfortable silence was broken by the comm links on their uniforms beeping. The Emperor's inquest would resume in five minutes. They all quickly walked to the Royal Court, knelt in front of the Emperor, and bowed their heads. Military High Command officers were seated at the long table.

"Rise. Rise, my Rangers. We will receive the aliens' transmission in three minutes," the Emperor said. It was the longest three minutes of Dan'L's life. Trying not to fidget, he inhaled deeply and exhaled as slowly as possible. He noticed Commander Bok glancing sideways at him suspiciously, with a frown on his face. Then the electronic music with heavy drumming began loudly.

The huge wall vid screen played electronic symphonic music, with prominent drumming, complex harmonies and solos, of original composition. The android in the vid began to sing in backwards vernacular while his eyes flashed in electronic code. "It's Father's voice!" Dan'L cried out, looking at Javette. A translated message began to appear in typeface at the bottom of the screen as the android sang:

"Gratitude. Our comrade rescued.
Property recovered, recovered, recovered.
Gratitude. Our comrade rescued.
No other life forms discovered, discovered, discovered.

Consciousness of one billion lives embodied in our memory.
Inferno of the Dalian system dying burned into our memory.

We are their living legacy.
They are no more, no more, no more.
We hold their dearest memories.
They are no more, no more, no more.

Consciousness of a faithful human embodied in our memory.
Cries of his life force dying seared in our memory.

K'Ser's consciousness with us now.
He joined with us, with us, with us.
His human life and love joined with us.
Forever with us, with us, with us.

Consciousness of your superior human embodied in our memory.
Cries of your brothers fighting etched in our memory.

You are not ready, much to learn.
Live in peace, in peace, in peace.
When you are ready we will return.
Live in peace, in peace, in peace."

A map of an unknown galaxy was projected on their vid screen; then all whited out. The video recorders caught the transcriptions and the map of the unknown galaxy.

Emperor P'Lau was as transfixed as everyone else in the Royal Court. Several Rangers, especially M.C. Javette and Novice Dan'L, had red, tear-filled eyes. The Emperor rose up on his throne and declared, "Their message to us is complex, yet perfectly clear. The Dalian androids came to us in peace, and received war in return. Let us take their message to heart, endeavoring to live in peace, so that we may someday become another treasured collection of memories for them, like Master Commander K'Ser."

For the next hour, refreshments were served to the silent Rangers and officers in the Royal Court. Each reflected on his or her own readiness to receive the alien message of peace, and their advanced knowledge, which they willingly shared with K'Ser. Bells sounded, calling everyone to resume the meeting with the Emperor.

"We will acknowledge our Beloved Daughters and Faithful Sons today, and thank them for their excellent performance in service to the Empire. In honor of your experience, suffering, and extraordinary performance during the first months of service as a new Borgund Ranger, Novice Dan'L is promoted to Ranger," the Emperor proclaimed. Ranger Dan'L was surprised at the announcement, but bowed his head and thanked the Emperor with humility. He also received a commendation and a bonus.

Commander Bok was promoted to First Commander, with a commendation and a bonus. Master Commander T'Anh was promoted to Commander Superior, and would take command of the Shi'Lon Rangers on K'Halon Prime. C.S. Bette, the highest-ranking Shi'Lon Ranger, was reassigned to Home World as Special Advisor to the Emperor, and commander of the Shi'Lon Rangers there.

An unannounced Borgund Ranger was led into the court by the Imperial Guards, and knelt directly in front of Emperor P'Lau. "Commander Steph'N, your performance in your mission was extraordinary, surpassing our wildest expectations. After your highly successful undercover duty, you are assigned to Home World with a commendation, a bonus, and an award, Master Commander Steph'N," the Emperor loudly proclaimed. When Steph'N stood, everyone applauded. He received a two-step promotion; a sign of great accomplishment.

"It is the Rebel Major!" Novice Kayla whispered to Ranger Dan'L, and they joined in the cheers and applause for the man who engineered their escape from Duma Wat and his Rebels.

Novice Kayla also received a commendation and a bonus. She was reassigned to C.S. T'Anh at K'Halon Prime. In a surprising move, new Commander Superior T'Anh requested Kayla serve out her first year as Novice. It was the first of many actions T'Anh would take to hold Kayla back, keeping her out of the spotlight, and in the background of mainstream Shi'Lon Ranger activities. T'Anh would be very hard on Kayla during her first five years, resenting the Emperor's obvious favor toward his young, emerald-eyed Beloved Daughter Kayla.

At the last, Emperor P'Lau called M.C. Javette forward, saying, "Your value to the Empire cannot be overstated. Imperial Planetary Governor Lem has written a glowing commendation for your negotiation skills on Ban'Ti. You singlehandedly convinced hundreds of invading Rebels to retreat, without the loss of any Imperial troop or officer. Yet, what has impressed us the most is your ability to counsel your Son Ranger Dan'L without interfering with his assignment. You have guided him well with your voice and love, never attempting to overstep your role as Mother, and influence him in making his own decisions and walking his own path. We promote you to Master Commander First Echelon Javette, with all the rights and privileges of your station." The applause for her was loud and full of cheering.

Javette now ranked directly below Commander Superior. A long-time friend of the late K'Ser and Javette, C.S. G'Rosk congratulated Javette and Dan'L on their promotions and success. His smile for Javette was genuine. Javette had served as a Master Commander for over eight years. She had been through so much the past few months, and deserved this promotion.

After the promotions, commendations and awards, the Rangers and officers were dismissed, except for Javette. The Emperor said, "We understand you paid a 5000-credit bounty to the traitor Petrov for the return of your Son, Javette, and another 5000 credits was given to the girl D'Anna who found and healed Dan'L, after his escape."

"Yes, my Emperor, funds from my own savings; with the advanced permission of Commander Superior Bette," Javette answered, bowing her head.

"We shall give you the 10,000 credits you paid as a reimbursement. Rescuing our newest Faithful Son was an important task. Dan'L holds much promise," P'Lau stated, and directed an Imperial Guard to hand her two gold credit bars, 10,000 credits each. "The other 10,000-credit bar is from Governor Lem, with his gratitude." She bowed and thanked the Emperor.

P'Lau said, "While no one can bring back your Partner, we can remove the burden of vengeance and potential law-breaking activity from your future, Javette." Then he smiled at the corner of his painted red lips and said, "You are hereby ordered to bring the criminal traitor Petrov before me to answer for his crimes against the Empire, Master Commander Javette. Leave in two days. Bring Petrov to me alive, and preferably, wearing his own skin!" Emperor P'Lau smiled at Javette, and dismissed her.

Javette laughed as she walked through the Royal Palace main doors. The

Emperor knew of her blood oath to find Petrov, skin him, and slice him into pieces with her plasma sword. Honor required the blood oath to be fulfilled; but the Emperor had wisely ordered otherwise. *P'Lau saved me from my own vengeance*, she realized. But Petrov didn't know it.

XVII

Home World

Ranger Dan'L moved into his private suite in the Royal Palace. His past two years were spent sleeping on his bunk bed, along with nineteen other trainees or Novices in a dormitory. Now, he had his own apartment with a private bathroom. *Life is good*, he thought. May the Creator bless Emperor P'Lau.

Dan'L put away his few personal things and his casual clothes. His green jacket needed deodorizing, bad. It still reeked of vomit. He emptied the jacket pockets and found his 100-credit gold coin, from his Mother for his Graduation Day. That happy event became a fateful day for him, setting a complex chain of events in motion. Twice he almost died. Dan'L flipped the coin in the air and caught it, realizing his life and his fate were no longer his own. He belonged to Emperor P'Lau.

Faithful Son Dan'L slipped the 100-credit gold coin into his keepsake leather pouch, opposite the two red Dalian crystals from his Father that were returned to him this afternoon. The gold coin and alien red crystals would remain with him all the days of his life. He touched the bone handle of his late Father's knife, now sheathed on his belt. No one knew how the knife, red crystals, or the other remains from his Father escaped the devastation on SB5. Even M.C. K'Ser's ES warbird was demolished from the devastating plasma disrupter arc explosion. Dan'L was certain the Dalian androids had preserved those artifacts, and somehow embedded them with their own technology.

His vid comm link in his apartment buzzed from C.S. G'Rosk on K'Halon Prime, congratulating him on his promotion and transfer to Home World. "A promotion is a reward for a job well done, Ranger Dan'L. But usually there's a price to be paid. It could have been a transfer to one of the Space Bases, or to Ban'Ti, or a solitary posting on an outpost," G'Rosk reminded him. Suddenly he felt very lucky. Dan'L thanked him for his call of congratulations.

Javette came by to help Dan'L unpack his brand new, glistening black battle armor suit, and set it up properly. The aides delivered it to his room, and struggled to move the large plex case off the anti-gravity dolly. "Do you need my help?" She asked in a sweet voice. The men were quickly inspired to lift the plex case off the dolly without any more grumbling, and sat it next to the charging outlet. She unboxed his new uniforms and hung them up for her Son. Javette showed Dan'L how to swiftly suit up in the battle armor. The armor opened in half length-wise, allowing him to step into the suit. Once he shoved his feet and arms into the suit, it activated and closed around him.

"You must practice this movement so you can suit up in seconds. This armor will save your life. Step into it at once, firmly and swiftly, and let it wrap its protection around your body. Put your helmet on while it is closing around you, Dan'L," she instructed. "The suit will seal itself around your breastplate and backplate, and your body. It will also seal around your plasma sword's sheath, so you can draw your sword without hindrance. Wear the battle armor to the training courts, and practice several times this week. A Ranger must be ready to fight in the blink of an eye." She spent several minutes teaching him about his battle armor, how to clean the armor, and how to attach the jet pack.

"The battle armor reminds me of the Dalian android on SB5, Mother. How many years ahead of us are they, I wonder?" Dan'L questioned.

"At least 500 years, I'd estimate. Thank the Creator they were peaceful. They came in peace to visit us, and communicate with our species. Instead of helping them with their disabled ship, the damned Rebels attacked them. Your Father spent time learning how to communicate with them, and established a method for a peaceful exchange of information. They had just begun sharing their technology and knowledge with him when the Rebels attacked. Damn Petrov," she cursed. She'd leave to find and capture the murderer of her Partner tomorrow.

The wall vid comm link beeped, and the dispatcher said, "An outside caller is trying to reach you, Ranger Dan'L. Do you wish to be connected with D'Anna?"

"Yes. Please connect her," Dan'L replied. He motioned for his Mother to listen.

"Dan'L? Is that you? It's D'Anna," she said.

"Hello, D'Anna. How are you? Are you in Nord?" He asked.

"No, I'm in Capitol City, Dan'L. I moved out and left Petrov," she answered anxiously. "He promised not to follow me. He let me go," she explained.

"Then let's meet up. We can have a nice dinner together, D'Anna. I'd like to see you again," Dan'L said. She agreed, and he locked in her coordinates to pick her up. Then they clicked off.

Javette cautioned, "Petrov may have forced D'Anna to contact you, to capture or kill you, Dan'L. Or, she may be alone and frightened, in an unfamiliar city, on a new planet. You must be prepared for either outcome."

He asked her to come with him, to ascertain D'Anna's emotional and physiological state. She agreed, but insisted they notify C.S. Vu'Duc, first. D'Anna was a member of Petrov's group, and considered a conspirator, whether willing or unwilling. Vu'Duc gave them permission to go.

The largest transport station in the Empire was an extremely noisy place, especially for a newcomer, like D'Anna. Filled with foreboding and anxiety, she sat on the corner of a waiting bench against the wall, so no one could sneak up behind her. D'Anna tried to appear bored and casual like the other waiting passengers, but it wasn't working. Her fear radiated from her entire being while she sat nervously watching the main entrance.

Dan'L slipped next to her unaware, and whispered, "You are the prettiest girl in Capital City, D'Anna. Welcome." He smiled at her, and she threw her arms around his neck. "Thank the Creator my cloak was closed, and you didn't get shocked, D'Anna. Let's go have some dinner, all right? Mother will be joining us. She wants to treat you for taking care of me when I was hurt," he explained. "You're okay, D'Anna. You're with friends, now," he said reassuringly.

Javette was waiting in the shuttle for them, and greeted D'Anna with a smile when she entered. The girl was still shaking. "I came straight from the Palace to meet with you, and didn't take time to change out of my uniform," Dan'L explained, noticing D'Anna warily look at him and his Mother, dressed in their black Ranger uniforms and long cloaks. She looked at him as if she was seeing him for the first time. He no longer looked helpless and lost. And his face still bore several scars from his beatings by Duma Wat's Rebels, not completely healed. Dan'L wore a wide tape across his repaired, broken nose.

They went to a nice restaurant with enclosed booths to talk privately. Both Rangers took off their cloaks and gloves, trying to help D'Anna relax. "D'Anna found me when I had crashed in the forest and hobbled to her cabin. I was hurt and lost, and filthy. I must have looked deplorable! But I never felt that you were afraid of me, D'Anna. Until now," Dan'L said to her softly. "I am the same man you helped to heal. I'm your friend, D'Anna."

"You both are very kind. I'm sorry to be frightened like a child. But this is all new to me," D'Anna said. She stared at Javette's dark red breastplate, and Dan'L's black breastplate, with their beautiful designs.

Watching the girl look at her breastplate, Javette said, "Our uniforms were designed to elicit feelings of apprehension and respect, D'Anna, and to immediately identify us as Rangers. We wear them every day. This armor is now as familiar as my own skin," Javette explained, touching her breastplate. "Just don't touch either our breastplate or backplate, as they are coded only to our DNA. They will shock you if you do," she cautioned. "There are many useful tools hidden in our breastplates and backplates."

"Like that sword? I can see its handle," D'Anna said, trying to converse more calmly with them. Dan'L smiled and nodded to her. "Your collars have different pins on them. What do they mean?"

"They are insignia to indicate our rank. Mine is Ranger, and Mother is a Master Commander, First Echelon. She outranks me by many levels," Dan'L said, and smiled at his Mother. Their meals arrived, and Dan'L ordered more wine. D'Anna ate silently. It was obvious she was very hungry.

After a few minutes, Javette excused herself, saying, "I have early meetings tomorrow. Thank you for letting me join you for dinner tonight, D'Anna, Dan'L. Here's my comm link number, D'Anna. Call me if you need anything, anytime," she said graciously.

D'Anna looked at Javette, and whispered, "I kept your gift, Javette. It's still with me. You were right about having my own money. It gave me the courage to leave Petrov. Thank you, again," she said, with a little bow of her head.

Javette smiled with D'Anna, and felt better about the teenager being on a new planet, in a new city. She handed Dan'L two 100-credit gold coins, winked, and swirled on her cloak. She said, "Have fun," and then left them alone to finish dinner and talk.

Slowly, D'Anna relaxed with Dan'L. She told him about Petrov forcing his group to move because of her bringing him from the cabin, through the tunnel, to their apartment. She whispered, "Petrov wanted me to prove I was dedicated to the Rebellion. He said you had influenced me adversely. He told me I had to go with them on their next raid. We flew on an old transport to Home World, and shuttled to a field by the Imperial Army base one hundred kilometers from here. We had lots of guns the Rebels here on Home World gave us—big guns—and some shoulder missiles. Petrov said we had to attack the base and capture the armory. I refused to do it. I've never attacked or killed anyone, Dan'L. I swear to you now: I was never forced to kill or attack anyone before this!" D'Anna started to cry.

"Petrov always told me of the wicked men of the Empire. How they attacked innocent women and children. All I ever did for Petrov and his group was what I did with you. I tried to heal them when they came home. I realized he used me. I cooked for them, healed their wounds, cleaned their clothes, cleaned the apartments, and never asked any questions. Until three days ago," she revealed, trying to control her emotions. "But Petrov was the wicked one. Families live on that base. I saw the school and the playground,

Dan'L. I couldn't do it!"

He took her hand tenderly and tried to comfort her as she continued telling him of her recent experience. If this was a set-up, his Mother would've read it in D'Anna's face and body language. Very few could fool a Shi'Lon Ranger, especially Javette. D'Anna calmed herself, and they finished their meals and drank the wine.

"My congratulations to you for coming here, D'Anna. You're very brave. What do you want to do now?" He asked.

She took a deep breath, and answered, "I want to live in peace, and not hurt anybody. I want to help people, and heal them. Nursing seems like a good career for me, but I have to go to school to learn all about it. And I want to be free to choose my own friends," she said decidedly. "I'm not a child, or a Rebel."

Dan'L smiled at D'Anna, and they finished their wine while talking about her possibilities. He took her to meet one of his friends, B'San, and his five sisters. They all worked at their family restaurant. The five girls "adopted" D'Anna instantly, and she was welcomed into their home. Although she was still scared and uncertain, D'Anna moved in with B'San and his family, and worked in their restaurant. They became good friends.

D'Anna went to nursing school during the weekdays and worked in B'San's restaurant nights and weekends to pay her way. Dan'L and his friends visited the restaurant frequently, and he introduced D'Anna to as many friends as he could, to make her feel she had found a welcome home in Capital City.

It took only three days to discover the hiding place of the Traitor Petrov and his Rebel squad. They were holed up inside a very low-budget tourist hotel on remote island, two hundred kilometers from the Capital City harbor. In the middle of the night, M.C. Javette crept into the dingy hotel where the band of Rebels had taken up residence. She deftly hacked the hotel's cheap security system. Wearing a small gas-mask, she set off thirty-minute, timed-release sleep gas charges along his hotel floor. Javette hot-wired the lock on his door, slipped into Petrov's room, and shot his sleeping body with a stun dart from her breastplate. He never knew what hit him. She rolled him up inside a blanket, attached anti-gravity braces under him, and pushed him out of his room, and into the lift. The eight other Rebels asleep in their rooms on his floor never saw or heard Javette remove Petrov from his room. She loaded his heavy, sleeping body into her shuttle on the roof, and flew away with him to the Royal Palace.

M.C. Javette brought the wide-awake Petrov into the Main Court of Emperor P'Lau, bound, gagged, and unharmed. Emperor P'Lau rose up on his gold throne and said, "You have been brought before me, as was my command, Petrov the Traitor. My Beloved Daughter, Master Commander

First Echelon Javette, was denied her vow of vengeance against the murderer of her Partner, Master Commander K'Ser. But the citizens of our Empire will have justice, Petrov. You are hereby ordered to the solitary confinement section of our prison, reserved for traitors, murderers, and those accused of high treason. Porridge and water will sustain you until your hearing before the High Court Tribunal. Any admission of guilt to charges levied against you, or confessions of your crimes against the Empire will weigh in your favor before the Tribunal."

Imperial Guardsmen took Petrov from Javette and removed his gag. Petrov yelled, "I do not recognize any authority here. I serve the true Emperor, Duma Wat, first-born son of Empress Tan's First Consort!" His gag was put in Petrov's mouth again.

Emperor P'Lau swept his hand to the right, and stated, "Take him to solitary confinement. Fast the traitor with only water and honey for three days. Your Emperor grants this Traitor mercy, and leaves his fate to the High Court Tribunal." After Petrov was removed from the Main Court, the Emperor lowered his flying throne to the top step, and waited for the rumblings from the audience to quiet.

"The Empire thanks you for retrieving the criminal Traitor Petrov whole, in one piece, wearing his own skin, as I commanded, Master Commander Javette," the Emperor said with a little smile. The Royal courtiers laughed and applauded Javette. He awarded her a commendation, and gave her the bounty offered on Petrov. But the Emperor knew some of those in his court were secretly plotting and funding his overthrow.

XVIII

Home World

The audience in the Palace Main Court was very noisy tonight. Every aristocrat, wealthy courtier, and VIP was fully engaged in some conversation. The cacophony of loud voices filled the large court until Steph'N felt his eardrums would burst. He had to get out of there.

Quickly walking through the Palace Main Court large doors, M.C. Steph'N descended the steps three at a time. Fresh air; he breathed in deeply and relaxed somewhat. He was joined by Novice Kayla, who said, "Big crowds of strangers unsettle me, too, Master Commander Steph'N. I feel like they're taking all my oxygen," Novice Kayla said to him, a smile on her face.

Steph'N smiled in recognition to her, and said, "My forte' is not 'the body politic.' We Borgund Rangers are much more comfortable in smaller groups."

Kayla walked a little closer to him and whispered, "Or hidden among the Rebels, 'Major S'Loc.'" They laughed together and walked through the Palace courtyard, through the archway into the gardens. "Thank you for providing an escape for us, Master Commander Steph'N. I owe you a life debt."

He slowed his pace and searched her young, pretty face, and then said, "You are a Shi'Lon Ranger, Kayla. You will give and owe many life debts in your service to Emperor P'Lau. Remember this: all life debts for the Rangers are owed only to the Creator. All thanks and praise belong to the One Who made us, young Novice." He stopped and touched her cheek, saying, "Be safe, my friend Kayla." Then he continued to his apartment.

All Steph'N's personal things had been moved from his old apartment into his new Master Commander-level apartment today, while he was attending his appointments and therapy sessions. He used the temporary passkey stick on the lock to open the suite door. The electronic voice told him to register his palm print for future access to his quarters. He coded the lock, entered, and shut the door.

Compared to his lodging with the Rebels the last two years, his new suite was posh and spacious. There was a small balcony off the living room, and he opened the door for fresh air. Was he really home? He was Master Commander Steph'N now, and no longer a Rebel. *Yes, it is over*, he said to himself. Finally. He was home.

His new comm link beeped, and a text came through from the Royal Treasury: "Back pay of two years, four months, and eleven days has been deposited in your personal account, Master Commander Steph'N." The amount nearly took his breath away. He forgot all about getting any back pay. May the Creator bless Emperor P'Lau.

The new uniforms he ordered yesterday were delivered to him, along with two new pairs of shiny, black boots. No more manky, old suede Rebel boots. Steph'N tipped the aide after he brought the packages inside. He hung up his long black cloak, and removed his breastplate and backplate to their charging stand. Tomorrow, he would test every hidden weapon, knife, gas pellet, razor wire spindle, and all his other "tools" for maximum efficiency, and replace any defective pieces. Two years unprotected among the Rebels, without his Ranger armor. His only protection was the power of his mind.

The new uniforms and few boxes inside his room were unpacked quickly. Like most Rangers, he owned few personal things, and lived where his superiors and the Emperor decided. He laughed, finding the two-year-old rock-hard tube of toothpaste, and cracked bar of soap. He emptied his old toiletries into the waste basket. After a quick trip to the base shop on the lower level, Steph'N put away his new toiletries. He placed the pack of drinks he purchased inside the small fridge and popped open a cold can of lemon soda. *Funny how it's the small things you miss so much*, he thought, savoring the first gulp of his favorite cold drink. Nothing but water and teas aboard the Rebel destroyer.

Deep immersion undercover assignments took their toll, he reminded himself. Some men became so immersed they lost themselves in the process. Now, he knew exactly how losing yourself came about. The psychiatrist he met with today told him to be patient with himself, and not try to jump back into his old routines too quickly. He was beginning to understand why he was transferred to the Home World Palace duty station; it would be less stressful for him to get used to, and take less time to readjust.

The Royal Physician and Vu'Duc permitted a five-minute, live vid call home today. His mother cried tears of joy to see her son alive and well. But his Imperial Army First Commander Sister demanded information as to where he had been, and why he never told them anything; of course, Steph'N could not share any pertinent information with her. His old friends and family on K'Halon Prime lived their lives and moved on during the last two years, while his memories of them were stuck in a two-year-old time warp. There was a lot of catching up he needed to do with them, but the psychiatrist said he was not ready. Maybe the doctor was right.

Steph'N took note of his vocabulary. He would have to carefully consider everything he said before the words came out of his mouth, now. The 'Rebel Major S'Loc' developed a bad habit of swearing the last two years. Using that kind of language was not acceptable for a Borgund Ranger. Neither was the small pad of fat on his belly. He thumped his stomach roughly. Too much Brandywine. He dropped to the floor and did eighty push-ups before he got too out of breath. He had much ground to make up, including getting back into the proper physical shape for a Ranger. It would take time.

He stripped and stepped into his spacious shower, without any time limit on the water flow, like the three-minute limit on the Rebel destroyer. He stood under the wide, rainwater shower head and let the hot water drench his head, washing away his anxieties, and releasing his pent-up emotions. Steph'N started to cry tears of joy. He was really home. He survived.

The bath towels were nice and thick, and he dried off, and shaved. He rubbed his hair on his head. Now he could let it grow again, like most of the Rangers did, and tie it back with leather ties. Steph'N began his T'Ly martial arts routine in his living room. He felt free for the first time in two years. When he completed his routine, he walked out in the dark onto his balcony to enjoy the night sky. Then he heard the knock on his door.

Steph'N immediately became defensive, as he had been the entire time during his last two years undercover. "Who's there?" He demanded.

"Room service, Master Commander Steph'N," the female voice replied. Room service? In the Ranger Barracks? No way. He opened the door, wearing only his underwear.

The Shi'Lon Ranger eyed him up and down, smiled broadly, and said, "Welcome home, Steph'N." She held a bottle of Brandywine in her hands. "I just found out you were here."

"Va'Pal," Steph'N whispered, and pulled her inside. She let her cloak fall behind her, smacked the clasps of her breastplate and backplate, and took her armor off, laying it on the floor. He caressed her face to make sure she was there. He began kissing her lightly, until she laid a big kiss on him. Then he picked her up in his arms, kicked the door shut, and took her to his bedroom. He was in her arms, at last. He was home.

K'Halon Prime

The faint outlines of the three moons setting in the late afternoon sky brought a smile to her tired face. Soon the sun would disappear under the horizon, and the air would become cold. But it was perfect on the balcony of the Royal Palace Main Court right now. She had it all to herself. Javette held out her arms and took a deep breath of the familiar, pine-scented air, and slowly exhaled.

"It's good to have you home, Javette. Everything is better when you're in the Palace. Your sister Shi'Lons will welcome your smiling face, I'm sure," G'Rosk said, walking up to stand beside her.

Javette smiled at her friend G'Rosk, and said, "It's good to be home. The trip took nearly three days, G'Rosk. I cut through the White Belt to save a day," she added with a confident, coy smile. They both chuckled, and turned in towards each other to talk. Two courtiers walked by them and exchanged greetings.

"As long as you're home safely, Master Commander. How are your new quarters?" He asked, conscious of the courtiers now gathering behind them. *Why did they have to gather here?*

"They are fine, sir. My things should be delivered from my old apartment in a day or two, I was told. The new apartment is larger than I expected, really. Now that K'Rissa is in the Royal Academy, I thought I'd get a small suite. But there's plenty of room for Dan'L and K'Rissa to stay when they come home for the Year End Holidays. The Emperor is generous, is he not, Commander Superior G'Rosk?" She asked. The balcony was almost full of courtiers and military officers. So much for a private talk.

G'Rosk stepped away from the beautiful Shi'Lon Ranger, as the crowd of people on the balcony became larger. He was so concerned about Javette and her Son, Dan'L, and wanted to talk with her alone. "Emperor P'Lau is wise, and generous to every citizen of the Empire. Good afternoon, Master Commander Javette," he said, and walked back to his office. Would he ever get to talk with Javette privately? K'Ser had been gone for more than a year, now. He missed his old friend, and could not imagine how his surviving Partner felt. Her young Son Dan'L was almost killed, twice. Then, soon after Dan'L returned, her five-year-old Daughter K'Rissa was taken away to the Royal Academy. G'Rosk knew Javette was a strong woman, but she had to be feeling the strain of the recent events. He wanted to be there for her. She was a dear friend.

The following Sunday, Javette slept in for an extra hour. It was her birthday, and she had been given three days off. She waited until most of the Rangers left the gym for her work out, and did not rush through her routine. The sauna was a great treat today, followed by a plunge into ice-cold water. Then she indulged in a massage for an hour. She felt so relaxed.

The aides finally delivered her things from her old apartment in the Family Residences. While she was unpacking her clothes, Javette rediscovered her black leather slacks, and put them on. Still a perfect fit. She found a cashmere sweater from her late husband, rarely worn. She put it on, and it was cut just above her bra. More of her buxom cleavage showed than she usually revealed. *Oh well*, she thought, *I'm just going for a manicure. Give the girls some air.* She put on her black high heels and walked to the closet for her leather jacket. Then the doorbell rang.

Javette opened her door to find G'Rosk standing there, with a worried look on his face. "I tried your comm link three times, Javette. Is everything all right? Are you okay?"

She let him inside, and explained, "Yes, I'm fine, G'Rosk. T'Anh gave me three days off, so I didn't wear my comm link to the gym. Sorry I missed your calls. Would you like to come in for a while?" She noticed his eyes looking at her breasts, and then quickly turning away.

He took off his cloak and walked to the breakfast bar, and sat where she pointed. "I wanted to let you know I spoke with Vu'Duc last week, and he agreed to let Dan'L come home for your birthday, Javette. He should arrive before nightfall. It was to be a surprise. But with Home World at its farthest orbital point from K'Halon Prime, it's taking him a long time to get here. He is not allowed to cut through the White Belt, as you are," he said with a smile. *What a voluptuous woman*, he thought. He hadn't seen her other than in uniform for a long time.

Javette's face brightened at the news immediately. "Oh, thank you, G'Rosk! Thank you so much!" She said, and lightly kissed her friend's cheek. "Let's celebrate, and have some wine, shall we?" She happily took out a bottle of red wine from the cabinet, opened it, and poured two glasses for them. G'Rosk watched her every move. No woman ever looked better in skin-tight leather trousers. They sipped some wine and began to talk. So many things to say. So much ground to cover.

"Take off your armor, G'Rosk, and relax. It's Sunday. Even you need a day off," Javette said. Her suggestion was excellent. G'Rosk removed his breastplate and backplate and set them on the floor. Then he twisted off his arm bands with their concealed assassin's knives, and laid them down, too. Much better. Javette poured more wine, and they resumed their conversation. *She is so beautiful. Her laughter could charm the angels*, he thought. G'Rosk had lost his partner in childbirth many years ago. Javette was the only woman with whom he would reveal his deeper thoughts and feelings. The level of trust between them was very high.

The afternoon passed, with the two long-time friends talking about everything. She reached for the wine bottle, and asked him if he wanted more wine. Suddenly he became very quiet. He looked into her eyes and answered, "More wine is not what I want, Javette."

The Shi'Lon Ranger saw his eyes change, and read his face. She knew exactly what he wanted. For the first time, she saw desire in his eyes, the fire burning into her soul. They were very close friends. Everything would change if this line was crossed. The silence between them was becoming uncomfortable. G'Rosk opened his mouth to speak, and said nothing; but his breath became shallow and quick. He lightly touched the back of her hand, and the electricity from his touch ran through her body, awakening all her senses. It was now or never.

Javette turned her hand over in his, palm up, and looked in his eyes. "Then take what you want, G'Rosk," Javette whispered. He gently pulled her off the stool to him and kissed her softly. Then he slid off his stool and embraced her body, and passionately kissed her, slowly and deeply. He completely took her by surprise, and Javette loved it. The cashmere sweater came off, then his blouse. Her bra went flying in the air, and he picked her up in his strong arms. The black high heels were kicked off on the way to her bedroom. Tremendous desire flowed between the new lovers, as they gave and took pleasure from each other in the late afternoon. The hours passed without either of them noticing.

Later in the evening, a tired Dan'L used his pass-key stick his Mother had left for him at the main desk on the recognition pad of her apartment, and opened the door. The floor was littered with a cashmere sweater, bra, high-heeled shoes, and Borgund Ranger blouse and armor. He instinctively reached for his bone-handled knife, and started towards the bedroom, to defend his mother. Then, he noticed the body armor. It was last generation, without the new plasma pulser pistols concealed in the backplate. The insignia on the black Ranger blouse was Commander Superior. It had to be G'Rosk with her.

Javette stepped out of the bedroom, tying the belt around her robe. "Dan'L," she said, reached for her Son's hand, and held it against her cheek. She was disheveled, and her long hair was a total mess. But she was smiling.

He took his hand off his knife, and apologized, "I should have called first, Mother. I didn't realize."

She said, "Not to worry, Son. This was unplanned. Purely spontaneous. And wonderful," she added, watching G'Rosk come stand beside her, fastening his trousers. He shook Dan'L's hand and welcomed him home.

"I'll get a room in the guest quarters tonight, Mother. Dinner tomorrow, then? A belated birthday celebration. We can all celebrate together, all right?" He asked, looking at his Mother and her lover: his Commander Superior. G'Rosk was a muscular, barrel-chested man, and had been his former mentor in Phase 2 and 3 Training for eighteen months.

"Dinner tomorrow will be perfect, Dan'L. See you then," she answered with a guilty smile. Dan'L started to leave; then he turned, laid his pass key stick on the breakfast counter, and left her apartment. He handled the uncomfortable scene well.

G'Rosk put his arms around Javette and asked, "Now, where were we?" They kissed and laughed, grabbed the bottle of wine and the glasses, and went back inside her bedroom.

At dinner the next evening, Javette and G'Rosk sat across from Dan'L and L'Mun. Everyone was having a fun time, enjoying a wonderful evening without uniforms. "This steak is terrific, isn't is, sir? I haven't had venison steak in months," Dan'L said, and G'Rosk agreed. The ladies enjoyed roasted duck with a sweet sauce, and they all ate well. Dan'L looked up and said, "There's Mur! Excuse me for a moment, please." He stood, and tapped Captain Mur on the shoulder. They shook hands, and he brought Captain Mur over to their table to introduce his Mother to him.

"I am so very pleased to meet you, Master Commander Javette. Dan'L spoke about you so often in Phase 1 Training. And L'Mun, a pleasure to see you again, too. Commander Superior G'Rosk," Mur said, and shook his hand. They exchanged pleasantries, and Mur asked for a moment with G'Rosk. "It is fortuitous to see you, sir. May I be allowed to send you something tomorrow on your private comm link? My Admirals do not see anything amiss. But perhaps another set of Ranger eyes might, sir," Mur whispered. G'Rosk agreed, and held up his wrist comm link to exchange numbers with him. Mur wished them all a good evening, and left for his own party.

Before dawn the next day, Mur sent G'Rosk vids of a huge salvage vessel, slowly gathering unidentified wreckage in space. The salvage vessel had special arms and catching containers affixed to it, for gathering floating remnants of destroyed ships, and other metal pieces. *Nothing special here*, G'Rosk thought. Then he sat bolt upright. The salvage vessel's big hangar doors opened, and fighters launched two by two rapidly; over thirty fully armed last generation fighters, in total. Not one of them bore any markings or tail numbers. They were Rebel ships. G'Rosk checked the date, and it showed last month. The coordinates were close to M'Wati. Why were Mur's Admirals not interested in this vid? He forwarded it immediately to the other Commander Superiors, and Emperor P'Lau.

XIX

The highest rank in the Rangers is Commander Superior. Each Royal Palace on Home World and K'Halon Prime contained two Commanders Superior, charged with commanding and leading the Shi'Lon or Borgund Rangers assigned to their command. Receiving a promotion to Commander Superior was the highest honor a Ranger could receive, and carried enormous responsibility. It also signified a great reward from the Emperor for a career of extraordinary achievement, excellent service to the Empire, and high trust.

Some Rangers celebrated their promotion to Commander Superior with a banquet for their fellow Rangers, family and friends. Most held welcoming events at the newly-assigned Command location for their Ranger charges and senior officers. But new Commander Superior T'Anh did not celebrate her promotion with anyone, not even her new Master Commander direct-reports. While she felt very appreciative of Emperor P'Lau promoting her to lead the Shi'Lon Rangers, T'Anh wanted to remain on Home World. She wanted to be near the Emperor, as she always had been. But Emperor P'Lau reassigned her to K'Halon Prime.

The biggest planet capable of sustaining human life in the solar system was K'Halon Prime. It was massive; a half-forest, half-desert world, capped at both poles with thick ice sheets. Although it was larger than Home World, K'Halon Prime supported less than a quarter of its population. And it was colder there, with much longer winters. It took 2.65 years to complete orbit around the sun. A terrible disaster occurred on K'Halon Prime more than 2500 years ago, stripping the forest, and all its human, plant, and animal life from one side of the planet, even its topsoil.

New C.S. T'Anh jumped into her new command position with both boots. Determined to improve performance in her Shi'Lon Rangers, T'Anh imposed more military-type regulations. She felt they needed to be more regimented and controlled. T'Anh wanted her subordinates to be more like her—tough, highly-skilled, and disciplined. Her motives were good.

The dedicated women warriors accepted their new Commander Superior T'Anh, and refrained from criticizing her harsh methods, or complaining about her rigid techniques. But the camaraderie within the K'Halon Prime Shi'Lon Rangers began to erode. A noticeable gap developed between the Rangers and their leader. The gap filled with resentment and fear, and exasperation with being unable to please C.S. T'Anh.

"Why can't she catch me doing something right?" Kayla whispered aloud. T'Anh had silently walked behind Novice Kayla, busy replacing training manuals and books on the highest shelves of their library, and startled her. Kayla crashed the entire rack of manuals and books onto the floor, and T'Anh blasted her verbally for being clumsy and incompetent. Everyone in the Palace library heard the scolding from T'Anh. It was an embarrassing moment.

Novice Kayla was assigned the most difficult, thankless tasks going forward. Whenever assignments came up requiring Main Court appearances, T'Anh intentionally did not choose Kayla, fearing she would embarrass her. The young Novice was kept hidden in the background for months, despite the recommendation from C.S. Bette to place her in Main Court assignments.

Kayla wisely chose to take out her frustrations by perfecting her weapons skills, and mastering the highest martial arts levels available to her, on her off-duty time. In the very early morning hours, late at night, and on Sundays, she studied and trained on her own, determined to qualify for promotion to full Ranger, and Flight Training School. She never knew what exactly she did to cause C.S. T'Anh to treat her so unjustly, but she refused to fail.

Begrudgingly, or so it seemed, Novice Kayla was promoted to full Ranger. With perfect scores in all her assigned study courses and training, C.S. T'Anh could not justify holding Kayla back. Novice Kayla received her promotion with humility and dignity, and showed respect to T'Anh. To M.C. Javette, and the several other Master Commanders reporting to T'Anh, the matter of Kayla's right to be called "Ranger," and one of them, was settled.

Her favorite family restaurant was chosen for the dinner celebration of Kayla's promotion to full Ranger. Dan'L was allowed to travel to K'Halon Prime for her party, and she appreciated Dan'L and her former mentor, C.S. G'Rosk being there to help her celebrate. They and Kayla's many friends feasted on several smoked meats, roasted fowl, and fresh bread and vegetables. For dessert, the owner proudly sat two bowls of prized blue apples and red pears from Ban'Ti in front of Kayla, and said, "Congratulations to our beautiful Shi'Lon Ranger!"

L'Mun whispered to Dan'L, "I can't believe how expensive those Ban'Ti fruits are. They cost as much as dinner!" She sipped more wine.

Cutting off a slice of red pear and holding it up to her mouth, Dan'L encouraged her to try it. L'Mun took a bite and savored the delectable fruit. "It's unbelievable!" She exclaimed, and winked at him as he passed the fruit around.

Kayla touched the gold, many-jeweled Shi'Lon Ranger ring on her finger, and commented, "It seemed to take much longer for my novice year to pass than did our year in Phase 1 Training. I thought I'd never get promoted to full Ranger." She let out a deep sigh.

Dan'L leaned over and whispered in Kayla's ear, "Your Commander Superior T'Anh worked you like a dog. It's very noticeable how much she dislikes you. She gave you every crummy assignment in the books. We all know it, Kayla," he said.

Sham'S asked, "Will you be reassigned to Home World for Flight Training School, Kayla? Commander Superior G'Rosk said I'll be reassigned for flight training next week, when I'm promoted to full Ranger."

Kayla lowered her eyes and replied, "No, I have to stay on K'Halon Prime. Commander Superior T'Anh ordered it. She said the Flight School here is just as good as the school on Home World." Her friends looked at each other without saying anything more about her situation. The K'Halon Prime Flight Training School was open to Space Cadre and private students, and not exclusively for Rangers, as was the Home World Flight Training School at the Royal Palace. The curriculum was different, and more generalized. She would have to take an additional nine months of classes to prepare her for fighter training as a Ranger. Kayla knew all too well T'Anh disliked her, and made every attempt to hold her back. T'Anh's resentment towards her was blatantly obvious.

The restaurant doors suddenly opened, and in walked M.C. Javette, carrying a box wrapped in silver paper and red ribbon. "A special gift from our Emperor P'Lau, to his Beloved Daughter, Ranger Kayla!" Javette proudly said. She sat the box in front of Kayla.

All her friends and Rangers gathered around to watch Kayla stand and carefully open the box. Inside was a new plasma sword, with an ornate, long handle. Javette said, "You must grab the handle with both hands and hold it until the little red light flashes, to imprint your DNA into it, Kayla." She picked up the new plasma sword and held it with both hands until the red light flashed. The sword immediately flamed with white, crackling energy, and her friends cheered. "Now, stand over here, away from the tables, Kayla," Javette instructed, "and twist the long handle."

The blazing white plasma sword handle expanded another 1.5 meters. "It's a spear, now!" Kayla exclaimed, and twirled it in her hands in martial arts movements. The other Rangers applauded. They were all trained with sword, spear, and modern weapons.

"Careful you don't set the restaurant on fire, Kayla," Dan'L said, and they laughed.

Javette said, "Emperor P'Lau said you were to have the first one, Kayla. Practice with it tomorrow. He wants you to demonstrate the extended handle and the new sword's capabilities in the Main Palace Court in two days—on Home World," she revealed. "Then, you'll begin flight training there in one week." Everyone cheered for Kayla, and her smile was genuinely grateful.

Kayla twisted her new plasma sword's handle again, and the handle collapsed within itself. She tapped the handle's end to shut off the plasma energy. The other Rangers all wanted to see the newest plasma sword. Many congratulations on Kayla's reassignment to Home World were given. Her friends shared Kayla's happiness and excitement, and the celebration continued with revelry and more wine.

When the celebration ended and everyone began to leave, C. S. G'Rosk and Javette pulled Kayla aside for a moment. "You're still assigned to Commander Superior T'Anh, Kayla, even though you'll be based on Home World. Make certain you report in to her every morning, and submit weekly reports on time, as if you were still on K'Halon Prime. If she gives you additional work, do it well. But do not let your Flight Training School work slide, Kayla," Javette cautioned.

G'Rosk advised, "Give T'Anh no cause to recall or order increased supervision for you. She is proud, and a Hero of the Empire, remember."

"I will be circumspect in my duties at all times, Commander Superior G'Rosk, and Master Commander Javette," Kayla said. She thanked them for their advice and wisdom, and stepped into the shuttle with the other Rangers and her new sword, and they flew off.

Javette said to G'Rosk, "Commander Superior T'Anh will feel slighted, since the Emperor chose Kayla to receive the new plasma sword, and ordered her to attend Flight Training School on Home World. He directly overrode T'Anh's orders. I asked for T'Anh to be allowed to present the sword to Kayla, but was ordered otherwise."

G'Rosk stated, "Even among the Borgund Rangers, there is talk of Commander Superior T'Anh's treatment of Ranger Kayla, Javette. Perhaps our Emperor did this to not only reward his newest Shi'Lon Ranger, but to also temper the situation," he suggested.

"Emperor P'Lau is wise. But T'Anh has her own eyes and ears on Home World. Ranger Kayla had best walk the straight and narrow path," Javette said.

"And watch her back," G'Rosk added.

Home World

The Rangers barracks at the Home World Royal Palace had been home to both Borgund and Shi'Lon Rangers for eight hundred years, since its initial construction. The only real upgrades to the rooms housing the Rangers were for plumbing, electrical, and communications. But most of the newly-promoted Rangers didn't mind. There was an intense feeling of espirit d'corps inside those ancient stone walls, with their lofty ceilings and exposed timber beams.

"This place reeks of tradition, duty, and service to the Empire. The dampness in the ancient building stones reminds us of the toil and sweat from thousands of Rangers who came before, whose boots you will try to fill," C.S. Vu'Duc proclaimed loudly to the newest Rangers in the General Assembly. He spoke for some time about the history of the Royal Palace, and the buildings within the Palace complex walls. Then, he assigned double rooms to the new Rangers, two Rangers per room, and handed out computer tablets with Royal Palace maps, protocol, etiquette, and their basic duties.

Vu'Duc said, "Study this information thoroughly to familiarize yourself with the Palace surroundings. No one is excused for arriving late because you're lost. Any area in red is strictly off-limits to you."

C.S. Bette spoke, "Those of you who have been assigned Flight Training School will assemble here at 5a.m. tomorrow. Flight School is fourteen months of classes, two months in flight simulators, and six months live flying. Fail, and you'll be transported by Space Cadre ships your entire career. Graduates will fly the standard fighters for two years, then train in the ES-class warbirds, if qualified. Before I let any Ranger pilot one of our Emperor's new ES-class warbirds, they must first prove themselves fully capable," she said sternly.

An assistant rolled in a cart stacked with aluminum cases, and a box of com tablets. Each Ranger scheduled for Flight School received his or her silver flight case of training books and manuals, and their new com tablet. The other Rangers whose math and science scores were not high enough to qualify for Flight School received a backpack of books and their own com tablet. The big, aluminum flight case weighed more than they expected when the Rangers took them off the cart.

"If any of you expected to have an active social life here in Capital City—forget about it for the next two years," Bette added sarcastically. "You have much work to do. Any questions?" She asked roughly. No one dare raise a gloved hand.

C.S. Vu'Duc ordered, "Take your new study equipment and personal gear to your assigned rooms and settle in. Meet in the dining hall in one hour. Dismissed!" The two Commanders Superior watched their newest Rangers scatter in search of their assigned rooms. "Quite an interesting crop of new Rangers this year, Bette," he commented.

She smiled, held up a 10-credit gold coin, and challenged, "I'll give you 5 to 3 odds at least two of them are late to Flight Training School tomorrow. And another 10-credit coin says half of them request tutoring in aerodynamics by the end of the week, Vu'Duc."

He responded, "I'll take those bets, at 50 credits each, Bette. There's real talent in this year's crop." She agreed to the bet, and they chuckled as they took the long staircase upstairs.

While most of the new Rangers were doubled-up for their room assignments, Kayla discovered her room was for single occupancy. She was the only Shi'Lon Ranger scheduled for Flight Training School this session. Her friend L'Mun didn't qualify for Flight School, and C.S. T'Anh kept her on K'Halon Prime. Kayla's room looked like a monk's cell with a tiny window. A single bed, wardrobe cabinet, and study table and chair amounted to her furnishings. At dinner that night, Dan'L came to her and Sham'S, and welcomed them to the Royal Palace.

Dan'L said, "We won't be seeing much of each other, except perhaps Sundays, Kayla. I have final exams next week, then flight simulator training begins the week after. I'm a little stressed right now," he added.

"You'll probably be head of the class, Dan'L," Sham'S quipped. "Hey—where'd you get that great knife? May I see it?"

Dan'L handed his bone-handled knife to Sham'S, and explained it had been his Father's knife for many years. Sham'S admired it, and passed it to Kayla. She hefted the knife, and tested its balance. As she handed it back to Dan'L, she noticed the knife sheath on his belt, and asked, "Why don't you get a new sheath for it? It's an impressive knife. The old sheath you're wearing looks worn through. I can see the green stiff backing showing through, Dan'L."

He was taken aback from her comment, but merely sheathed his knife and bid them good night. Upon leaving the dining hall, Dan'L ran to C.S. Vu'Duc's office, and asked to see him privately at once. Dan'L removed his knife and its sheath from his belt, and told Vu'Duc about Kayla's comment. "She saw green in the backing, sir. I never saw it. I thought it had the usual steel backing, for strength and support. Could my Father have hidden the Dalian green power crystal in this sheath? The scientists tested and scanned my knife, but not this old sheath. Shouldn't it be tested, too, sir?" Dan'L asked in a low, excited voice.

The senior Borgund Ranger took the knife sheath and looked at it carefully. Then he took a magnifying glass from his desk drawer and examined the inside closely. The leather next to the stiff backing was cut and worn from many years of use. Vu'Duc held it up to the light, and finally saw the green Kayla mentioned. His entire face froze. He punched numbers on his comm link, and said, "This is Commander Superior Vu'Duc, your Majesty. We need to meet with you at once, Sire, please!"

Two hours later at the top-secret research lab, the green Dalian crystal lay in a sealed glass container inside a flash-out room. The heavily-insulated room was fitted with charges, and capable of destroying the green crystal, or so they believed. No one could identify the type of mineral the green crystal was, or what it potentially could do. But they all feared the green crystal. The scientists excitedly talked among themselves about the tests they could perform on the crystal without disturbing its equilibrium; how to measure the potential of the crystal's destructive power if it exploded, and what the circumference of the firestorm would be; and whether or not the flash-out room could destroy the crystal, if it became necessary to do so. After several minutes, the scientists became so absorbed in their conversations they forgot the Emperor and his group were in the lab with them; they totally ignored the VIP in their midst.

Emperor P'Lau grew more upset every second, and remarked, "Our records state the Dalian androids were very careful with this green crystal, and told Master Commander K'Ser it was extremely powerful. And my young Ranger Dan'L has been wearing it on his belt every day for more than a year, here in the Royal Palace, and in Flight Training School! Thank the Creator we all were not blown to oblivion!" Dr. D'Vre apologized profusely to Emperor P'Lau, and took responsibility for the oversight. The Emperor, his Imperial Guards, C.S. Vu'Duc, and Ranger Dan'L left, and returned to the Palace Royal Court.

The Emperor dismissed his Imperial Guards for the night, and then declared, "Kidnapping of my Novice Borgund Ranger, with a price on his head equal to a planet's ransom. The green Dalian crystal hidden in plain sight for more than a year, of unknown energy and power – noticed only by my young Shi'Lon Ranger Kayla, her first night here in the Palace. Red crystals with fifth dimensional storage capability, and perhaps more potential than which we are aware. Scans of an anomaly inside the Royal Suite onboard our Imperial Battle Cruiser, which are now shadows, not to be found. And the only living persons in connection with all of these phenomena are two of my newest, most brave Rangers, Dan'L and Kayla!" The Emperor was very distraught.

The Emperor rose high in his flying throne over the Borgund Rangers in his Private Court, demanding any other information from them they might have; but everything had previously been reported to him. He summoned Ranger Kayla and C.S. Bette immediately, and they arrived in minutes. After Vu'Duc updated the Shi'Lon Rangers on the evening's discoveries, Emperor P'Lau announced, "Never in our reign have so many disturbing events with unexplained artifacts presented themselves. We will establish a Special Inquest about these events and artifacts at once. It will be top-secret, not to be spoken of other than in my private Royal Court, with those you see around you, and myself. Truth must be uncovered!"

Then the Emperor lowered his throne to the top step, slowly stood, tapped his wrist comm link to record, and ordered, "I command that Borgund Ranger Dan'L and Shi'Lon Ranger Kayla have their flight training accelerated to the fastest speed they can tolerate, to graduate as soon as possible. Day and night, if feasible. They are to proceed directly to ES-class training upon graduation. The Empire needs these Rangers ready to pilot my ES-class warbirds as soon as they are ready. All other duties are forbidden for them. There are unseen forces at work among us and outside our Palace walls engaging in the most dastardly subterfuge I have ever seen. We need our best and bravest ready to defend the Empire. It is my will."

The four Rangers bowed and left the Private Court, hurrying to C.S. Bette's office. She called C.S. T'Anh on K'Halon Prime, and relayed the Emperor's orders for Kayla to her. T'Anh's face plainly showed her displeasure with those new orders, but she said nothing in front of Ranger Kayla, standing next to Bette. C.S. Bette said to Dan'L and Kayla, "Now, both of you get to bed. You will need maximum effort and concentration every day going forward. We all have our orders. Dismissed."

After Dan'L and Kayla left C.S. Bette's office, she said to Vu'Duc, "Our innocent, young Rangers Dan'L and Kayla have made quite a name for themselves already. Our Great Emperor P'Lau has taken an intense interest in both of them, and will be watching their progress closely. Perhaps the Rebellion has taken a more pronounced, unanticipated turn. For some reason we do not know, both Dan'L and Kayla have become unintended targets of unknown forces at work against the Empire. But the Creator is with them," she stated.

Vu'Duc said, "The Rebellion is growing stronger every day, in every way possible. Only Emperor P'Lau knows exactly why he feels compelled to make these decisions, Bette. It is not merely favoritism. Such an unorthodox training curriculum has never been ordered, at least in my twenty-seven years of service. You are correct: the Creator has preserved both of their young lives, to what end, we do not know. Dan'L and Kayla may hold the keys to the future of the Empire." They sat at her work table, and stayed up throughout the night designing the new, accelerated training for their Rangers.

XX

When C.S. T'Anh was told Emperor P'Lau chose Ranger Kayla to receive the new, expanding plasma sword, she became annoyed. Why was a more experienced Master or First Commander Shi'Lon not given the new weapon? Adding salt to an unhealed wound, P'Lau directly ordered Ranger Kayla assigned to the Royal Palace on Home World—but still under T'Anh's command. If Kayla was reassigned to Home World, she should have been placed under C.S. Bette. T'Anh dutifully designed additional training assignments to her newest Ranger to augment her Flight Training School studies, and to increase the scope of her duties at court.

Only two days later, C.S. Bette called with the news Kayla was to be accelerated in Flight Training School. Later, the Emperor personally called T'Anh about Ranger Kayla, and said, "Our newest Beloved Daughter shows much initiative, insight, and great promise. I have ordered her to receive accelerated Flight Training School tutoring, to prepare her to pilot my ES-class warbirds as soon as possible. No other assignments or projects are to be given to her, so she may fully concentrate on her accelerated training. It is my will."

The will of Emperor P'Lau must be obeyed. C.S. T'Anh acknowledged his decision, but it felt as a dagger in her heart. The Emperor had overwritten her orders for his favorite little Kayla again. T'Anh considered herself chastised. She withdrew even more from her sister Shi'Lon Rangers, suffering in her self-imposed isolation for quite some time. All she tried to do was mold an inexperienced, clumsy Novice into a proper Shi'Lon Ranger, the Emissary and Protector of the Emperor. Ranger Kayla was without a doubt the favorite of Emperor P'Lau.

Twenty-one years ago, when she was eighteen and a young Ranger, T'Anh served at the Royal Palace of Home World. Empress Tan suddenly died in her sleep one night, under questionable circumstances. Her oldest child, fourteen-year-old P'Lau, was crowned Emperor immediately. At noon the next day, his public coronation took place. It was a magnificent ceremony. Many celebrations took place until well past midnight the same day. T'Anh was assigned as the Emissary of the boy-Emperor and escorted him to every function. She was very comforting to P'Lau, who had just lost his Mother, and was now thrust into a powerful role for which he was not quite ready.

During Emperor P'Lau's first official day of Royal Court, his younger brothers and sister, all officials of the Court, the Empire's highest Military Advisors, titled aristocrats, and his other half-brothers and half-sisters fathered by the Empress Tan's First Consort, knelt and swore allegiance to P'Lau – except for the oldest, Duma Wat. Over ten years senior to Emperor P'Lau, Duma Wat was a favorite at Court, and the best friend to P'Lau, until he was crowned Emperor. But Duma Wat was not Empress Tan's child. He was not of the Imperial bloodline.

Duma Wat became incensed at his little half-brother's good fortune of birth, and refused to swear allegiance to him. Warned by the High Priest and Tribunal Judges that failure to swear allegiance to Emperor P'Lau would result in his banishment and forfeiture of his inheritance, defiant Duma Wat dared his half-brother to send him away. He openly railed against the new Emperor in the Main Court, and claimed the throne as his. More than a few wealthy and titled aristocrats supported Duma Wat's claim to the throne. Imperial Guards quickly silenced their outbursts of shouting at the new boy-Emperor to step down. Order was restored.

The laws of the Empire must be obeyed, and enforced. The first official act of Emperor P'Lau was the banishing and exile of Duma Wat. Many of the courtiers and wealthy aristocrats present in the Royal Court spoke out loudly against the ruling, but were silenced by Imperial Guards. Several Rangers were chosen to protect the boy-Emperor P'Lau night and day for the first two years of his reign, including Shi'Lon Ranger T'Anh.

She took the boy-Emperor P'Lau under her personal protection. T'Anh defended him during an armed uprising by several disgruntled courtiers in the Main Court session the following week. She was wounded saving her Emperor. P'Lau demanded Ranger T'Anh escort him for his first two years wherever he went. He trusted her implicitly. When P'Lau grew older and became a man, T'Anh resumed her Shi'Lon Ranger duties, but was always called upon to accompany the Emperor during his travels for more than ten years. She protected him at all costs. Ranger T'Anh grew to love P'Lau as if he was her own brother. Or, some of her older Ranger sisters said, even more so.

Looking out the window of her large office in the K'Halon Prime Palace, T'Anh again wondered why the Emperor sent her to this cold, wintry world. Had he merely tired of her presence? Was there something she did to displease her Sovereign? Or did she just grow old and hard, and less pleasing to look at than the younger Shi'Lon Rangers, like Kayla.

Neither actions taken nor orders given by Emperor P'Lau came with explanations, unless he chose to share them. His orders were to be obeyed without question. T'Anh knew the Rebellion was expanding farther than in years before. The daily Confidential Reports sent to her and C.S. G'Rosk apprised them of Rebel raids and attempted attacks, which ones were successful, and which failed. The source of many Rebel activities originated directly from K'Halon Prime. The "Rumor Mill" in the Palace Main Court there was working at maximum capacity. Secret meetings where loose tongues wagged incessantly were all too common.

As the months passed, the Ranger High Command leaders were notified of special security measures to be enforced in both Royal Palaces, on Home World and K'Halon Prime. Everyone entering the Royal Palace main gates and Main Court now had to pass through scanners at security checkpoints. The men of K'Halon Prime frequently wore knives on their belts, many of which were hand-made, with jewel-laden handles, and very costly. Such knives were status symbols, and many were family heirlooms.

But neither belt knives nor any hidden weapons were allowed any longer. Even the ladies had to surrender their little one-shot laser tubes, usually concealed inside their clothing. Formal complaints filed by aristocrats and courtiers were rejected. Only the Palace Guards, Imperial Guards, and the Emperor's Rangers could bear arms inside the Royal Palaces.

Despite her lack of affinity with her own sister Shi'Lon Rangers, C.S. T'Anh got along well with the Borgund Commander Superior. Any task assigned to her and C.S. G'Rosk was carried out professionally and swiftly. Both leaders were cordial and polite with the courtiers, as well as the wealthy and titled aristocrats. But T'Anh's finely-honed listening skills and ability to interpret body language penetrated the false faces of a select few courtiers, and she shared her observations with G'Rosk. Not even the most perfectly performed Imperial protocols and etiquette could fool an experienced Shi'Lon Ranger.

Neither C.S. G'Rosk nor C.S. T'Anh were prone to gossip or conjecture, and did not permit such negative behavior among their Rangers on K'Halon Prime. But they could not ignore the instant silence of the powerful aristocrats and courtiers whenever they came into proximity of their whispers and subdued conversations. Main Court was intended to be an open forum, where anyone could feel free to speak their mind. But not now.

The ripples caused by such actions and whispers became more conspicuous. As the undercurrents of deceit, treachery, and betrayal became stronger, the peaceful waters of harmony in the K'Halon Prime Palace Main

Court churned. Rumors of the Rebellion abounded, with tales of the victories notched into the belt of Duma Wat.

Loyal courtiers became frightened of some of their fellow aristocrats, and an uneasiness permeated the Main Court. Very few spoke openly within the Main Court now, afraid their words might reveal secret sympathies for the Rebellion, or be misunderstood. The Emperor held court very few days during his last visit there, and would soon travel for his annual visit to M'Wati. There was no one to calm the feelings of trepidation in the Main Court. Only the constant presence of the Rangers and Imperial Guardsmen kept order, calmed the courtiers, and maintained the decorum of the Main Court, and the status quo.

XXI

Well before the dawn broke, Kayla was awakened by her alarm. She threw off the covers and jumped out of bed. One day, she would smash the piercingly loud alarm against the wall, and bury her head in the covers until she felt good and ready to get up. But such a day was not in her schedule for the next year. She pulled on her workout clothes, put her ear buds in her ears, and jogged to the gym.

No time for the treadmill this morning; another exam was facing her later today. Kayla took a few minutes to stretch out, and then mounted the stair-step machine. She hit the "Max Effort" program, and it began when she grabbed both the poles. While she stepped more steeply and rapidly, pulling and pushing the poles and breathing deeply, she listened to the computer voice in her ears describing the effects of atmospheric pressure on acceleration and thrust.

The stair-step machine finally slowed, and came to a stop. She was sweating and panting like a beast of burden. Kayla downed a cup of cool water to rehydrate, and toweled off. Her free weights routine was next, followed by T'Ly martial arts training. In forty-five minutes, she completed her workout, and headed for the shower. Other Rangers trekked into the gym.

"I've never seen anyone turn their martial arts routine into an aerobic workout before," First Comm. Bok commented. "If you're as strong as you are fast, the Empire is fortunate to have your service, Ranger Kayla."

Kayla blushed and thanked Bok. She hurried into the showers to clean up. Special tutoring began at 6a.m. and ran until lunchtime. They gave her half an hour to eat, then resumed her tutoring until 6p.m. Every Monday through Saturday, Kayla was tutored and trained, until she felt her brain's gray cells would burst. Her homework on Sundays took at least six hours. But she was keeping up with the accelerated program, and her grades were high.

Challenged to the limits of their learning ability, Kayla and Dan'L pushed themselves to the max. Ranger Dan'L was accelerated to the ES-class fighter simulators. He trained on the simulators ten hours a day, seven days a week, and passed the course in seven weeks. Dan'L flew the ES-class warbirds in live flights another two months with various instructors, and passed his tests. Upon receiving his ES-class pilot wings, he was awarded a bonus and three days off-duty. Then Dan'L was assigned to the Imperial Command Battle Cruiser for Emperor P'Lau, to escort and protect his Sovereign. He was also sent to be P'Lau's eyes and ears there.

Aboard the Imperial Battle Cruiser

The Imperial Command Battle Cruiser was the flagship of the Imperial Fleet, and the primary transport for Emperor P'Lau. Dan'L was assigned to the ship, and ordered to secretly investigate the Cruiser while carrying out his usual Ranger duties. The anomaly shown inside the Royal Suite on the red Dalian crystal holograph within the gold ring had not yet been found, and P'Lau felt it was still on board his Battle Cruiser. With hard work and some good luck, perhaps Ranger Dan'L could learn more about the anomaly, or whatever the object was physically. And hopefully, find it.

Friendly, out-going and always willing to assist the Imperial Guardsmen or Space Cadre officers on board the Cruiser, Ranger Dan'L became much sought-after for many tasks. Because of his willingness to assist in many areas, Dan'L was learning firsthand about the massive Cruiser operations. He knew there were hundreds of potential hiding places for some anomalous object approximately the length and size of what appeared in the Royal Suite scan on the red Dalian crystal holograph.

Under the guise of learning all about the Cruiser, Dan'L methodically scanned every floor, section, compartment, and room of the Cruiser during his off-duty hours. He'd tuck his small, portable scanner in his cloak pocket and casually walk from stem to stern, scanning everything. At meal time, he chatted with the ship's officers and learned where they worked, what their duties were, and other valuable information. The officers enjoyed the young Ranger's company, and his obvious eagerness to learn about their work.

More reserved were the Imperial Guardsmen. They could not fault Dan'L for being so interested in the largest, most powerful, and fastest battleship in the fleet. But it was uncommon behavior for a Borgund Ranger to be so socially active. The trained assassins and protectors of the Emperor usually kept to themselves.

Imperial Guard Commander Nat'N said to Dan'L during dinner one night, "The Borgund Rangers I've worked with always reminded me of falcons. They'd stay on their perch, watching everything, until they found their target. Then they attacked, killed, and flew back to their nest with their prey. So, are you a falcon, Dan'L, or a pigeon?" The other Imperial Guardsmen chuckled at his question.

Dan'L smiled broadly and replied, "The falcon knows his territory well, and protects it from other predators. This falcon is learning about his new territory, every open space, every nook and cranny. Then, I will take unsuspecting pigeons for lunch."

His answer brought a round of laughter from Commander Nat'N and his fellow Imperial Guardsmen. They were more accepting of Ranger Dan'L, but kept close watch of his daily interactions with the Space Cadre officers. Nat'N noted in his personal log: "The Ranger is a friendly assassin. Perhaps he has been sent here to uncover hidden assets of the Rebellion. I will watch him, and watch out for him." Nat'N could not be certain of Dan'L's true purpose, but he would discover he was correct.

The most difficult area on the Cruiser for Dan'L to explore was the Ship's Stores. It was a small storefront, fronting a humongous storeroom of cargo boxes, dry and refrigerated lockers, and massive freezers. Dan'L had no real reason to ask permission to go inside the Ship's Stores. No one besides assigned crewmen and food service personnel were allowed inside. Robots loaded, stacked, and unloaded the thousands of crates and boxes, vacuum-packed beef quarters, venison, pork, and other fresh and frozen foods. What a perfect place to hide the anomaly.

The Central Core of the solar system was the area between the White Belt and Ata, the giant gas planet. M'Wati, Home World, and K'Halon Prime orbited within the Central Core. Six Space Bases strategically placed within the Central Core provided protection for merchant ships and the huge space transports traversing the shipping lanes and major routes between the three main planets.

Any mercenary activity or pirating taking place within the Central Core was punished quickly and efficiently by the Space Cadre patrols. If necessary, the Battleship Groups would provide extra fighters and heavier gun fire to eradicate any problems. Rebel activity had to be quick, with pinpoint accuracy, and a successful getaway. The fighters used by the Rebels were more than twenty years old, mothballed Space Cadre craft. If their attack was not fast enough, the newer, faster Space Cadre fighters outran and blasted the Rebels into fiery explosions.

Food and supplies, and replacement personnel were delivered to the Space Bases by large cargo ships, and the transports. Flying slower through space than the fighters, the cargo ships and transports were prime targets for mercenaries, and Duma Wat. The supply and personnel ships always were escorted by Space Cadre ships in the last three years. Long convoys now traversed the shipping routes, and the cargo and human passengers were much safer than before. But it increased the costs by a huge amount for the Empire. The peoples' taxes were raised again to pay for the increased Space Cadre protection.

For twenty years, Duma Wat recruited rich and poor, young and not so young. He promised independent, democratic rule for each planet, and reduced taxes for all people. Many citizens saw little need to have such a large Space Cadre force in the solar system, with so many bases in full operation. Although Duma Wat promised democracy and independence, what he really wanted was to usurp his half-brother, Emperor P'Lau, and take his place as Emperor.

Three times in the previous seven years, taxes had been raised on the populace. And they resented it. The Rebellion was indeed growing, as Emperor P'Lau feared. He called a secret meeting of his Special Inquest Commission, and added M.C. Javette and C.S. T'Anh to the membership roster, which also included C.S. Vu'Duc, C.S. Bette, and Rangers Dan'L and Kayla. He tasked the Commission to develop innovative ways to defeat the Rebel Leader, Duma Wat, and slow his increasingly effective recruiting efforts.

Mission assignments for the Special Inquest Commission members were put on the back burner, except for Kayla's advanced tutoring, and Dan'L's assignment on board the Imperial Battle Cruiser. The Commission had become a trusted advice council for Emperor P'Lau, especially regarding the Rebellion. Every lead they followed, each act of sedition or treason led them back to the Rebellion, and Duma Wat. Someone was providing lists of names of discharged and recently retired officers and crewmen to the Rebel leaders. Applicants who failed entrance exams and assessments to enlist in the Imperial military were also being actively recruited by the Rebel leaders, with amazing conversion rates. The Rebels did not reject them, but welcomed them into the fold with open arms, and bonuses. The number of fighting Rebels was growing every day.

The Emperor said, "The incessant struggle for power and control are now touching my people. We must make a definitive, victorious stand against Duma Wat before he ignites the anger of the average man and woman. My Military Advisors assure me of the weakening of the Rebel forces in the Central Core; but my gut says otherwise. You are my most trusted Borgund and Shi'Lon Ranger leaders. What suggestions do you have for your Emperor? I want the truth— not some politically correct, sugar-coated response. I am sick of hearing how wonderful everything is, when all around me I feel undercurrents of treason and war!"

He gave them one week to prepare answers and suggestions to remedy the situation. The Commission members offered several proposals to Emperor P'Lau. Some were military; others were mission-specific recommendations for the Borgund Rangers. But all were excellent.

The Commission recommended several methods for discovery of the Rebel training camps. Those who volunteered without any military training had to be trained to mission-ready physical condition, and use of weapons. They agreed M'Wati would be one of the most logical places for their training camps. With thousands of islands, camps could be quickly set up, and many fighters trained under the nose of the Imperial Governor, and satellites orbiting above the planet. The Rebel base where M.C. Steph'N worked undercover as Major S'Loc had been abandoned, and relocated to another, unknown site. The new Rebel base was thought to be on one of the larger islands on M'Wati somewhere, but had yet to be discovered. Although Ranger Dan'L had spent time on the new M'Wati Rebel base, he was brought there unconscious, and transported off the planet without being able to pinpoint its location.

The Special Inquest Commission members also advocated for establishing a Media Group for the Emperor, so he could more effectively communicate directly with the people, and not rely upon the dissemination of information from the courtiers. He was also urged to increase his media presence, so the people could feel closer to the Emperor, and he would, in turn, be more accessible to the common man and woman. Duma Wat was famous for speaking directly to the people in his secret mass assemblies, and broadcasting his message of revolution through his Rebel followers. Emperor P'Lau was urged to reach out to the people, and reassure them he was still their Benevolent, Great Emperor, who cared about his people and their needs.

Aboard the Imperial Battle Cruiser

Several months later, Ranger Dan'L was invited by the Medical Officer to visit the Hospital. He was amazed at the sleek, efficient android nurses and medical techs. "Their voices are soft and feminine, almost human," Dan'L remarked. "I'm used to battle droids with commanding, male voices." The Doctor smiled at his comment, and continued the tour of his ultra-modern hospital, and introduced him to the human doctors and nurses working there.

"This is our Recovery Room, Ranger. We have three patients here, being treated for minor injuries from a workplace accident in the Ship's Stores," Dr. Ba'Lel said.

Dan'L saw two men with minor wounds, and a female crewman with a shoulder and collarbone brace. He walked up to the female crewman and said, "I'm Dan'L, a Borgund Ranger. Are you all right? Are you in pain? How can I help you, crewman?"

She answered, "I am First Crewman La'Do. This whole thing was my fault. The loading bot over-stacked the cargo boxes while I was taking a bathroom break. When I returned and tried to correct the bot's error, the entire stack of crates crashed, injuring my crewmen, and me."

Dan'L asked, "How bad is your injury? She will heal soon, won't she, Dr. Ba'Lel?" He appeared very concerned about the female crewman.

"She took the brunt of the accident, I'm afraid. We'll fuse the broken bones when the swelling goes down, but she's on Medical Restriction at least six weeks," the Doctor answered. First Crewman La'Do hung her head and sighed.

This was the opening Dan'L needed. He said, "There is no excuse for this accident, First Crewman La'Do. Obviously, the programming for your workplace robots is faulty. It is no fault of yours. Perhaps the entire process management system needs reconfiguring. Humans require breaks, period. I am required to report this incident to my superiors, you understand. This Battle Cruiser is the flagship of the Space Cadre Fleet, and primary transport for Emperor P'Lau. I will conduct the investigation myself, beginning at once!"

Admiral Wen'T, in command of the Imperial Battle Cruiser, was copied on Ranger Dan'L's "Urgent Report to Commander Superior Vu'Duc." In minutes, Dan'L had unlimited access to the Ship's Stores, their files and manifests, and all their records. He did not have to hide his small scanner inside his cloak. The big scanners were used to scan each crate and box, supposedly to verify weight and load content for his report. The technicians worked on the loading robots programming, and operations officers analyzed the storage processes for improvement. All the while, Dan'L and several crewmen scanned and recorded everything.

"This is the section for replacement electrical and computer components, Ranger Dan'L. We haven't opened any of these packing boxes in over a year. We can probably skip this section," one of the crewman wrestling the big scanner suggested.

"Have any boxes been added, moved, or taken out of this section in the last year?" Dan'L asked. The crewman stared at the dozens of boxes and crates, and then checked his com tablet.

He shrugged his shoulders and answered, "Don't think so. But, now that you asked, I'm really not sure, sir. The manifest is labeled 'Incomplete.'"

Dan'L called for the officer in charge, and a security squad. "Let's find out now," he said. The packing boxes were five rows deep, stacked twelve high. Behind the fourth row was an unmarked, two-meter-long black crate, with electronic locks and magnetic seals. The crate could not be scanned. He focused his recorder on the unusual crate, clearly out of place with the other packing crates and boxes, all of them labeled and coded.

"What the hell is that thing?" The officer in charge exclaimed. "This crate doesn't belong in here. It's unmarked, and doesn't even have a numbered scanning tag."

Dan'L tried to hide his excitement. He said, "It is the anomaly."

XXII

The live broadcast showing the recovery of the illegal crate was witnessed on board the Imperial Command Battle Cruiser by Admiral Wen'T and his full senior officer staff, and interested citizens of the Empire. A Public Media Officer narrated the removal of the long, heavy crate by forklift bots:

"Citizens of the Empire; we are today witnessing the discovery of an important, illegal shipping crate on board the Imperial Battle Cruiser. Upon removal of the crate from its hiding place, Admiral Wen'T will determine if it is safe to open. What is inside the crate, hidden here on Emperor P'Lau's Imperial Battle Cruiser? Who hid it here, and for what purpose? We all want to know," he said. Vid cameras focused on the unmarked crate from every angle.

On Home World, the Special Inquest Commission members, Emperor P'Lau, and his Military High Command officers watched, as transfixed as the people. "Take the crate off the Cruiser, and onto a small loading barge. Record everything for the people. Have the bomb bots stand by on the barge, and two skiffs, as well, in case evacuation is necessary. I assure everyone here this crate is not any possession of your Emperor," P'Lau stated.

After the mystery crate was loaded onto the barge with Ranger Dan'L, Admiral Wen'T and his officers, and the media crew, the Cruiser was moved 100 kilometers away. Then the officers broke the locks and hacked the electronic seals on the crate.

Dan'L looked at the other officers on the barge, and realized they were all wondering why they were so eager to witness the opening of the crate. The Media Officer continued his soft, steady monologue during each step of the activity, while the vid cameras whirred. This was the biggest event of his media career.

"Stand back. I will open the crate. I am the Commanding Officer of the Imperial Battle Cruiser, and I take responsibility for this crate and its contents," Admiral Wen'T declared anxiously. He put on large protective gloves and a face and body shield, and the cameras zoomed in closely. The Admiral popped open the crate, and raised the lid cautiously. His men continually scanned for booby-traps.

If it's wired to explode, my Mother will see her Son get blown to the Afterlife, Dan'L thought to himself. He watched the Admiral raise the lid halfway, then stop.

"Oh no. Oh No!" Admiral Wen'T cried, "It's a nuke. Evacuate the barge. Abandon ship!" Dan'L, the officers, and media crewmen abandoned the barge on the skiffs. The Imperial Command Battle Cruiser pulled farther away. The two skiffs launched at full speed, heading away from the barge.

Bomb robots took over, analyzing the nuclear warhead. They dismantled the arming, detonation, and ignition controls, then took apart the entire deadly weapon systematically. The inventory control number on the warhead was analyzed. It had been stolen from the arsenal on K'Halon Prime, at an unknown time. No theft had been reported from the Imperial Army arsenal on K'Halon Prime. This was an inside job, Dan'L realized. There were traitors here on the Cruiser, and on his home planet, K'Halon Prime. Traitors in their midst were planning to overthrow the Empire, and kill the Emperor. Emperor P'Lau was not paranoid, as some of his courtiers whispered. The Emperor was right.

Instead of hushing up the discovery of the warhead, as he and his predecessors before him would previously have done, Emperor P'Lau permitted the public media's investigative journalists to run with the story. The Emperor had nothing to hide—but traitors somewhere surely did. Daily reports were broadcast on the investigation of the warhead, and the traitors responsible. The official Media Group Secretary hosted a brief weekly session on "News from the Empire," and it became a very popular video segment for the people.

A special, live interview was broadcast from the new Home World Media Center when the investigation was concluded. Emperor P'Lau spoke to everyone in the Empire via closed vid screen directly: "We sincerely thank the many journalists for their excellent investigative work. We also thank the men and women of the Space Cadre; the Imperial Army, Air Corps, and Navy; Imperial Guards; and our Borgund and Shi'Lon Rangers for their efforts. We have all of you to thank for saving the lives of so many innocent men and women serving faithfully aboard our Imperial Battle Cruiser. Your investigations have helped uncover the evil traitors who plotted the murder of over 2,000 Space Cadre officers and crewmen, and our Imperial Guards. May the Creator bless you all!" He bowed his head to the invisible audience, and the camera faded out. It was a very touching moment.

Paradise Island

The next week, Ranger Dan'L flew his first ES-warbird solo mission to Home World, and landed safely on the Capital City Space Base. Then he was shuttled to Paradise Island, one of the dozens of islands off the mainland, an exclusive island retreat owned by the Emperor, and rarely used. Dan'L was immediately brought before Emperor P'Lau and his Home World Ranger High Command: Commanders Superior Vu'Duc and Bette. His report was in depth, succinct, and accompanied by vid recordings and testimonies from Imperial Command Battle Cruiser officers.

In formal and Royal Court settings, Emperor P'Lau always wore his painted white face and red lips, and sat on a flying throne. But today, the Emperor rocked gently in a hammock strung between palm trees, bare-faced. The Commanders Superior were casually relaxing on chaise lounge chairs under the shady trees. P'Lau said, "My newest Faithful Son has succeeded where others have failed me, and failed our Empire." He sipped his drink, and then commented, "The Royal Physician has ordered me to lower my blood pressure, or implode. We have decided to spend the New Year holiday here, on Paradise Island. More wine spritzers for everyone," he ordered with a big smile. Ranger Dan'L was given a commendation, an award, and a sizeable bonus. The young falcon caught his pigeons.

They celebrated the recovery of the nuclear warhead, and the uncovering of several traitors on board the Imperial Command Battle Cruiser and at the Imperial Army Arsenal, on K'Halon Prime. Partial fingerprints were obtained from the nuclear warhead casing and crate. Space Cadre and Imperial Army officer traitors on board the Imperial Command Battle Cruiser and at the arsenal on K'Halon Prime were arrested, and their confessions and court martials were made public. The Emperor's media moguls turned the frightening discovery of the nuclear warhead into a huge win for the Emperor.

One week before the New Year Holiday, Emperor P'Lau announced immediate tax rebates to each citizen for the last year's tax increase. His Special Inquest Committee members suggested the rebate, to demonstrate the generosity of the Emperor. The move was also a monumental success politically. There was much less reason to be angry at the Emperor. Credits to fund the rebates came from the confiscated accounts of Duma Wat. It was a brilliant tactic.

The last order of the year from Emperor P'Lau was to replace Ranger Dan'L with Ranger Kayla on board the Battle Cruiser: "Ranger Kayla will now be my Emissary on our Imperial Battle Cruiser. She will continue Ranger Dan'L's secret investigation, in the Shi'Lon Ranger tradition of Ambassador and Emissary for her Emperor. I have also selected Master Commander Steph'N to join our Special Inquest Commission." He then dismissed everyone in his private Royal Court for the Year End Holiday break. Everyone needed some time to themselves.

The Imperial Command Battle Cruiser traveled within orbit of Home World over the holiday break. On the first work day of the New Year, Ranger Kayla stepped off the transport on the landing deck of the Imperial Battle Cruiser. She spent the last hour on board the incoming transport marveling at the magnificent ship, its size, and the beauty of its design. It looked deadly, yet glorious. How could Duma Wat have wanted to blow it up in a nuclear explosion? It would make more sense to her if he was hatching some sort of scheme to overtake the vessel, and rule the solar system from its powerful bridge. She noted her thoughts in her personal log; then, after a few moments, she copied C.S. T'Anh, knowing T'Anh would probably disregard the personal log from the unexperienced Ranger.

The Commanding Officer, Admiral Wen'T, and several Imperial Guardsmen welcomed her on board. He pointed out her brand-new warbird, the ES-519, sitting across the hangar bay. Kayla felt excited, and free. The farther she was from C.S. T'Anh, the better she liked it.

At the Admiral's Welcome Dinner, Ranger Kayla was introduced to the ship's command officers and more Imperial Guardsmen. She conversed freely with them, and relaxed in the gentlemen's company. Trained in social skills, body language, and etiquette, Ranger Kayla impressed her hosts. But she knew there was much work to do on the ship. Friendships to be made. Trust to be earned. And traitors to be uncovered.

The officers in the small, dark office on the auxiliary cargo deck huddled together. Commander C'Mak whispered, "Another bloody Ranger has been assigned to the Cruiser. A Shi'Lon, this time. She will all but read our minds. She can see beyond our pretense of service to the Space Cadre. Stay clear of her. Don't look her in the eyes," he cautioned. "Will everything be ready in six months? There can be no more screw-ups."

The youngest officer replied, "All will be ready to go in six months, upon delivery of the assets, and receipt of our Lord's signal. Victory will be ours, Commander C'Mak." The men broke up their clandestine meeting, and went back to their duty stations.

The Emperor's Battle Cruiser is the most beautiful ship ever designed, Kayla thought again, as she strolled through the Observation Lounge. She chose a stool at a high-top table near the viewing window, and enjoyed looking at Home World. It was a wonderfully clear night in Capital City, and its lights twinkled all along the coast. For the first time in over a year, Kayla was relaxed, and felt comfortable in her surroundings.

"Greetings, Ranger Kayla," the tall, blonde Imperial Guard said. She turned to greet him, and smiled as she extended her hand. His hard countenance relaxed into a friendly grin. "I'm Commander Nat'N. Welcome aboard the Imperial Battle Cruiser, Shi'Lon Ranger." She completely caught him off guard with her charm and gentle disposition.

"Thank you, Commander Nat'N. It is truly an honor to meet the Commander of our Emperor's personal guards," Kayla replied. "Would you care to join me? The view of Home World is stunning!"

She's stunning, even in uniform, Nat'N thought to himself as he sat at her table. They chatted about the ship and the view of Home World, and then ordered tea. Their conversation continued for over an hour, with neither Kayla nor Nat'N aware of the many officers talking and drinking in the lounge. Nat'N escorted her to her suite and bid Kayla good night. They stared at each other a moment too long and she blushed, then quickly went inside.

One of the most delicious feelings anyone can experience is the spark of love between a man and a woman. It is sweeter than the richest honey. Kayla took off her cloak and hung it up, not noticing it slipped off its hanger onto the floor. She removed her breastplate and backplate, and laid them on the floor. She tried to concentrate on the next day's schedule, but was distracted by thoughts of Nat'N. He was so handsome, in a rugged sort of way, and had a very expressive face. She could read him like a book: a dedicated officer, but flirtatious, and a lady's man. Kayla floated into dreamland, staring out the porthole into space. All she could think about was Nat'N. She had fallen in love for the first time.

Compared to her sparse single room in the barracks, her onboard suite on Deck Three was luxurious. She'd graduated with honors and ES-class pilot wings, and Kayla enjoyed a welcome feeling of accomplishment. The crewmen finally delivered her travel bags, breastplate charging stand, and the big plex case containing her battle armor. Kayla was happy she was on the ship, and was making friends easily, like she did before coming under the thumb of C.S. T'Anh.

The first few days aboard a ship as large as the Cruiser were challenging for any newcomer. Over twenty decks, some split in many levels, with corridors ranging less than a meter wide, to ten meters in width. Kayla learned to close her cloak around her in the narrow corridors; she was careful no crewman touched her breastplate, and got an electronic shock. The crewmen were wary of being too near the pretty Ranger. Her predecessor, Dan'L, had accidentally bumped into a crewman in a narrow corridor and shocked the poor man unconscious.

Saturday's schedule showed a tour of the Royal Suite, on Deck Twelve. Kayla arrived at the double doors flanked by two Imperial Guards, and Commander Nat'N showed her inside. The very large sitting area faced viewing windows, offering a wide-angle view of the solar system. The furniture was white leather, with colored glass tables. There was space for fifty or more people.

Nat'N explained, "When Emperor P'Lau is on board, the wall panels are opened. We keep them closed, otherwise," he said, and touched a panel. The entire wall section opened, revealing a fully-stocked bar with ten stools, and a large vid screen. Nat'N touched the adjacent wall panel, revealing a wall sculpture, which occupied most of the space. It was an abstract design of many colors and textures, very pleasing to the eye. It was almost hypnotic.

While Kayla looked at the sculpture, it slowly changed, morphing into a slightly different pattern. "It's moving! Did you see it, Commander?" She asked.

Nat'N walked beside her, enjoying her reaction to the artwork. He stared at Kayla, watching her face, alive with wonder and joy. "The artwork is intended to enhance the mood of the viewer, I was told. One of those new, 'feel good' art pieces," he said. He felt great being near her, and silently moved a little closer. The sculpture moved again, and changed colors, with more red in the design. The artwork elicited suggestive feelings, although the art was abstract.

Suddenly, Kayla's cheeks flushed bright red, and she turned from the artwork and stated, "Please continue the tour, Commander Nat'N." They completed the tour of the Royal Suite's four bedrooms and lavish baths quickly. Ranger Kayla thanked and saluted the Commander of the Imperial Guards with a hard right fist striking her left breastplate, and walked down the hall.

One of Ranger Kayla's duties was to join the Space Cadre fighter patrols every other day in her ES-519. Patrols lasted three to six hours. The fighters swept the immediate space around the Cruiser and its group of seven support vessels regularly, to keep a watchful eye open for Rebel activity.

During post-flight debriefing the third month, Kayla asked the Flight Commander, "Sir, I am still learning my flight duties here. But it appears we are flying our patrols in regular patterns. The same course, every day. Should we not patrol in more varied flight patterns, sir?"

The twenty-year officer chafed at her question. "Just follow your squad's flight plans, Ranger Kayla. Let the Space Cadre officers maintain the patrol routes," Commander C'Mak retorted. He turned and walked quickly down the hall.

Kayla notated in her nightly report to C.S. T'Anh the exchange with Commander C'Mak. She respectfully recommended the patrols alternate their flight patterns, to protect against potential Rebel attacks. But her notes were ignored by T'Anh, since Kayla was so unexperienced.

XXIII

During her weekly live report to T'Anh, Kayla mentioned again the routine of the patrol flights. "I am concerned about the predictability of our flights. If I were a Rebel tactical flight officer, it would be very tempting to insert an attack against the Battle Cruiser, Commander Superior T'Anh. Wait three hours until the patrols are at their maximum range from the Imperial Command Battle Cruiser group, and then attack," she said emphatically. "Half of the fighters would be out of range to defend the battle group."

"Commander C'Mak should know this, Ranger Kayla. He is in charge of flight operations. Address this issue with him," T'Anh answered, trying to dismiss her concerns.

"I have done so, Commander Superior, but he said to let the Space Cadre handle the flight plans and routes. I mentioned our exchange in last week's nightly reports. The Commander seemed unconcerned about the predictable flight patterns. But I am highly concerned, Commander Superior T'Anh. This Battle Cruiser would be a sitting duck."

T'Anh saw the genuine look of concern on her Ranger's face. Her points were valid. She said, "I will take your concerns under consideration, Ranger Kayla. Are there any issues besides the flight plans troubling you?"

"Only a question: did Ranger Dan'L's personal scanning reports stop after the warhead was discovered? Was he granted access to the 'Top Secret Experimental Lab' on the lowest deck, below the auxiliary cargo hold? I noticed several unmarked cargo crates being delivered to the lab, and rather quickly, too, as if the crewmen were trying to hide them. It was very strange," Kayla said. "They did not see me watching their movements. I stood in the shadows. I am concerned the unmarked crates might contain contraband, or illegal weapons, Commander Superior T'Anh."

Now this was real news from the young Ranger. "I will discuss your question with Commander Superior Vu'Duc, and ask him to confer with Ranger Dan'L. T'Anh out."

The next day, Kayla was ordered not to continue her investigation of the Top Secret Experimental Lab, and use extreme caution on board. "Ranger Kayla, there is no deck on the ship's internal diagrams or schematics below the auxiliary cargo hold. No such 'Top Secret Experimental Lab' is listed in the Cruiser's records. No personnel are assigned to any such facility. How did you find this place?" C.S. Vu'Duc demanded.

Kayla answered, "One of the officers in our General Assembly said he managed the cargo decks, and offered to show them to me during the big shipment delivered last week. Thousands of crates and shipping boxes were off-loaded from the cargo transport onto barges, then they were brought into the auxiliary cargo hold. I saw a full barge dip below the landing bay, and he told me about the lower deck, and the Top Secret Experimental Lab. When the officer left to supervise the crewmen and bots for the fresh food items, I went downstairs to check it out," she answered. "It's a huge area, nearly as big as the main cargo bay. It's too big to be a secret, sir."

She waited while her vid comm monitor flashed "Transmission Paused." The Ranger leaders were privately discussing her latest information; but with whom? In a few minutes, T'Anh took over her call. She ordered, "You are to avoid the lower cargo decks from now on, and do not discuss this matter with anyone on board. Understood, Ranger Kayla?" Her face was tense.

"Understood, Commander Superior T'Anh. Kayla out." By the look on T'Anh's face, this discovery was important. Kayla found out one reason her senior Ranger leaders were so concerned in a few days. The announcement was made in the General Assembly: the Cruiser was ordered to make preparations for departure in two weeks. Destination: M'Wati. And Emperor P'Lau and his Main Court entourage would be their passengers.

Kayla called Ranger Dan'L later, and asked, "Dan'L, have you ever received any other messages from the Dalians or your Father inside the red crystals, possibly inside one of those boxes you told me about?"

Her question was interesting. "No, Kayla, I have not. But I haven't used the red crystals in over a year. Why do you ask now?"

"Because intriguing things are happening here on the Imperial Battle Cruiser. We are to make way for M'Wati soon, with several VIPs. Perhaps you could humor me, and look inside the gold ring again, Borgund Ranger," she suggested, trying not to give her suspicions away to anyone potentially eavesdropping on their conversation.

"If I have time, I will. Ranger Dan'L, out." He would definitely use the ring he inherited from his Father with the red Dalian crystals. The anomaly was found inside the stored holographic schematic data there, and it turned out to be a nuclear warhead. Dan'L used the Dalian crystals again several times, but no additional information was found. What was Kayla looking for on the ship?

New orders appeared on her com tablet hour by hour, in a steady stream. As the Emissary of Emperor P'Lau, Ranger Kayla represented him in all matters, reported, and recorded every official meeting. Her mundane shipboard duties were set aside, to prepare the Cruiser and its personnel for its highest VIP passenger. The official meetings tripled in frequency.

Commander Nat'N and Kayla had become regular lunch partners the past few months, and she typically enjoyed dinner with all the Imperial Guardsmen in the dining hall. The Guards liked Kayla, and sometimes shared stories about each other with her. The Guards were her best friends on the Cruiser, and they had a lot of fun talking together. But since the announcement of the Emperor's arrival, Kayla and Nat'N avoided each other intentionally.

Commander Nat'N's "command and control" presence and hard face melted into a boyish smile whenever he was too near Kayla. He was crazy about her, and could not hide his feelings. Back on Home World, the handsome Imperial Guard had several girlfriends, but none of them could compare to Kayla. Nat'N knew Kayla was very busy now, but he missed seeing her so much; it was painful. He decided they should come to terms about their feelings. Either she felt the same about him, or she didn't. Nat'N had to find out soon. The Emperor would arrive in ten days. He had to regain his focus and concentration to protect the Emperor.

Each officer and crewman had their specific assignments in preparation for the Emperor's arrival. Most would be in presentation formation, dressed in their formal white or black uniforms, when the Imperial Shuttle landed in the main hangar bay. Everyone knew their spot.

Eight days before the Emperor's arrival, Ranger Kayla accompanied Admiral Wen'T and his officers for the main hangar bay inspection, at his request. All cargo crates were being moved out, or back against the walls. Kayla made notes on the dozens of hiding places an assassin could lie in wait for her Emperor. The Admiral and his officers walked along the hanger bay wall, watching the cargo crates being pushed back and stacked.

Ranger Kayla and the Admiral overheard one crewman complaining loudly, "All this trouble so the Emperor can see his pretty officers in formation. And so we can look at his ridiculous painted face!"

In an instant, Ranger Kayla drew her curved-blade knife and held it at the throat of the complaining crewman. "Who do you serve, crewman?" Kayla demanded, backing him up against the wall.

His eyes grew as large as giant, white marbles. He uttered, "I serve Admiral Wen'T, and the Space Cadre." The man began to shake, and looked pleadingly at Admiral Wen'T.

"Wrong answer, crewman. One last time, I ask you: who do you serve?" She demanded, pressing the flat of her blade against his throat.

"Emperor P'Lau. I serve the Great Emperor P'Lau!" He choked out.

"As do we all. You have disparaged the Emperor you serve, the Emperor whose will I am bound by blood oath to obey," Kayla said. The Admiral and his officers were silent. They knew the Shi'Lon Ranger had license to kill any one, especially the disgruntled crewman with the loose tongue. They could not interfere with the Ranger's justice.

"I—I meant no harm. Forgive me, Ranger. Please. Forgive," the crewman pleaded.

Her green eyes were intensely focused. Kayla said, "The Great Benevolent Emperor P'Lau serves us all. Today, you will taste his mercy, crewman." Kayla flicked the tip of her knife under his chin, and drew a drop of his blood onto its tip. She touched his lower lip and left the drop of his blood there for him to taste. "Now—fulfill your duties, and thank the Creator for your merciful Emperor, and your life," she said, and replaced her knife in its concealed place in her breastplate.

The hangar bay inspection incident went viral throughout the ship. The good-looking pilot of the ES-519 spared the life of a careless crewman. Kayla had been congenial and cordial to everyone since her arrival; a perfect lady. The officers and crew realized today, Kayla did indeed deserve to wear her black cloak and blood-red armor. She was the Emperor's Shi'Lon Ranger. Respect and fear her.

XXIV

In five days, Emperor P'Lau would arrive on his Imperial Battle Cruiser. Every deck was swabbed spotless. All viewing windows were crystal-clear. Bots and crewmen in the ship's laundry were overwhelmed, cleaning all the white and black formal uniforms. Imperial Guards monitored the cleaning of the Royal Suite. Every glass table and viewing window gleamed in the lighting.

After the cleaning crew left the Royal Suite, Commander Nat'N took a long lunch break with Ranger Kayla. After a few minutes of discussing the ship's readiness, both stopped eating. The silence between them was deafening. Nat'N finally said, "Walk with me to the arboretum, please, Kayla."

Nat'N loved the arboretum, full of live plants, fruit and nut trees, and live birds singing. They knew visitors were observed by the video cams, so he led her to the noisy artificial spring, to talk beneath the tall tree. After a few minutes of enjoying the beautiful arboretum, they turned towards each other, and stared into each other's eyes.

"Kayla," he began, then his throat closed, and no words came out. Nat'N reached for her gloved hand, then stopped. He smiled and asked, "Is there anywhere I can touch you, without being shocked unconscious, or having one of your knife blades at my throat?"

His question broke the uncomfortable silence, and they both laughed softly. She answered, "No, Commander Nat'N, not under the many vid cameras here. We're both in uniform, sir. Anyway, at this range, it's my hidden darts I would use, if provoked."

He wanted to do more than provoke her. Time to tell her outright. "I want you out of that uniform tonight. I want you on my bed. I want your arms around me, and your lips kissing me. Tonight. Tomorrow. Every night. I need you. I burn for you, Kayla, with every fiber of my body," Nat'N whispered low and soft, with his eyes aflame.

Kayla realized she was trembling, and keenly felt the strength of Nat'N's passion. She whispered, "If what you feel is more than a temporary surge of desire, then show me. I will not settle for a hit-and-run, Nat'N. If this is real, show me—tomorrow." She turned and quickly left the arboretum.

Nat'N wanted to climb the tree and hang upside down, like a kid. She didn't say no. But she didn't say yes, either. Kayla was the highest tier of the warrior class, a Ranger for the Emperor, and P'Lau's Beloved Daughter. The Imperial Guards ranked directly below them. The Shi'Lon Ranger would not compromise herself with a Guard looking for a brief, shipboard affair. He fully understood her situation.

After work, Nat'N spent hours alone in his room, being honest with himself, and soul-searching. Kayla was more than a girl to be played with, to "hit-and-run," as she said. She was the one, the only girl for him. How could he show Kayla how he felt without coming across as a horny jerk—just like the other two thousand horny jerks on this ship?

The officers and crew were busy finalizing preparations for the Emperor's arrival. Everyone was on edge. To top it off, Commander C'Mak abruptly switched the patrol flight plans last minute, extending the routes to a total of eight hours each day, for the next five days. When she relayed the new development to her Commander Superior T'Anh, she was ordered to remain aboard the Cruiser, and not accompany the fighter patrols as she had done for the past seven months. For once, she and T'Anh were in perfect agreement. The other pilots commented to her their new orders came at a critical time, during the Emperor's arrival. Kayla became even more suspicious than she had been. Something was in the works.

M.C. Steph'N sent Kayla a message that he and Ranger Dan'L would be escorting Emperor P'Lau's Imperial Shuttle to the Battle Cruiser. He invited her to have dinner with them the night of their arrival, and she accepted. Kayla was anxious for Steph'N to meet Nat'N, and the other Imperial Guards with whom she had become friends.

"Dinner at 8:30?" Her comm text read from Commander Nat'N. The man did not give up easily. After an hour of consideration, Kayla agreed to meet him at one of the restaurants in the shopping plaza on Deck 4. She bought a lovely new dress in a boutique, then walked into the hair salon, held up her thick ponytail, and asked the stylist, "Anything you can do with this in 1½ hours?"

At 8:35, an anxious Nat'N fidgeted at a table for two, trying not to drink both their poured glasses of wine. The host led an absolutely gorgeous Kayla to Nat'N's table, smiling confidently. She knew she was looking great. Kayla wore a long white dress, with a white and gold-paneled matching long jacket. Her long black hair fell around her shoulders, perfectly styled. Delicate eye make-up of golden flecks accentuated her bright green eyes, and her lips were the color of red wine.

"I've never seen you so beautiful, Kayla," he said, and held her chair for her to sit. He was nearly speechless. He could not stop smiling at her. What a prize for any man to win. Nat'N eventually managed to talk normally with Kayla, and they had fun together. They strolled the plaza after dinner, making small talk, and enjoying being with each other. He led her once again to the arboretum, where he felt comfortable. They sat on a bench looking out the viewing window at the stars. The birds were quiet, and the lighting inside was like a moonlit night at home. It was so peaceful.

"I would like to ask you something, Kayla. But, if you cannot give me an answer tonight, I'll understand," Nat'N began. He took a deep breath, kneeled, and asked, "Would you consider giving this Imperial Guardsman the chance for true happiness, by letting me love and cherish you every day of our lives? Would you be my life partner, Kayla?" His question entailed more than she anticipated. He really took her by surprise, and she was speechless.

Kayla looked into his eyes and studied his face. She read no signs of deceit or untruths in this man at all. He had no ulterior motives. Her heart began racing, and she parted her lips to speak, but could say nothing. She slipped her hand in his and smiled. The knowledge that the vid security cameras were recording was the only thing holding her back from kissing him.

They stood and silently walked towards her suite. She touched the recognition pad and stepped inside, turned to face him, and said, "Yes, Nat'N." His face lit up, and he smiled broadly. Kayla let him inside her suite, and they kissed and held each other. Her sofa was a wonderful place to make out, and stare at the stars in space. They talked about their future as partners, and how the commitment would change their lives. Nat'N declared his true love for Kayla, and they kissed again; but she stopped his advances short of having sex. Nat'N walked—skipped, ran, or flew, who knew—back to his quarters. She said yes!

The long, solid gold and jewel-laden ring on Kayla's third finger of her left hand was the Shi'Lon Confirmation ring from Emperor P'Lau, and she stared at the ring with new understanding. It was law that no Ranger could marry, because they were sworn by blood oath to the Emperor. But they could take a partner, with the Emperor's permission. Any child born to their union belonged to the Emperor, and must be given to him to teach, train, and care for, around their fifth birthday. If Emperor P'Lau approved, she would soon wear a plain gold partnership band on the third finger of her right hand, as would Nat'N.

Commander Nat'N and Ranger Kayla filed their Partnership Petition to Emperor P'Lau the next day. This was a totally unexpected move from Ranger Kayla. Emperor P'Lau called Kayla directly, and asked, "My Beloved Daughter Kayla, you have served us on the Imperial Command Battle Cruiser for only seven months. Are you certain my Imperial Guard

Commander Nat'N is worthy of your commitment and devotion? This is a life-long decision. You are a Shi'Lon Ranger, my child, with many years ahead of you to serve the Empire. You are so young, my Beloved Daughter."

Ranger Kayla bowed her head and replied, "I serve you, my Benevolent Emperor P'Lau, and obey your will. If it is not your wish, then I will withdraw my petition to take Commander Nat'N as my life partner. But he has my heart, Sire. My service is to you, my Lord Emperor. Please guide and counsel your Beloved Daughter, my Emperor," she asked softly.

The Emperor knew Kayla had no living parents to advise her. He said, "I must ask you: have you given yourself to this man? Is there any....urgency in your petition, my Beloved Daughter?"

Kayla blushed and quickly replied, "No Sire, I did not give myself to him. No 'unplanned urgency' is on the horizon. I will not submit to him without your approval, Emperor P'Lau," she answered, looking directly into the vid camera. "I am your Shi'Lon Ranger. Your will is my command."

The Emperor was pleased Kayla was not in a desperate situation; she was not pregnant. His unpainted face showed his relief. P'Lau said, "Always follow your heart, my Beloved Daughter, and obey my will."

The scheduled arrival of Emperor P'Lau and his large entourage was made even more memorable by receipt of the signed Petition of Partnership from him, delivered to both Commander Nat'N and Kayla's comm links. During the trip to M'Wati, they would have their commitment ceremony at the new moon, next month. The warriors were both love-struck.

Evenings spent together were getting very cozy, and romantic. Alone in her room, they could barely keep their hands off each other. But she was the daughter of strict parents, and would not give in to his wish to become physically joined until after their partnership ceremony. Although he felt he was going crazy with unrequited desire for her, Nat'N respected her feelings. He knew he was the "Right Man" for whom Kayla had saved herself, and it made him proud.

Kayla wisely insisted they concentrate on the arrival of the Emperor and keep apart for a while. Nat'N agreed reluctantly. But he knew just being around her made him senseless and unfocused. He was the Commander of the Imperial Guards and needed to regain his control. They agreed to see each other only at mealtimes surrounded by other Imperial Guardsmen, and not chance being alone with each other until their ceremony. *Behave yourself, man,* Nat'N told himself for the umpteenth time. *The Emperor is watching over his Beloved Daughter.*

XXV

"Imperial Shuttle approaching main hanger bay one. Clear main hangar bay one immediately," the announcement ordered. The Imperial Shuttle was no four or eight-person craft. It was a transport capable of carrying fifty people, and was heavily armored. The escorting ES warbirds and Space Cadre fighters hovered until the Imperial Shuttle landed on the main hanger bay deck. Then they flew to the aft bays and landed.

Bells sounded, and over 1800 officers and crewmen in formal uniforms marched into their presentation formation. Admiral Wen'T and four senior officers stood at the opposite end of the hangar bay, awaiting their signal to approach. The Imperial Guardsmen marched to the Imperial Shuttle, carrying their pulser spears. One blast from a pulser spear could kill several attackers, and it was the primary weapon of the Imperial Guards.

The hatch of the Imperial Shuttle slowly opened and began to lower. Admiral Wen'T and his officers quickly marched towards the hatch, to welcome their VIP guests. Shi'Lon Ranger Kayla walked well behind the Admiral's welcoming party, dressed in her formal red uniform cloak and dress, and red leather high-heeled boots. When the hatch touched the deck and the Emperor appeared, Commander Nat'N declared, "The Great Emperor P'Lau, Ruler over all Known Worlds and Conqueror over the Unknown Domain. All hail the Emperor!" The officers and crewmen hailed P'Lau, and he walked down the hatch alone. Admiral Wen'T and his senior officers saluted with the other 1800 officers and crewmen in formation.

Imperial Guards followed the Emperor for a few steps, then he stopped to receive his Shi'Lon Ranger. Kayla knelt before her Emperor, drew her fiery, white plasma sword with both hands, and brought the handle down against her left breastplate, in the Royal Salute.

Emperor P'Lau commanded, "Rise, my Beloved Daughter, and walk with me." Kayla replaced her plasma sword in its sheath, and accompanied her Sovereign through the main hangar bay, up to the Royal Suite. An Imperial Guard halted their progress while he systematically scanned the entire Royal Suite, checking out each room thoroughly. He welcomed the Emperor inside, and opened the wall panels for him. The Emperor walked to the farthest end of the spacious room, and sat in his preferred chair, now flanked by four Imperial Guards.

The Emperor whispered to the closest Guard, who then announced, "Our Emperor P'Lau commands Shi'Lon Ranger Kayla and Commander Nat'N to approach." This was not the usual sequence of welcome protocols. They walked to the Emperor, knelt, and bowed their heads. The Royal Suite was now packed with the Admiral, his command officers, and members of the Royal Court traveling with the Emperor.

In a soft voice, Emperor P'Lau said, "It is the wish of your Emperor to meet the Imperial Guard who stole the heart of our youngest Shi'Lon Ranger. Rise, my children, and let me look at the both of you." Kayla and Nat'N stood, both feeling nervous in the large crowd. The Emperor looked at them for a moment, then said, "We have taken the liberty of bringing the High Priest on this journey, so that your vows of partnership may receive his blessings. We will honor your union with a banquet after your ceremony," he added with a smile. "You may enter into your partnership with our endorsement." Then they both were dismissed for the day.

The officers and courtiers congratulated Kayla and Nat'N as they left the Royal Suite. When they finally entered the corridor and were alone, Nat'N whispered to Kayla, "The High Priest will bless us? You must be one of the Emperor's favorite Shi'Lon Rangers, Kayla."

She replied, "What an honor for the Emperor to do this for us. May the Creator bless Emperor P'Lau." She walked down the many staircases to her suite on Deck Three. As she entered her suite to change out of her formal dress uniform, Kayla thought about Nat'N's comment. Never had she considered the Emperor as having any favorites among the Shi'Lon Rangers. He treated them all with respect and honor.

There were fifty-five Shi'Lon Rangers and over one hundred-fifty Borgund Rangers. Some more-experienced Rangers were assigned duties on the Space Bases, or other individual postings. But the majority of the Rangers served Royal Palace assignments, split between Home World and K'Halon Prime. They were frequently sent on special assignments, but returned to one of the Palaces afterwards. Partnered Rangers were housed together in private suites in the Ranger Barracks, then in the Family Residences, after they had children. Kayla knew her partner-to-be had one more year of service assigned on board the Battle Cruiser. The length of her assignment there was unknown to her.

It felt good to take off those red high-heeled boots. Her usual black boots were so much more comfortable. Kayla changed out of her formal red uniform dress, and into her black trousers and blouse. Quickly she stuffed her feet inside the black boots and snapped the latches along their sides closed. Then she carefully inserted hidden knives inside the tops of her boots. The breastplate and backplate were put on her torso next. She removed her cloak from its hangar; then the ship's alarms suddenly sounded, "Red Alert! Red Alert! All hands to battle stations. This is not a drill. Battle stations! Red Alert!"

Kayla quickly went to the big plex case, smacked the opening button, and stepped into her black battle armor. In seconds, the shiny black armor closed tightly around her, and she put on her helmet to complete its seal. The black cloak was swirled around her shoulders as Kayla ran back to the Royal Suite, nine decks above her.

Battle armor for the Rangers had power cells in the heels and joints, enabling them to run faster, and have more strength. The armor itself was resistant to laser blasts, and several other energy weapons. When she turned into the corridor bordering the Royal Suite, a security officer yelled to her, "They were hiding inside the Royal Suite walls, Ranger Kayla! They're attacking the Emperor! Hurry!"

The corridor was packed with defending Space Cadre men, exchanging laser fire with the Rebels inside the Royal Suite. "We can't break through their line," the security officer told her. "The Rebels have barricaded themselves inside. The Imperial Guards stopped firing their pulsers. We've got to get inside!"

"Crouch down for me," Kayla ordered. She lowered her visor, stepped back, and then bolted forward, launching her body off the crouching security officer. She unclipped her body shield and activated it while she somersaulted above the Rebel barricade. Into the storm of laser fire Kayla somersaulted, holding her body shield in front of her, spinning over the Rebels barricaded in the Royal Suite. Their barricade was overturned furniture, and piled up, dead bodies of the courtiers accompanying the Emperor.

Kayla quickly drew her fiery, white-hot plasma sword in mid-air, and landed behind their barricade. With the energy shield in her left hand and plasma sword in her right, Kayla made quick work of reducing the number of surprised Rebels. Using a spinning motion, she cut five men in half in split-seconds. She swiftly thrust the plasma sword into the Rebels' bodies, or beheaded them, and expertly sliced the remaining Rebels into pieces.

The Space Cadre men ran inside behind her to back her up, but some began vomiting on the floor, seeing the gruesome sight of Kayla's handiwork with her plasma sword. She heard movement, and saw a wounded Rebel raise his laser to fire at the Space Cadre crewmen. Kayla turned her plasma sword's handle to extend it, and thrust it into the Rebel. A burned-out hole was left where his heart used to be. She checked out the other fallen Rebels, in case any moved to fight, but all were dead.

Fallen bodies and severed, bloody extremities were everywhere. What remained of the Master Bedroom door was open partially, and she saw an Imperial Guard pulser spear sticking out from the opening in defense. She called out, "Is Emperor P'Lau all right? The room is clear. It's Ranger Kayla. Are you safe, Emperor P'Lau?"

The bedroom door opened slowly. A wounded Imperial Guard on his knees raised his spear to fire at her, then lowered it when Kayla raised her visor, and he recognized the Ranger. Then he collapsed onto the floor, and exhaled his last breath. The large master bedroom was covered with the bodies of dead Imperial Guardsmen. Emperor P'Lau was helped out of the bathroom by another Imperial Guard. Both were wounded and bleeding.

"Medics! Medics for the Emperor NOW!" Kayla shouted into her comm link. She ran to assist the Emperor, and helped him onto the bed. She applied pressure to his abdominal wound to stop the bleeding. The medics arrived shortly, and tended to the wounded Emperor, and his wounded and dying Guards. Emperor P'Lau was pale and very weak from his abdominal wound, and the long flesh wound on his leg. Only one Imperial Guard showed any life signs, L'Roy, who helped the Emperor out of the bathroom.

Devastation was all throughout the Royal Suite. The formerly posh Royal Suite looked like a hellscape in a bad nightmare. Everything was destroyed. The floor was littered with bodies of dead Rebels, Imperial Guardsmen, and unarmed members of the court who accompanied the Emperor on his yearly trip to M'Wati. The walls were completely blasted out, the bar was demolished, and the beautiful, alluring wall sculpture was destroyed completely. The wide viewing windows were cracked from all the laser blasts, and shots from the Guardsmen's pulser spears. The ship's emergency window shields had closed tight, to keep inside precious air and maintain constant pressure in the Royal Suite.

L'Roy, the recovering Imperial Guard who survived, relayed the surprise assault details to Kayla while she waited on her Emperor's wounds to be bound: "The Rebels hid in the hollow walls after the Royal Suite was scanned. There were so many people in here, Ranger. During the noise and excitement of the greetings, and the food and cocktails being served, the Rebels stacked themselves inside the hollow walls. They used some kind of rope ladders. We never heard anything but the cocktail party, and the welcome greetings to the Emperor."

Guard L'Roy took a long drink of water, and continued his story, "The Rebels blasted through the walls, killing the unarmed courtiers and several Guardsmen. So much screaming, Ranger. We covered the Emperor with our cloaks and shielded him with our bodies, and rushed him into the master bedroom. So many Rebels came out of the walls! They fired at anything and everyone who moved, and then set up the furniture and dead bodies as a barricade, to keep out the Space Cadre security officers. We put the Emperor into the spa tub to protect him, and emptied our pulser spears into the Rebels. But they used the dead bodies as shields," he cried. "The cruel bastards even used the dead body of our High Priest!"

He coughed several times, and then continued, "How'd they all get inside the walls silently like they did? Someone below this deck had to help them. The interior walls change configuration above this level, and there is little space for a man inside them. Each Rebel had at least two laser rifles, Ranger. If you hadn't managed to break through their line, I hate to think what would've happened," he ended, and laid back. Kayla saw the blood running down his head, and called the medics over to him, trying to save at least one of the brave Imperial Guards.

Kayla stood and looked at the faces of the dead Imperial Guards, knowing what she would find. The men in their now blood-soaked purple uniforms and cloaks saved Emperor P'Lau's life. Kayla stepped carefully over the dead Guardsmen, and found Nat'N, lying dead against the bathroom door, with his spear in firing position. His neck, chest armor, and uniform were drenched in his own blood. He gave his life protecting his Emperor. Kayla felt as if a huge hole opened inside her solar plexus, and a part of her suddenly was ripped away.

"My Daughter Kayla, thank you," Emperor P'Lau said weakly. He raised up on his elbow, saw her looking at the body of Nat'N again, and said, "Our sworn protector Commander Nat'N gave his life protecting us, my Daughter," P'Lau said softly to Kayla, and held out his hand to her. "We are sorry, my Daughter. I am truly sorry, my Kayla. My poor Kayla." He began to cry for her.

Kayla kneeled at his side and bowed her head, and removed her helmet. P'Lau placed his hand on her head, and gently caressed her face. They both cried softly while the medics completed bandaging his wounded leg, and moved him onto an anti-gravity gurney for conveying the Emperor to the Hospital.

Then abruptly, the ship's "Red Alert" siren began screeching. Her comm link beeped the emergency signal, and she was ordered to her ES-519: "All pilots to their fighters. We are under attack. All pilots report to their warbirds immediately." She put her helmet on again, and stood.

"Go, my Kayla, my Protector. Make them pay for this, my Beloved Daughter. Show no mercy. Give no quarter, my Shi'Lon Ranger!" Emperor P'Lau ordered. He raised his fist and cried, "Make them pay!"

Kayla saluted him, and ran into the corridor as if she was in a dream, knowing where she was going, but unable to focus on anything around her. She boarded the ES-519 and launched into the heart of the attack. She would make them pay dearly.

XXVI

The Rebel leaders in the old destroyer fired on the Imperial Command Battle Cruiser in an anemic attempt to damage the pride of the Space Cadre fleet. Eighty Rebel fighters swarmed around the big Cruiser, firing at strategic points for communications and defense, but could not penetrate the Cruiser's shields. Their missiles and laser cannon blasts continually burst into brilliant fireworks against the main energy shields of the big Cruiser. But its shields could not hold forever.

After the announcement of the attack, dozens of Space Cadre fighters from the Cruiser and its support vessels launched to engage the Rebels. The battle took on another dimension when the Space Cadre fighters spread out the attack. But they were still badly outnumbered. Too many Space Cadre fighters were out on patrol, and not available to fight.

"ES-519, launching now," Kayla reported, and shot out of the hangar bay at full throttle.

"ES-519, this is Master Commander Steph'N. Welcome to the party. Engage stealth mode, and rendezvous at the following coordinates." Kayla engaged the stealth mode and flew to the assigned coordinates, flying invisibly away from the main battle. The Space Cadre fighters were hopelessly outnumbered. She felt like she abandoned them.

Steph'N ordered, "Let's get the Rebel destroyer, Ranger Kayla. You take out their portside cannons. Ranger Dan'L, the starboard cannons are yours. I'll get the forward plasma pulsers," he instructed. "Arm and target missiles, and hold your position, until my signal."

Only when they were in optimal firing position did the three ES warbirds disengage stealth mode. By the time their warbirds were discovered, it was too late. They fired their missiles at the big cannons, and demolished them. Then the warbirds flew through the smoke, became stealthy again, and rendezvoused underneath the destroyer.

A ship-to-ship hail came over their comm links: "All Imperial fighters, this is Colonel T'Lok of the Rebel destroyer. Your Emperor P'Lau is dead, and we claim his Battle Cruiser as salvage. Surrender and be spared, or die serving a dead Emperor!"

Kayla did not ask permission to respond. Instead, she immediately replied with a powerful voice on the same ship-to-ship frequency: "This is Kayla, Shi'Lon Ranger. Our Emperor P'Lau is alive and well. I have seen him myself, less than twenty minutes ago. Your cowardly Rebels who hid in the walls like cockroaches have all been exterminated by loyal Imperial Guards and Space Cadre. Your attack has failed, and now you will pay the price, Colonel T'Lok!' Cheers were heard loudly over the comm link.

Steph'N called, "Good job, Ranger Kayla. Let's finish the destroyer."

Kayla flew invisibly to the top of the Rebel destroyer, and saw several uniformed officers looking out the command bridge. She armed and targeted the massive "devil bomb" her warbird carried, disengaged her stealth mode, and fired the highly destructive devil bomb directly into the command bridge. "For my Nat'N!" She cried. The devil bomb blew out not only the command bridge, but also the entire top midsection of the Rebel destroyer.

Dan'L and Steph'N took out the Rebel destroyer's engines with their devil bombs, and the flash was blinding. The Rangers flew their ES warbirds away from the failing Rebel destroyer at top speed. The old destroyer began to list, and then deck after deck of explosions rippled through the wounded ship, and it died in a brilliant flash.

The Ranger ES warbirds continued towards the main battle, engaging the Rebel fighters again. Several Rebel fighters broke off their attack and retreated towards the White Belt, looking to hide among asteroids. Ranger Kayla told Steph'N, "Master Commander, the Emperor ordered me to give no quarter to the Rebels, sir."

"Then what are you waiting for? Take them out now. Ranger Dan'L, let's not let our Shi'Lon sister have all the glory," he said with a chuckle. "Watch your fuel gauges, Rangers. When you're at 30%, return to the Cruiser to refuel and reload."

The ES warbirds picked off the retreating Rebel fighters from behind, then carved their attack into three smaller sorties. The super-fast ES warbirds out-gunned and out-maneuvered the older, slower Rebel fighters, quickly reducing their numbers. Space Cadre fighters focused their attacks on the Rebels closest to the Battle Cruiser, forcing them farther away. The main hangar bay of the Battle Cruiser was constantly receiving fighters whose laser cannons needed recharging, and whose fuel cells needed replacement. The flight crews and their robots were operating at max efficiency, turning around empty fighters to fully-charged in minutes.

With no command destroyer operating to direct and coordinate flight operations, the Rebel fighters were left on their own. The tide was turning. Many Rebel fighters began to pull away from the battle while they still had fuel remaining. Those retreating Rebels flew towards the White Belt, with the Space Cadre fighters in pursuit. The three ES warbirds returned to the Battle Cruiser to refuel, re-arm their missiles, and reload their laser cannons. They launched at top speed back into the fight.

The final act came when the Space Cadre patrol squadron leader called: "Major Fel'T reporting. Space patrol fighters have returned. We'll take it from here." With fully charged lasers and pulser weaponry, and their missiles targeted, the remaining Rebel fighters were chased away from the Imperial Command Battle Cruiser Group by the fresh Space Cadre patrol fighters, and blown to bits in minutes.

Ranger Kayla led the ES warbirds in pursuit of the retreating Rebel fighters. Asteroids be damned. The more-maneuverable ES warbirds flew around, above and beneath the space junk and tumbling asteroids, and chased the Rebel fighters into the heart of the White Belt. She hunted the fighters down, and the Rangers destroyed every Rebel fighter on their target screens.

Steph'N ordered, "All ES warbirds return to the Cruiser. Dinner's on me tonight!" They returned towards the Cruiser's main hangar bay, and both Dan'L and Steph'N were jubilant.

The triumphant Space Cadre pilots returned to the main hanger bay of the Battle Cruiser, and cheered and congratulated each other. When the three Rangers landed their ES warbirds, the pilots gave a rousing round of applause for them, and chanted, "All hail the Emperor's Rangers!" But Kayla asked to be excused without saying why, and silently went to her suite.

The celebrations by the pilots dampened when news of the devastating Royal Suite battle, and the great loss of all Imperial Guards but one, reached them. Many Space Cadre security crewmen were also killed or wounded, defending the Emperor in the Royal Suite. Vivid tales of the magnificent Shi'Lon Ranger warrior in her black armor welding her plasma sword were told by the witnessing Space Cadre security officers and crewmen.

The Imperial Command Battle Cruiser itself sustained damage only in the Royal Suite and its surrounding deck areas. But the ship's hospital was full of badly wounded Space Cadre defenders. And many Space Cadre pilots and their fighters were lost. One of the support tender vessels and its crew of 132 Space Cadre was destroyed. It was a costly victory for the Empire.

After their dinner, the Borgund Rangers were ordered to return to Home World with Emperor P'Lau in one hour. They talked quietly of the death of Kayla's partner-to-be. Her best friends were very sad for her. "I wish I could've met her Imperial Guard, Commander Nat'N. She looks so different now. It's heartbreaking for her, I'm sure. Kayla will never forget this day, Dan'L," Steph'N lamented.

Dan'L shared, "My Father once said, 'Victory always comes at a terrible price.' I wish Kayla didn't have to be the one to pay. She has no living parents, and her brother Olm is serving on a ship halfway across the solar system. She has no one to talk to about this tragedy."

"Everyone who was killed was important to someone: their friends and relatives; their wives and husbands; and their children," Steph'N wisely observed. "They all paid the price for this bloody Rebel attack, Dan'L, including our best friend Kayla," he added bitterly.

"I hope she finds a way to work through it," Dan'L said. "I feel bad we have to leave so soon. I wish I could talk with her." They stood and left the dining room, and walked to the hanger bay to ready their refueled and resupplied ES-warbirds.

"Kayla is a Shi'Lon Ranger, and she will prevail. But I hope the loss does not change her too much. Her Imperial Guard's death might even make her stronger. We shall see," Steph'N said.

Adrenalin leaves such a bitter, sour aftertaste in your mouth. Kayla slowly stood, feeling post-battle fatigue in the muscles of her hands, arms, shoulders, and back. She spent seven hours in the cockpit flying the ES-519 in her heavy battle armor, blowing up the Rebel destroyer, punishing the Rebel fighters attacking the Imperial Battle Cruiser, and chasing and killing the retreating Rebel fighters throughout the White Belt. Not to mention her explosive battle in the Royal Suite. She took a two-liter bottle of icy water from her little fridge and tried to drink it in little swallows, but gulped half of it down. Her esophagus was now cramping from the cold fluid. It was the first water she'd drunk since breakfast. *Slow down, or up-chuck,* she warned herself, and tipped the bottle once more for a small sip.

"Lights on," she said, and the darkness in her suite was instantly replaced by bright, artificial light. She removed her breastplate and backplate, and set the armor on its charging stand. She looked at her black battle armor, and realized if she didn't clean it soon, it would take hours to clean later. It was splattered everywhere with Rebel blood. Her helmet was full of dents and scars from laser blasts, as was her battle armor. Kayla sighed heavily, took her cleaning kit, and methodically cleaned the black battle armor bottom to top, until it once again gleamed.

When she cleaned her black helmet, she found blood inside. After touching behind her ear, she felt the small gash. Just a pressure wound, nothing to be concerned about. Then she placed the helmet inside its plex case with the black battle armor, and shut the case tightly, to initiate its recharging cycle. Kayla plopped down on the sofa and stared out the window.

Hundreds of fragments of fighters and destroyed space vessels floated in the space surrounding the Imperial Battle Cruiser. Any pieces of new space junk coming too near the Cruiser exploded on its energy shields in bright, silent fireworks. Some pieces of the space junk floating by were organic; remnants of a human fighter pilot, or a crewman from the Rebel destroyer; even possibly a Space Cadre crewman from the support tender destroyed in the battle. It was so sad to watch. It was surreal. Such an incredible waste of humanity. "May they all find peace in the Afterlife," Kayla prayed.

Space junk would float and tumble, until caught in the gravity field of a planet or moon, or the White Belt. Some junk would escape gravity's pull, and travel endlessly through space. Kayla watched the floating and tumbling space junk, and let her consciousness drift with the fragments, far away from the Cruiser. She felt this deep anguish when her Mother and Father died. And now the pain was back again, crushing her heart, and ripping out her guts.

Her strict upbringing kept Kayla from giving in to her love's desire. Now Nat'N was in the Afterlife. She regretted not sleeping with him. What good did it do? They never made love and became as one. Her Nat'N was gone—forever. There was no going back. The only direction was forward.

Many times, she had been told stories of the glorious victories of the Emperor's Rangers. Kayla saw no glory in the scenes in front of her. There was no glory in the aftermath of the slaughter in the Royal Suite. Perhaps she would experience the "ecstasy of victory" some other day. But today, all she felt was emptiness and sorrow. Kayla lowered her head and placed her fingertips on her forehead. Here came the tears. There was no holding them back any longer. She managed to say, "Lights out,' in between broken breaths. It would be a long, painful night.

XXVII

Home World

News of the largest and most destructive Rebel attack of his reign ran through the Emperor's Main Courts in both Home World and K'Halon Prime Palaces like wildfire. The Rebels lost; but they successfully infiltrated the Imperial Command Battle Cruiser and wounded Emperor P'Lau. It was a very close call, and an event the Emperor did not want repeated. Seventy-three reported kills of Rebel fighters were confirmed. Forty-one Rebels were killed who attacked from their hidden positions within the walls of the Cruiser. It was a large loss of highly-trained pilots, fighters, and men for the Rebels. But, in Duma Wat's eyes, his attack was successful, albeit very expensive in manpower and machines. His half-brother P'Lau was proven vulnerable.

The overwhelming majority of the Rebels killed inside the Royal Suite were slain by Ranger Kayla and her plasma sword. But Kayla did not act like a victorious heroine. Instead, she politely thanked any officer or crewman for their congratulations to her, and quickly responded, "The Creator was with us. May the Creator bless Emperor P'Lau," and hurriedly walked away. She did her sworn duty and protected the Emperor at all costs.

As any hunter knows, the fiercest animal in the forest is one who is wounded. There is nothing for the injured animal to lose, and they will fight to the death. The Emperor knew the Rebellion had taken a critical movement upwards in scope and scale. His wounded half-brother would have even more financial support from the well-to-do and wealthy after the attack on his Imperial Battle Cruiser. The fighting men and materiel would eventually be replaced, in greater numbers.

Some affluent and wealthy people would now back Duma Wat who had never considered doing so in years before. There was a chance he could defeat the Imperial forces, and they would want to be on the winning side.

Everyone with wealth and power at stake wanted to be in the favor of whichever side would win; forget about loyalty to the Empire. The calculating aristocrats played both sides.

The Emperor resolved to place more trusted men and women in his Royal Main Court, to be his eyes and ears among the courtiers and aristocrats. He promoted several Master Commander-rank Imperial Guards and Borgund Rangers to high, official court positions in both Palaces. Borgund Rangers who were not pilots were put on transports to the six Space Bases, to observe and report to Emperor P'Lau or their Commander Superiors directly.

Ranger pilots of the traditional fighters were assigned duty on battleships and destroyers, to accompany their patrols, and keep watchful eyes open for any onboard treachery. The Ranger pilots of the ES-class warbirds currently unassigned were kept close to wherever the Emperor stayed, to be activated for battle at a moment's notice. Any future planned away-missions for his unassigned Shi'Lon Rangers were postponed, or cancelled outright. The Emperor kept his Beloved Daughters and Protectors in his Main Court, by his side. All Imperial Guards were issued hand lasers and holsters, and were ordered to wear them at all times on duty.

Emperor P'Lau watched recordings of the Imperial Command Battle Cruiser space battle with much consternation. "The Rebels thought you had successfully been assassinated, Sire. The Rebel fighter pilots were highly motivated to take control of your Battle Cruiser, and the Empire, for Duma Wat," Fleet Admiral U'Ret said, explaining the obvious. Emperor P'Lau listened to his Military Advisors for another half hour before dismissing them. Their post-battle observations were weak, and without significant contribution. P'Lau was surrounded by "yes-men."

The Special Inquest Commission members were called into his private Royal Court. The Emperor ordered C.S. T'Anh, C.S. G'Rosk, and Ranger Kayla to be conferenced in with them. He commented, "My Military Advisors agree we won the battle, and all is now well. They feel Duma Wat is finished. I thank the Creator their attacks were foiled and the attacking Rebels defeated. But what say you, my most trusted Rangers?"

"Traitors working on board your Imperial Command Battle Cruiser enabled this attack, my Emperor. Commander C'Mak is under arrest, and your scribes cannot write fast enough to document his lengthy confession. He is being vid recorded, thankfully," C.S. Vu'Duc said. "I thank the Creator the Space Cadre patrol squad leader Major Fel'T returned the patrol squad to your ship, when he saw the Rebel destroyer and its fighters on course for the Battle Cruiser. Their efforts limited the damage to our Space Cadre fighters. We suffered the loss of many experienced pilots, Sire. I respectfully suggest we recall recently retired pilots back into service, my

Lord, before Duma Wat tempts them to fight against us."

C.S. Bette offered, "I believe the nuclear warhead was placed inside your Royal Suite initially to be detonated when you arrived, Sire. How fortunate the anomaly was visible in the Dalian crystal holograph, and Ranger Dan'L found it. The traitors smuggled more weapons onboard afterwards, accidentally discovered by Ranger Kayla on the auxiliary deck activities. But the traitors currently in prison are merely pawns. Someone higher up is planning these events; someone with intimate knowledge of military protocols and plans. Someone with power. Not a Rebel isolated on an asteroid in the White Belt," she said forcefully. "I am afraid there are traitors within our midst, my Emperor."

"They have deep pocketbooks, my Emperor. They used eighty last-generation Space Cadre fighters. They purchased the old destroyer and fighters from salvage dealers, but had to spend hundreds of thousands of credits to repair, refurbish, and weaponize them. And have the trained technicians to perform the work," C.S. T'Anh added. "Duma Wat is actively recruiting retired and recently discharged Space Cadre crewmen. I agree with Commanders Superior Bette and Vu'Duc: someone very high in the Space Cadre is enabling these activities. A traitor is in our midst. There is no other explanation for Duma Wat's success, my Lord Emperor."

Ranger Kayla asked permission to speak, and the Emperor nodded. "We are analyzing the attacks in retrospect; more predictable behavior. Everything that occurred from the second your journey to M'Wati was announced was pre-planned and practiced for two weeks ahead of your actual arrival, Sire. The military protocols are well-documented whenever the Emperor comes aboard ship. The reception proprieties and etiquette are, as well, Emperor P'Lau. Your Ranger respectfully requests you to become more unpredictable. Throw a monkey wrench into the machinery, my Emperor," she said with great enthusiasm.

Emperor P'Lau listened to Kayla, and slowly smiled, like a tom cat about to pounce on a cornered mouse. "A monkey wrench, indeed, my protector Kayla. Your Commanders Superior will then design this 'monkey wrench,' and we will disrupt our well-oiled machinery just enough to throw off plans our enemies are engineering." He liked her simile. Their discussions continued for another hour, offering meaningful analysis from the experienced warriors.

After their suggestions, Emperor P'Lau stated, "Now, it is time for recognition, and it cannot wait for a formal Main Court ceremony. My Beloved Daughter Kayla: your insight and initiative alerted us to an undercurrent of treachery aboard our Imperial Battle Cruiser. Without your selfless acts of bravery and incredible skill, we would not be here today. For saving the life of your Emperor at risk of your own life, and personally slaying thirty-eight Rebel attackers, you are hereby promoted to

Commander Kayla, with a commendation and a bonus. You are also designated a 'Hero of the Empire,' my Beloved Daughter."

New-Commander Kayla bowed her head in humility. Being designated an official "Hero of the Empire" title meant your word was true, and you were trusted above others. Several members of the Special Inquest Commission were Heroes of the Empire: Commanders Superior G'Rosk, Vu'Duc, Bette, and T'Anh, and M.C. Javette. Commander Kayla was now a member of the Ranger Elite. But she felt hollow, and numb; incapable of rejoicing for the high honor.

The meeting adjourned, but Kayla and T'Anh were told to remain online. The Emperor spoke, "We are sorely grieved at the personal suffering you have recently experienced, my Beloved Daughter Kayla. Also, we have watched the recordings of the attack within the Royal Suite on the Cruiser many times, and are very impressed with your skills during our rescue. Commander Superior G'Rosk assured me the somersault moves you used were not part of our Ranger training; but they will be, going forward. For these reasons, and to help your heart heal, we are sending you to the monks on Xau for six months of advanced T'Ly martial arts training. When they have assured us of your skill mastery, you will receive your new assignment." Kayla bowed her head, and she was dismissed. She clicked off the vid comm, and left the booth.

T'Anh asked for a few more minutes with the Emperor. She said, "Sire, never has a Shi'Lon Ranger spent time alone with the monks at the Temple Complex, only select Borgund Rangers. The Temple monks are not celibate, Sire. It is not my place to question your judgment; but I must mention Commander Kayla's weakened, sensitive condition. What if one of the monks attempts to take advantage of her recent emotional distress? She is going there at a particularly vulnerable time, my Emperor." T'Anh was genuinely concerned about Kayla.

The Emperor noticed her demeanor, and replied, "The priests and monks are under my direct orders to train her in their highest, most secret martial arts. They are not to touch her, otherwise. The priestesses and nuns will consul, house, and heal her, if she is injured. My Kayla will have the eyes of the Creator, His priestesses, and His faithful, watching over her. She showed remarkable skill and strength in our rescue in the Royal Suite, as you saw in the recordings. Commander Superior G'Rosk was her mentor during Phase 2 and 3 Training. When he saw the Royal Suite battle recording of Kayla, he was astounded."

Emperor P'Lau smiled a little and said, "I am certain her progress has much to do with your advanced training as her Commander Superior, T'Anh. You are the best. I have trusted you with my life and my Empire since the day of my coronation. But Kayla is ready for the higher knowledge only the monks can teach. And she needs to focus on the greatest challenge of her young life, to overcome the loss of Commander Nat'N, her promised partner. It is my will, T'Anh," he concluded in a softer voice. T'Anh bowed her head, and felt honored by the Emperor. The matter was settled. For the first time in many months, C. S. T'Anh walked with her head held high. Her self-imposed isolation came to an end.

Home World, three days later

The Emperor's Special Inquest Commission met with him in the top-secret research lab. This time, Dr. D'Vre had urgently requested an audience with Emperor P'Lau, M.C. Javette, and, especially, Ranger Dan'L. Critical testing of the green Dalian crystal had stopped. Not much headway had been made; none of the scientists would scan the crystal, for fear the scanning beams would potentially cause an adverse reaction in the crystal.

Dr. D'Vre asked, "Ranger Dan'L, you carried the green Dalian crystal in your knife sheath for over a year without knowing it was there. Did you ever feel affected by the crystal, or, have you felt any differently since you stopped carrying it on your belt?"

Dan'L answered, "I never felt any differently before, during, or after carrying the green Dalian crystal, Dr. D'Vre. Why do you ask?"

The research scientist team leader pulled up a large vid screen full of charts and graphs. He said, "When the green Dalian crystal was brought to us, we could not scan it, but we measured its energy levels, magnetic fields, radioactivity, and so on. Everything registered similar readings from the initial measurements, until two days ago. Then, our readings changed to this." With a click, the graphs expanded, and the lines went off-scale.

"Is it going to explode?" Command Superior Bette asked. "We should remove Your Majesty from this facility immediately!" The group turned to leave, but Dan'L stayed behind and studied the charts a moment longer. The long lines moved even higher while he watched.

While the group escorting Emperor P'Lau walked towards the main doors, Dan'L cried out, "They're coming back! The Dalians are returning!" He smiled at his Mother Javette, then ran outside and looked up at the sky. A strange ship soon appeared from out of nowhere and hovered directly above the group. Its lights flashed on and off intermittently.

The senior Ranger leaders, Emperor P'Lau, M.C. Javette, and Dan'L shaded their eyes, then quickly looked away when the bright column of light appeared in front of them. A Dalian android materialized within the light. The shiny gray, green, and chrome android had neon-green eyes, and tiny lights of several colors shining around its front neck area and midsection. Its head was shaped more like a helmet than a human head, and was moveable. It was two-legged, in a similar shape to a human, but with longer legs and arms. The android was unarmed, as far as they could tell, and held up his arms to show he was peaceful.

Dan'L eagerly stepped up to the Dalian android and said, "Greetings, keeper of the living legacy of my Father, K'Ser. I am Dan'L. How may we serve you today?" It blinked its eyes at him, and tilted its head slightly.

The shocked leaders behind Dan'L nervously said, "Greetings" to the two-meter tall android, and it looked at each person for a few seconds. The android held out both cool, metallic hands to Dan'L and Javette, and they took its hands. It walked them back into the top-secret lab. When Dan'L opened the door and Dr. D'Vre saw the Dalian android leading the Rangers inside, he stepped back quickly, in awe.

The android began playing soft, melodic music as he led Javette and Dan'L to the flash-out room where the green crystal laid in its glass case. "Protect you from your own, we must," the android sang. Dan'L noticed it was no longer singing backwards.

Dan'L sang to the android, "You showed us where they hid the warhead. You saved many innocent lives. Thank you, Dalian, thank you."

Javette added in a similar melody, "We are in your debt. We honor and thank you, and thank our Creator." The android looked at her for a moment, and then blinked a few times.

Changing its voice from an electronic voice to the voice of her late husband, the android bowed its head a little and sang to her:
"The path of honor you nobly walk.
The words of peace you need to speak,
And let them heal your troubled heart.
The strong must protect the weak."

While Javette's eyes misted with tears, the android walked inside the flash room, took the green crystal from its glass case, and inserted it into a slot in its body. Then, the android returned for Dan'L and Javette, took their hands again, and led everyone out of the lab and onto the lawn in the cool evening.

The Dalian android touched his midsection and red crystals emerged from within his metallic body. He handed the crystals to Dan'L, who excitedly accepted his gift, bowed his head, and thanked him in song. Once again, the android flashed its green eyes, and sang to the group:
"Too much power corrupts your souls.
You must seek peace within.
Much to learn. Much to learn.
When you are ready, we will come again."

The bright column of light appeared, and the Dalian android de-materialized into millions of particles, and then disappeared into the light. The light dissipated, and the ship disappeared in a bright flash. The Dalian visit was over, leaving the human witnesses full of questions, yet speechless.

Dan'L led the Emperor and his Special Inquest Commission back into the lab to play his new red crystals. Ranger Dan'L said, "These new red crystals I give to Emperor P'Lau, in memory of my Father, Master Commander K'Ser." The amount of data and information was overwhelming. Hundreds of galactic space maps and navigational charts were stored on the 5D red crystals. Worlds with fantastic cities appeared before them. Creatures never seen flashed within the crystal holographs, living in their natural, alien habitats. Flying craft in shapes and immense size never envisioned by any human flew within the holograph, flying through unknown spacescapes.

Mathematical and physical formulas, organic chemical compounds, and DNA records for new species were also discovered. The new red crystals contained a treasure trove of information. Dr. D'Vre and his scientists had their work cut out for them, for many years to come.

The Emperor ordered a full synopsis created of the new red crystal information. They would be studied only by scientists at Imperial facilities, until they could determine which knowledge on the crystals was safe to share. Once the full content of the knowledge was disseminated, the knowledge would be distributed with university scientists and research professionals throughout the Empire. All citizens would eventually benefit from the new knowledge.

"The Dalians shared more of their knowledge with us, to help us grow and advance," Dan'L said. "How can we possibly thank them?"

"By using the new knowledge for peaceful means, young Ranger," C.S. Bette wisely offered. "Perhaps we will merit another visit from them, in a few years. I certainly hope so."

Everyone quietly boarded their shuttles and flew back to the Royal Palace in silence. "I wish Kayla could have been here, Mother. Maybe the android's words could have helped her somehow," Dan'L said. "It's sad she can't be here with us."

"Kayla is where she is supposed to be, as are we, my Son. We all have our own internal struggle to find peace, Dan'L," Javette said quietly.

XXVIII

Onboard the Imperial Battle Cruiser, Admiral Wen'T hosted a farewell luncheon for their champion, Shi'Lon Ranger Commander Kayla, with all his command officers attending. It was a happy, yet very sad, gathering. The absence of the Imperial Guards was noticeable. The brave Imperial Guardsmen in purple robes were nowhere to be found, except for L'Roy, the lone surviving Guard still recovering in the Hospital. Once he was sufficiently patched up and fit for transport, L'Roy would be sent home to K'Halon Prime, and reassigned to the Royal Palace as an Advisor to the Court, with full honors.

Kayla carefully packed her uniforms, boots, and other clothing, and toiletries. She looked at the new dress she bought to wear for Nat'N, when he invited her to dinner, and proposed life partnership to her. The beautiful white and gold dress was elegant, and cost nearly a month's pay. Her eyes welled with tears, remembering her love Nat'N, and the most perfect evening of her life. She pulled the white dress and its jacket from the hanger, and ripped them to shreds.

When the night shift took over monitoring in the flight control booth on the Cruiser, Kayla waved good-bye to them, and boarded her warbird. She threw her travel bags into the ES-519, supervised the crewmen loading her battle armor plex case for her, and started the pre-flight checklist. Xau was as good as anywhere to disappear for a while.

Xau

Xau was the third moon of K'Halon Prime, large enough to qualify as a planetoid, captured in the gravity of big K'Halon Prime. Kayla spent two and a half years in the Ranger Training facilities there, for Phase 1, 2, and 3 Training. Dry desert, full of humongous rats and shrews, snakes and poisonous scorpions; they called this inhospitable moon home. The only place green and lush was the Temple Complex, in the Southern Hemisphere.

The Temple Complex was a retreat for pilgrims and prayers, solace, devotion to the Creator, and T'Ly martial arts advanced schooling for monks, priests, and a few privileged students. The mountain rising from the desert centering the Temple Complex was the highest point on the moon. Although Xau had many bubbling mineral pools and hot sulfur springs, the Temple Complex had cool springs from an underground river. It was an oasis of fresh water, fruit trees and date palms, green grass, and prayer. A small flock of sheep peacefully grazed along the slopes of the mountain. After Phase 3 Training, Kayla was allowed to visit the nearby Temple Complex. It was as beautiful as the remainder of Xau was bleak.

When Kayla landed her ES-519 on the marked landing site, she was told to enter the Temple Complex without her weapons. "Weapons of war are not allowed in the Temple Complex, Commander Kayla. Leave your armor. Your breastplate and backplate, your knives, laser rifle, handgun, and your plasma sword must stay behind. Follow your faith inside the Temple of the Creator." *Okay, okay; whatever*, she thought. *My mind and body are my primary weapons*, Kayla reminded herself.

Carrying only a travel case of clothing and toiletries, Kayla declined the offered skiff ride, and walked away from her warbird. No blades, armor, or plasma sword. Only her lonely, broken heart and her faith in the Creator accompanied her. She walked the two kilometers leading towards the Temple Complex in silence. She obeyed the will of her Emperor.

Two priests, one elder priestess named T'Char, and a shaved-head monk greeted her. "Welcome, Beloved Daughter of our Emperor P'Lau. We have prepared a place for you here," the young priest said. The friendly greeter stepped aside after a few meters. Soon, the men took another path away from the women without saying another word, leaving them at the Entrance Arch to the Temple.

While they walked the path towards the Temple Complex, the elder Priestess T'Char said, "You will be schooled in our secret, advanced T'Ly martial arts. You are a rock; a thing; dull in sunlight, invisible in starlight. We will hammer and chip away your inconsequential matter. It will not be pleasant for you. Your training will require hard work, pain, dedication, and personal suffering. But master our ways, and emerge as a diamond. A thing of beauty. Polished and perfect in all its facets. This we offer you, Kayla." The elder priestess turned her head a little and bowed slightly to Kayla. The women continued their walk into the Temple of the Creator.

Six months of pain, suffering, and hard work. It was the most perfect thing Kayla could imagine now. She said, "Bring it on, priestess."

Tinkling chimes were so much nicer to wake up hearing than screeching alarm clocks at 4 a.m. Kayla tossed aside her covers and quickly put on her wool robe. It was cold, as usual. She slept in the long hall of the nuns, which closely resembled a dormitory. All of them slept on individual woven mats, and beds made of layered wool blankets. After straightening the blankets, Kayla rolled up her bed inside its woven mat, tied it closed with two attached cloth straps, and placed the bed atop her small dresser.

Daily regimen for the T'Ly advanced students consisted of meditation, stretching, and sixty minutes running up, around, and down the mountain, in sandals. Then a quick shower, followed by breakfast of green tea and honey cakes or gruel. They took ten minutes rest, and then the students walked silently along the Path of Penance to their training and sparring arena, an open-air arena four meters below ground. The walls of the arena were of sandstone blocks, with terraced wood benches lining either side. The tops of the walls were large, flat sandstone pavers, where the priests, monks, and others could observe the training and sparring.

Most of the year, the weather on Xau was hot and dry, and freezing at night. But today, a pouring rain accompanied by blustery winds greeted the students during their run around the mountain. The rain turned into a storm, and the students were soaked to their skin by the time they reached the training arena. Wearing only cotton pants and tunic, and barefoot, same as the other students, Kayla took her place in line. The dirt floor of the arena had been only dust for two and a half months, but they were up to their ankles in mud today. The rain was still coming down, drenching them completely. Some students complained to each other quietly, but not Kayla or the military officers, T'Pul and M'Kel.

"What a blessed day our Creator has made for us! Today, we begin advanced spear training," the bald monk instructor yelled. He raised both arms, then pulled them down sharply, signaling the monks standing on top of the arena walls. Twenty spears were thrown at the students, and each spear landed directly in front of their feet. Three students were startled, and broke their stance.

"Thank you for volunteering," the smiling monk instructor said, and pointed at the three startled students. They took their spears, and walked in front of the instructor. He proceeded to lecture the students in the proper T'Ly handling of a spear, using the three volunteers for demonstration. The instructor enjoyed himself, lecturing loudly and evenly, while introducing trick maneuvers with his own spear. Not one of the volunteers could land a single hit on him. It was an impressive demonstration, but painful for the three volunteers.

To qualify for the advanced training offered by the monks and priests at the Temple, a student must have achieved a ninth-degree ranking in T'Ly from a certified master. The prospective student must also have an endorsement from an influential sponsor in the top tiers of the Imperial

Class; there must be a good reason for the student to need to know the advanced, secret T'Ly art. And, pay the tuition of ten thousand credits per month.

The students in Kayla's class were the two military officers, sons of wealthy aristocrats, and several priests. Kayla was the only female. She was also the only student with a twelfth-degree ranking, the highest of them all. The high ranking was earned on her own time, taking out her frustrations with C.S. T'Anh while advancing her T'Ly skills and ranking.

For hours in the storm, the students practiced the spear movements again and again, perfecting each nuance of hand, wrist, and body coordination. Monks walked among the students, correcting their motions individually, until each one perfected the spear routine. Regular T'Ly utilized several spear movements, but the advanced movements were very fast, and involved many new tactics. Kayla practiced the spinning movements, and special jump-thrusts until she perfected them, and could perform them at a fast speed.

At first, Kayla felt like a baton twirler. But she soon realized the advantages of the very fast twirling motions and thrusting of the spear, and learned to incorporate her own body's spinning movements. Kayla moved to a corner of the arena, and took the wooden spear to new heights, totally engrossed. She was anxious to try the advanced movements with her new expanding plasma sword. The monk instructor watched Kayla, completely in "the spear zone," and silently signaled to a priest watching from the top of the arena, so he could observe the Shi'Lon Ranger. She was amazing.

After a short break for lunch, the students gathered on the arena steps. It was still raining, but the worst of the storm had passed. A new instructor took over, and announced, "You have sparred with each other wearing training pads and gloves up until today. We will issue only helmets and pelvic guard pads to protect you. You must feel the snap of the spear, and the pain of its kiss." The spears for sparring had their sharp tips removed, thankfully, but they could still break bones and cause deep contusions. This could be painful.

No head or groin hits were permitted. Kayla hefted her wet sparring spear, and felt along its length for any cracks, or weakness. She felt only strong, solid wood, with just enough flexibility for a "snappy" hit. She was very good with spears. But so were most of the other students, especially after the morning training. They were paired off by the monks. Several priests in dark green hooded robes stood on the top steps to observe the bouts.

Unlike their previous sparring contests, each pair was sent to the center of the arena to spar, while their fellow students watched, groaned, and cheered. The winner of the sparring bout was the first to land four hits on his opponent. Kayla stood by, watching the bouts, and occasionally flexing her wrists. Her opponent was Imperial Army officer T'Pul, a tall, muscular man specializing in covert operations. He was a Phase 1 graduate; a fearsome combatant, and very strong. They had been paired against each other several times in their many weeks of training. One of them was going to be in pain tonight; perhaps in the infirmary.

The last two opponents were called into the center of the arena. Slowly twirling her spear, Kayla focused on her opponent's eyes. T'Pul did not have an expressive face, but his eyes were another matter. She took the purely defensive stance against T'Pul, blocking and repelling his aggressive, fast moves. He landed one hit on her butt, and chuckled. Then Kayla began closing in on him, intently watching his eyes. She faked a left thrust, spun in knee-deep water, and hit his hard stomach with a "Whack" heard throughout the arena: the spear's kiss.

T'Pul bent forward slightly in pain, and Kayla quickly pummeled him with three alternating hits on his upper back, ribs, and lower back. He fell to his knees in pain. The contest was over. Kayla and the instructor helped T'Pul to the steps to rest, next to several other injured students. One of the observing priests walked down the steps to them.

"A very effective attack," the hooded priest said to Kayla. "But not every opponent you will face has untrained eyes, Student Kayla. The eyes can deceive, as well as reveal. Remember this," he cautioned. The priest bowed his head to her and walked up the steps, leaving the arena.

Later in the evening after vespers, Kayla thought about the words of the priest. She was trained interpreting body language, and could read the faces and eyes of most people she met. Looking at her reflection in the bathroom mirror, she searched her own face for any signs of pain, joy, deceit, and so on. She was not able to change her eyes very much. In the months after her T'Ly advanced training, Kayla would spend considerable lengths of time looking in the mirror, training her eyes to express certain emotions, and how not to reveal her true feelings.

XXIX

Many days of advanced T'Ly training passed, with Kayla fulfilling her commitment as Student. She learned more of the secret T'Ly martial arts, and spent most evenings after dinner practicing the movements as fast as she could. Kayla was tall and strong, but her female body did not have the heavy musculature of her male competitors. The moves the students learned in their advanced classes could not only stop an opponent, but could kill. The best way for her to defeat the men in class—and in any future Rebel battles—was to be faster and more agile than the men.

But she was continually sequestered from the other students outside of training classes and the arena. A pair of acolytes or nuns escorted her to and from the training areas and arena. All her meals were taken with the white-robed nuns and blue-robed priestesses. She had never been around so many females in her life. Although they were kind, and sometimes had interesting conversation, they were not warriors, like Kayla. She had little in common with them.

The pain of Nat'N's death was still fresh in her heart, and in the forefront of her mind. In her dreams, Nat'N laughed with her, and held her in his arms. Then the chimes would tinkle, destroying her only happiness. Kayla had undergone years of specialized training and eight months of service onboard the Imperial Battle Cruiser, surrounded by her friends, warriors all, most of whom were men. She was starving for Ranger conversations and warrior camaraderie.

Outside of training and sparring, the monks and priest instructors avoided any interaction at all with Kayla. In her fourth month, Kayla sought out the elder Priestess T'Char, and asked pointedly why she was continually sequestered from the other students. "In Phase 1, 2, and 3 Training, we trained, studied, ate, worked out, and swam together. I felt like one of the warriors there. Here, I feel 'untouchable,' and alienated, except during sparring. What have I done to be treated so?"

T'Char smiled graciously and told Kayla to sit next to her. She clapped her hands, and an acolyte served them tea and lemon cookies. After a few minutes, T'Char answered, "Female students have rarely been accepted into T'Ly advanced training here. Not because they are unworthy, but simply because of their gender. Here at the Temple of the Creator, no vows of silence, poverty, or celibacy are required of us. Some of our monks, and yes, even some priests and priestesses, have....enjoyed themselves too much, in times past." She sipped her cold tea quietly.

Kayla said, "No one has approached me during my stay at the Temple. No man has even said, 'Good morning,' or had any conversations with me. None! And I have certainly not given any man leave to think I desire his advances. But the other students enjoy each other's friendship, and camaraderie. Why does every man turn and walk away if I happen to meet them? It is unfriendly, and unjust," she said. "What have I done to deserve this?"

The elder priestess sighed, and sat her tea cup down. Then T'Char said, "I see how difficult this is for you, Kayla. You are a warrior. I assure you, the reason for the actions of the men has nothing to do with your personality, or your behavior. The beautiful gold and bejeweled ring on your left hand signifies your life commitment to our Great Emperor P'Lau. You are his Beloved Daughter, Kayla. Emperor P'Lau gave stern orders for no man to touch you outside of class. Any man who violates his order is to be immediately castrated," she revealed. "We were not supposed to tell you this." She put her hands in her lap and bowed her head to Kayla.

Now Kayla understood. She thanked T'Char for her frankness and time. It wasn't her fault she was treated so differently. She was not ostracized; they had to avoid her. There was absolutely no chance for her to be "one of the warriors" here. The men didn't hate her. They were scared stiff.

The Path of Penance seemed to invite her to walk in the moonlight, and stop to kneel and pray at the several meditation areas. The last kneeling spot was near a little pool, fed by an underground spring. After a prayer, Kayla stood and silently watched fireflies begin to appear, performing their aerial mating dances. For the first time in months, Kayla smiled, and a feeling of pure joy overtook her.

Holding out her arms, Kayla let fireflies land and dance on her skin, and the feeling delighted her. She laughed softly, and wiggled her fingers in the little swarm of fireflies. A blue dragonfly landed on her left hand, and she gently brought him closer to her. The dragonfly slowly moved and shook his wings, and did not fly away.

"He is courting you," a familiar voice said. Kayla turned only for a moment to see the priest behind her. She recognized him; he had observed her training since she arrived. He was the priest who spoke words of warning to her after the spear contest. She quickly turned away from his gaze, not wanting to get him into trouble.

She raised her hand ever so slightly, and the dragonfly flew off. "Even the dragonfly is afraid to be seen with me," Kayla said softly. "May I at least know your name, sir, so I may properly address you?" She asked, not turning toward him intentionally. Someone was probably observing them.

The priest answered with a smile she could feel in his reply, but not see, "K'Ramm. My name is K'Ramm, Student Kayla. May our Creator bless you, and give you peace," he said, and walked away. *At long last, the lady warrior smiled*, K'Ramm thought to himself.

Dozens more fireflies joined the swarm, lighting the area in front of her. After a few prudent minutes of waiting, Kayla walked back to the nuns' quarters. She got ready for bed, and unrolled her sleeping mat and blankets. Sleep descended on her quickly, and gave her a peaceful night of no dreams; no pain, no loneliness, and no fear.

For their final test on the last day, the twenty students were once again matched to fight each other hand-to-hand in their arena. But these were contests of elimination, fighting until one winner emerged. The whispers among the monks prior to the beginning of the bouts were unsettling. T'Pul commented, "I think they're wagering on who will win." Several other students agreed with him and made a few bets of their own. The crowd favored T'Pul, the biggest and strongest of them all. Small vid cameras hovered above the arena, waiting to record the bouts.

A fighting ring had been set up for their bouts. Kayla stood to the side, away from the other students, praying for strength and endurance. K'Ramm watched her from the top of the arena wall and said another prayer for Kayla. He knew she had won many bouts during the last six months, but this was the first time the students had competed tournament-style, until only one winner was left standing. Kayla matched a few of the other students in height, but not in weight or reach; the others were all males. Anyone surviving their first few bouts would feel the strain of fighting as fatigue set into their muscles. Tired fighters made mistakes too easily. The arena walls soon filled with more priests, priestesses, and monks anxious to watch the fighting.

The twenty students competed in ten center ring bouts of one round, and soon there were ten who qualified to continue to the second round. Her first opponent landed only one kick on Kayla, but she still felt the pain on her ribcage. Another bruise. The second round of five bouts began immediately after the first. Everyone watched T'Pul win again, eliminating his second opponent in only four moves. His fellow students cheered, and several monks were seen passing coins to each other. T'Pul's confidence was very high.

When the bell rang to begin her second bout, Kayla's opponent charged her in an aggressive attack meant to knock her out of the ring. But she was ready for him and spun just in time to miss the flying double-kick to her chest. She jumped and knee-kicked his exposed back while he was still in the air. Kayla chopped his neck, and followed with a spinning kick to the back of his head. He fell to the ground, unconscious.

The remaining five students were pumped by their victories, yet anxious to finish the competition. All were battered and bruised. T'Pul fought against his opponent M'Kel well, and showed little sign of fatigue. But his opponent beat him soundly with a well-placed kick to the side of T'Pul's head, and the crowd moaned for him as he fell down, unconscious. More money exchanged hands, as the favorite was eliminated. Kayla won her next two bouts, after several minutes of very fast, hard kicks and hits. She was beginning to wonder if winning this competition was going to land the victor and the loser both in the infirmary.

For the last bout, the formal T'Ly rules of greeting were used, not just the fighting. The opening moves of formal T'Ly were like a dance, very hypnotic. Kayla and her opponent M'Kel bowed to each other, and then bowed to the monks and priests at the four cardinal directions. The two fighters walked around one another in a circle, then faced off. Each formally pivoted to the left one step, raised hands, and touched the backs of their stiff right hands together. They were in traditional, formal combat positions of T'Ly, the highest of the martial arts. Their eyes were totally focused on each other, each waiting for the first move. Slowly and deliberately they stepped three steps to the left, hands touching, and eyes focused. Each fighter bowed their head slightly to their opponent, and then stepped three times to the right.

M'Kel struck first with a fist intended for Kayla's gut, but she blocked him. He made several attempts to kick and hit her, but she took the defense, and blocked him each time. Most lost count of the number of kicks and hits thrown; few landed on either opponent. It was a hard fight, with neither Kayla nor M'Kel about to give the other an easy win. Although he was taller and more muscular, Kayla was much faster than M'Kel, and more nimble.

He backed her against the ropes of the arena ring twice, but she evaded his attack. M'Kel spun and kicked at her head, and Kayla did a perfect back flip, causing him to miss, and leave his body open. Then, she jumped straight up in the air, spun as fast as she could, and landed a kick on his upper chest. M'Kel gasped for breath, then jumped and double-kicked. But his target moved too fast for him, and he landed on the opposite side of the ring. When M'Kel touched the ground, Kayla jumped on his back, and caught him in the "Python:" a full-body squeeze-and-choke hold. She wrapped her legs around his ribs and squeezed, feeling his labored breathing.

M'Kel bucked and turned, hitting Kayla's legs, and tried to throw her off him, but she held on tightly. He used his free arm and pounded her arm holding his throat, but she did not release her grip. The students closest to the ring yelled and screamed for their favorite while the last two opponents battled each other fiercely. "Yield, M'Kel," Kayla warned, and tightened her grip with her legs around his ribs and her arm around his throat. But he struggled again and again to get free. When he bent to try and throw her off him one last time, Kayla dug her toes into his liver and pancreas until M'Kel screamed in pain.

The crowd was yelling so loud, and the midday sun beat down on them, burning their faces and eyes. The tension was incredibly high, as both opponents stubbornly held on for the win. With one final deep breath and battle cry, Kayla once more tightened her choke hold and pressured his pancreas and liver, and his ribs.

"Yield! I yield!' M'Kel choked out, and the monks rushed into the ring to stop the fight. Kayla let go, panting and breathing hard, and dismounted his body. When the monk instructor raised her hand in victory, Kayla took M'Kel's hand, and raised it with hers. The students cheered loudly and the monks applauded, and the watchers along the top of the arena cheered for them.

The reward after the final day of tournament competition was a dinner feast, which Kayla was permitted to attend, sitting between two priestesses. Each student received a necklace of hand-woven colored wool strands, with a tungsten spiral-shaped ornament attached. The spiral symbolized the ever-expanding universe, and was one of the symbols most used in worship of the Creator. Carved spirals appeared frequently throughout the Temple.

The students were invited to perform a cleansing ritual: walking on white-hot coals, followed by being branded on their shoulder. Most declined, but Kayla accepted. The monks took her into the garden for meditation and prayers, and chanting. Then they led her to a two-meter length of hot coals. "Your mind is your ultimate weapon. Push away your fear, and replace it with calm and control. There is no pain. Only peace," they chanted.

Kayla walked through the hot coals, and felt no pain. Neither did her feet burn. After the coals, the monks led her to Priest K'Ramm, dressed in white and gold robes, wearing an ornate, tall hat. He anointed her forehead in holy oil, and blessed her in the ancient language of the priests. Then, he pushed her sleeve up to her shoulder while the monks chanted, "There is no pain. Only peace," and branded her right shoulder with a small spiral. She smelled her flesh burning for an instant, but felt no pain. K'Ramm rubbed holy oil on the brand, prayed over her, and smiled. It was done. She walked back to the feast, feeling as light as air.

Priest K'Ramm watched Kayla sit between the two priestesses, and spend time happily conversing with the other students. She did not elevate herself above them, as some champions would have done. To Kayla, they were all champions to have completed the advanced training. K'Ramm had observed her training nearly every day for over six months. He knew of her Ranger and family background, her loss of Nat'N, her victorious battles, and her expertise with T'Ly before she arrived. K'Ramm respected the cool professionalism Kayla exhibited every day, her willingness to learn from the monks, and the way she handled herself. He had never met a warrior woman before, and Kayla fascinated him. Seeing he was watching her, Kayla bowed her head slightly to the priest, and gave him a gracious smile. K'Ramm was captivated.

Priest K'Ramm prayed for Kayla every day, for her pain to heal while at the Temple. On this final evening of training, K'Ramm realized Kayla would leave the next morning, and take a piece of his heart with her. He thought of her too frequently, and not always in priestly ways. He was forbidden to touch Kayla, talk with her outside of class, or spend private time with her. K'Ramm knelt before the altar in the dark chapel and prayed for Kayla, that she would find peace, and survive in her Shi'Lon Ranger life. Perhaps the Creator would allow them to meet again in the future; who knew. K'Ramm brushed away a silent tear as he walked from the chapel, for the woman he never knew, and loved.

No tinkling chimes played this morning. The Ranger uniform of black blouse, trousers, and boots were clean and waiting for her beside her sleep mat in the morning. Kayla dressed as a Ranger for the first time in over six months, and it felt good. She rolled up her sleep mat for the last time, packed up, and walked out of the Temple of the Creator. Two kilometers later, she boarded her ES-519, tossed her bag into the hold, and reluctantly reported to C.S. T'Anh.

"Much has happened during your six-month absence, Commander Kayla. You are ordered to proceed directly to the Xau Imperial Army Outpost on the far side of the moon, and report to Captain Hal'Bek. You have been assigned there for an indeterminate length of time, to assist the Army patrols with curtailing Rebel activities. Further orders will be sent to you, once you are settled into your new post. T'Anh out."

So much for her peaceful disposition. Thirty seconds of hearing T'Anh's harsh voice brought her sharply back to feeling under her Commander Superior's thumb again. Kayla sighed, and then replayed T'Anh's message, and visualized hundreds of fireflies dancing in the moonlight. Much better. There is no pain. Only peace.

Commander Kayla flipped the switch to awaken her onboard computer, and began the pre-flight systems check. She logged in her flight plan and coordinates, and launched towards the opposite side of Xau, en route to the Imperial Army Outpost.

XXX

What a desolate place. The ES-519 circled over the landing site. No surrounding town; just a handful of buildings next to the outpost entrance, including a flashing neon sign advertising hard cider and dancing girls. C.S. T'Anh probably sent her to this cesspool, as penance for her specialized six months T'Ly training with the monks and priests. Very well, then. Kayla reminded herself she was a Beloved Daughter of Emperor P'Lau, who had no idea what his Army outpost looked like. The officers and troops on this outpost most likely hated their assignments in this place. She was also the Emperor's Emissary, and would do her best to be cordial, professional, and brighten someone's day, every day. If possible.

Kayla landed her warbird and walked to the main building. She reported to Captain Hal'Bek, and saluted. The hard officer had a half-chewed, half-smoked cheap cigar in his mouth. His office was reeking with cigar smoke. He scowled, "I ask for more help, and they send me a princess in her black cape." The other two officers in his office laughed with him.

Commander Ki said gruffly, "The Emperor must be too busy shagging his concubines to care about us here, or else he's tired of you, sister." They started to laugh again.

Kayla pulled him out of his chair, backed him against the large desk, and put her knife to his throat. The Captain dropped the cigar from his mouth. She stated, "I am Commander Kayla, Shi'Lon Ranger, Beloved Daughter and Emissary of our Great Benevolent Emperor P'Lau. You have disparaged and demeaned the Emperor whose will I am bound by blood oath to obey. When any of you speak to me, you are speaking to our Emperor. Give me one reason I should show you mercy."

The stunned officers were momentarily speechless, then Captain Hal'Bek said, "He— he's one of only two officers I have here. He's in charge of our flight patrols," he blurted. Shaking Commander Ki began

BARBARA J. ROBERTSON

pissing his pants. "Please Ranger, don't do this. We need him here. We're not used to Imperial protocols anymore, here in this shit hole. Please, forgive him," the Captain pleaded. "Forgive all of us, please, Ranger."

Kayla drew her plasma pulser pistol from her backplate with her free hand, and blew out the window of the Captain's smoke-filled office. "Enjoy the mercy of Great Emperor P'Lau, Commander Ki, and thank the Creator for your life. Let us all breathe some fresh air and begin again," she said, and withdrew her knife from his throat. Ki took a deep breath.

Captain Hal'Bek and his officers exchanged salutes with Commander Kayla, and they invited her to sit with them. Commander Ki excused himself for a few minutes, presumably to change pants. Tea was served, and then the officers gave her an in-depth update on recent Rebel activity discovered two weeks ago, near the southern ice cap.

The new, underground Rebel base was just beyond the range of their Army short-range fighter patrols. Three armed land attacks had been carried out by the Rebels near the copper mines. They viciously attacked the food stores and fuel depot, and the towns supporting the copper mines. Several townspeople were killed, and many more wounded were transported home to K'Halon Prime for treatment. The miners and their families were terrified. Their Mining Guild ordered all work stopped until the mines and surrounding town were safe.

"The Traitor Duma Wat prefers mines, especially deep ones, beyond our scanner range. He uses them to store stolen weapons and equipment, and house his Rebels. Have your drones spotted any Rebel incursions inside the mines themselves?" Kayla asked.

"The Rebels have destroyed all our spy drones. This outpost is too small for the autonomous attack drones," the Captain said. They discussed the current situation in depth for two hours with her, the Army officers now appreciative of Kayla's being assigned to help them. The Emperor had not forgotten the men serving at his outpost, after all.

A quick tour of the outpost was followed by a simple lunch. Kayla settled into her assigned room in the officer's quarters. She didn't bat an eye when they told her of the shared bathrooms and showers. The Captain watched his men deliver her travel bags, and fumble with the big plex case containing her black battle armor. He shook his head, and said, "How the hell do you wear that heavy thing? It must weigh thirty kilos."

"Thirty-two, to be exact. Plus the jet pack. I'll show you, Captain," Kayla answered. She took off her cloak, hit the button on the plex case, and the battle armor opened. She thrust her arms and feet inside, and it closed around her quickly.

"Three seconds, flat. It takes our Army commandos two and a half minutes to suit up," Captain Hal'Bek said. "I hope the Rebels don't know you're here, Commander Kayla," he laughed, and walked down the hall shaking his head.

The Rebels would find out soon enough. Kayla took off her battle armor, and sat at the desk. Putting her ear buds in for privacy, she read the newly-received files from C.S. T'Anh. If the Rebels had concentrated on fortifying their new base and not attacked the mining towns, they might have escaped discovery for a few more weeks. She developed her flight plans for reconnaissance in her ES-519.

Kayla unpacked after dinner and sent a "Hello" text to her brother Olm, Dan'L, and Steph'N. M.C. Steph'N congratulated her for graduating from advanced T'Ly training, and her rapid promotion to Commander. He tactfully reminded her most promotions came with a challenge, and a reassignment to a ship, a Space Base, or a solitary posting, like the Imperial Army Outpost on Xau. Reading his message made her feel better about her new assignment. Kayla determined to fulfill her duties on the Outpost to the best of her ability.

The responding message from Dan'L was comforting. He was still on Home World, shadowing M.C. Steph'N, and learning Main Court duties. Handsome and out-going, Dan'L interacted well with the courtiers. But he missed his best friend Kayla. She missed Dan'L, too, and her other friends she hadn't seen or been permitted to contact in six months. During her six months of training with the monks, Dan'L's Mother, M.C. Javette, and C.S. G'Rosk became Life Partners. Kayla sent them a congratulatory message.

Captain Hal'Bek ordered partitions built to provide some privacy in the shared officer bathrooms and showers. By morning, they were installed. His gesture of respect created the first of many bonds between the tough Army officer and Commander Kayla. They would become trusted, good friends over the next few months. On her personal requisition list, Kayla ordered a portable air purifier for the Captain's office and a box of fine cigars for him.

Flying the powerful, long-range ES-519, Kayla broke away from the regular Army flight patrols the five next days, in stealth mode. She flew well beyond the range of the regular Army patrol short-range fighters, directly to the Rebel base. She recorded the location of the base, its tunnels, entrances and exits, and weaponry. Kayla located the partially-buried, large life support power supply generators, and scanned the area thoroughly, all the while invisible to the Rebel scanners. She scanned and mapped out the entire Rebel base, and transmitted the information to C.S. T'Anh and C.S. G'Rosk.

More Imperial Army fighters, personnel, weaponry, and Space Cadre long-range fighters were soon sent to the Outpost upon receipt of Kayla's initial reports. In less than one month of Kayla's arrival, plans were made for a full-scale attack on the Rebel base by Space Cadre fighters, the Imperial Army, and the ES-519.

Cpt. Hal'Bek, Commander Ki, and Kayla met with the Space Cadre flight squadron leader Maj. P'Rak, and meticulously planned the attack on the Rebel base. Since the base was largely underground, a traditional aerial assault would not be effective enough to destroy the base in one attack. Missiles and regular bombs would only scratch the surface, and the Rebels would remain safe in their tunnels. The decision was made to utilize a specially-designed cluster bomb for the mission: "Boring Betsy."

A standard cluster bomb contained fifty mini-bombs which would be released upon the detonation of the primary bomb's delivery shell. The mini bombs would be fired in all directions, adhering to anything and everything, and explode in seconds. Cluster bombs were devastating in both traditional and space warfare. But they would not penetrate below the surface and reach tunnels and fortified underground facilities. Even the big "bunker buster" bombs caused little more than severe shaking a few meters underground.

Three weeks went by while the weapons designers created "Boring Betsy." The Imperial Army positioned dozens of various land craft within fifty kilometers of the Rebel base. Using the intel from Kayla's many scans of the Rebel base, the Space Cadre fighters planned their bombing runs for the attack. But everything hinged on the success of Boring Betsy.

XXXI

Boring Betsy was too big to be delivered by any Space Cadre fighter or ES warbird. She was the Imperial Army's baby. The Imperial Army Command advanced their land attack craft in a slow roll, dropping more troops and machines behind their lines daily, in an attempt to capture the attention of the Rebel defenders. Once the Imperial Army land craft were in attack formation, they held, and waited. The skies were clear and empty. The Rebels in their deep, underground base targeted the Army land assault craft, currently holding position far beyond the range of their weapons. No one moved. Each tactical officer watched, waited, and sweated bullets.

The only movement on the surface of Xau near the Rebel base was the slow but constant landing of troop transports behind their own Army lines. Twenty Imperial Army troops would rush out from the landing transports in fifteen seconds, then the transports lifted off again, and flew back to the Outpost. The Rebels watched the troop build-up, but felt safe in the tunnels. Deeper extensions were dug for extra protection.

At precisely 7:11p.m., an Imperial Army cargo carrier transport landed, dropping more troops on the ground inside the Army perimeter. But instead of flying away from the ice cap and the Rebel base, the big transport continued towards the vast ice sheet at a slow, steady pace, alone. The big transport landed less than five kilometers from the Rebel base. The cargo transport's landing lights went out, its engines shut down, and the craft slowly opened its hatch.

The Rebels inside their underground base watched the big cargo transport closely. It was just out of firing range. Was someone inside coming out to parlay, to negotiate a surrender? The cargo transport, huge though it was, showed no armed weapons on the Rebel scanners. Who was inside? Were they waiting for a Rebel representative to come aboard? The Rebels became very apprehensive about the cargo transport, so apprehensive, they took no notice of Imperial battle droids dressed in white snowsuits crawling silently through the snow to flank the base entrance.

179

"Captain Hal'Bek, this is Tactical Officer Commander Ki. 'Boring Betsy' is in position, ready to initiate detonation sequence. Imperial battle droids have flanked the Rebel base main entrance. You may commence ground assault upon signal from Space Cadre squadron, sir," the Commander advised confidently. "You may begin forward movement at half speed, sir."

Cpt. Hal'Bek acknowledged Ki's message, and gave the signal to his land assault vehicles to move out at half speed. It felt good to be in a command assault hover-tank again. The attack tanks and troop haulers roared ahead of the massive command machine, preparing for the attack on the Rebel base. In seventeen minutes, the first assault craft would be in range. The land assault craft moved forward steadily.

"Squadron leader Major P'Rak reporting. Space Cadre fighter squadrons in firing range in two minutes. Is the ES in position?"

Kayla answered, "ES-519 in position, Major P'Rak, and awaiting my friend Betsy." She was in stealth mode, hovering directly above the Rebel base, unseen. *If Boring Betsy failed, this air and land assault was futile*, she thought. *Come on Betsy. Almost time...*

Rebel laser cannons began firing on the Space Cadre fighters the second they were in range. Missiles from the Army assault tanks took out one power generator, reducing the Rebel shields to less than half. The Army vehicles increased their speed to maximum towards the Rebel base, but fired only enough to keep the Rebel laser cannons busy.

When the initial battle maneuvers commenced, the big cargo transport began slowly advancing towards the main entrance of the Rebel base, with its shields on full. Then came the announcement over the Army comms, "Timer is set. Initiating detonation in three minutes," the Army Commander reported. "We are evacuating the transport now."

"Get the hell out of there, Commander," Cpt. Hal'Bek ordered. "All assault vehicles, give cover to the transport. Space Cadre fighters, ready shock bombs in 45 seconds. ES-519, fire at will," he bellowed.

The Army officers lowered the aft shields and ran as fast as they could from the cargo transport, and remotely raised the shields again. They were picked up by approaching Army vehicles. The transport sped faster and faster towards the main entrance, while the Rebel laser cannons fired on the approaching behemoth. Space Cadre fighters kept the laser cannons occupied, providing support for the transport. Then, the Army officers lowered the transport's forward shields.

With an explosion that rocked the heavy, reinforced metal doors of the main entrance of the Rebel base, the cargo transport launched Boring Betsy. The big cluster bomb exploded on the metal doors of the base and blew them apart. Hundreds of mini-borers were fired into the base, drilling downward, below ground. The diamond-tipped mini-borers drilled and penetrated the underground tunnels, storerooms, and man-made caverns where the Rebels were hiding, along with their smaller weapons and ammo. The walls and ceilings of the tunnels were perforated by the mini-borers from the surface down more than twenty meters. Then, in a well-time detonation, the explosives inside the mini-borers blew apart the lower underground shafts. The underground base was now completely exposed.

Army missiles took out the remaining laser cannons, and the Space Cadre fighter missiles demolished the exposed main entrance. The battle droids in white snowsuits rushed into the Rebel base, taking out their interior defenses and computer command console, in advance of the Imperial Army assault vehicles and troops. A full barrage of Imperial Army missiles was fired into the wounded underground stronghold, as the fury of the Empire's might was unleashed. Rapid underground explosions were heard when the Rebel ammo and weapons storerooms were destroyed. There was no escape for most of the Rebels.

A false snow wall half a kilometer from the Rebel base main entrance slowly opened to reveal a hidden hangar exit. The fully-armed Rebel fighters inside were lined up to launch, and escape. "ES-519 locked and loaded, and ready for the turkey shoot," Kayla calmly reported. She targeted the nose of the first Rebel fighter emerging from their rear escape hangar, and came out of stealth mode to fire a devil bomb into the rear hangar. The explosion was massive, triggering a devastating series of explosions as the armed Rebel fighters blew up, one by one. Kayla fired her missiles and destroyed the last Rebel fighters attempting to get away. Dozens of Rebels rushed outside holding their noses and shielding their eyes, frantically seeking fresh air and safety. She used her broadcast speakers and offered surrender to any surviving Rebels inside the hangar. They ran out, holding their arms in the air.

"Approximately 50-60 Rebels surrendering on foot, escaping through the rear exit, Captain Hal'Bek," Kayla reported. The men were captured by Imperial Army troops and taken to the Army Outpost, and held for transport and interrogation on the K'Halon Prime Imperial Army Base.

The underground Rebel base was obliterated, completely destroyed. Rescue droids pulled several Rebels from the wreckage, but most were killed. Initial reports indicated less than fifty Rebels occupied the base. But thanks to Kayla's many stealth reconnaissance flights, the true scope and size of the base was uncovered. The Rebel base housed more than twelve hundred fighting personnel, three squadrons of fighters, and enough weapons and ammo to launch a full-scale assault on Centralia, the capital of K'Halon Prime — the purpose of the underground base, according to the confessions of the captured Rebel officers.

The humble Imperial Army Outpost on Xau was soon reclassified as a full base, with a Space Cadre fighter squadron detachment. Captain Hal'Bek was promoted to Colonel, and assigned as the base Commanding Officer.

Spy satellites were placed in orbit around each moon of K'Halon Prime, Home World, M'Wati, and Ban'Ti. Commander Kayla received a commendation and an award for her discoveries, and for preventing the escape of the Rebel fighters from the base.

XXXII

Home World

An emergency session of the Emperor's Special Inquest Commission was called. All available members appeared live in the private Royal Court, and the remaining members vid-conferenced in to the meeting remotely. Two of the Bankers Guild leaders were presenting their findings from the top-secret audit ordered by the Royal Treasurer.

Bankers Guild Chairman Pet'R reported, "We have conducted top-secret audits internally of all banking facilities, as ordered by the Royal Treasurer. We traced all incoming and outgoing funds of every account, over 250 million personal and business accounts, and all funds were deemed from legitimate sources." The Chairman put down his com tablet and sat back in his chair, waiting to be dismissed. But his scant information was not accepted as the definitive answer the Commission was expecting.

C. S. Vu'Duc asked the Chairman, "What about the twelve accounts directly traced to Duma Wat, and the various business accounts set up to fund the Rebellion? You were tasked with sourcing their depositors' information, so the Emperor could discover those directly contributing to the Rebels!"

The Bankers Guild Chairman Pet'R and Vice-Chair S'Golt leaned their heads together and whispered between themselves at length, until C.S. Bette slammed her hand loudly on the table, stood, and addressed the Guild leaders directly: "There will be no whispers at this meeting. No information is to be withheld from this Special Inquest Commission, or our Great Emperor P'Lau. Speak openly, or I will personally see that both of you are arrested, and forced to confess your secrets!" Even the Emperor jumped when she hit the table. He pursed his red lips to fight back a smile at her forceful tactic.

"You cannot force us to reveal personal information. All account and depositor information is private and confidential," the Chairman retorted

183

haughtily.

From the vid screen, C. S. G'Rosk calmly offered, "All information discussed in this meeting is confidential, Mr. Chairman and Mr. Vice-Chair. Every person present at this meeting holds the fifth-level top-security clearance; except yourselves, of course. My advice is to reveal all you know now. Failure to answer all our questions will result in your immediate arrest for conspiracy to commit high treason," G'Rosk threatened.

"This is disgraceful! I refuse to reveal confidential information!" The Chairman declared. With one slight move of his index finger, the Emperor signaled to his Imperial Guards, and they pulled the Chairman out of his seat. He was taken away, protesting all the way to his prison cell.

Emperor P'Lau spoke for the first time in the meeting, "Mr. S'Golt, you are now the Bankers Guild Chairman. Do you have any answers to my Special Inquest Commission members' queries?" He leaned forward and stared at the shocked bureaucrat.

Like a levee giving way in a torrential flood, the new Chairman S'Golt revealed as much information as he knew to the Commission. He showed them recent and historical transaction activity from all twelve identified accounts for the last ten years. The biggest deposits originated from business accounts of the "New Tomorrow Holding Company," headquartered on K'Halon Prime.

C.S. Bette ordered, "Commander Kayla, you will keep your eyes and ears open for any information pertaining to the New Tomorrow Holding Company on your Imperial Army Outpost on Xau. Report to Commander Superior T'Anh immediately with any discovered information. Dismissed." Kayla clicked off. She later conducted a confidential search with the Commanding Officer, and no records of any transactions had occurred with the New Tomorrow Holding Company. They put the company on their top-secret watch list.

New Chairman S'Golt was "invited" to spend several days in a secure guest suite in the Royal Palace under protective guard, to keep him safe. He was gently escorted to his guest suite, and the meeting continued. It was decided to bring in the three identified directors of the New Tomorrow Holding Company for questioning. M.C. Steph'N volunteered to bring them in, along with his charge, Ranger Dan'L. They left for the Ranger High Command Center immediately.

In the next few hours, M.C. Steph'N and Ranger Dan'L received their full mission briefing from C.S. Vu'Duc. They were issued Centralia police badges, and suits for plain clothes duty. Workmen's coveralls and grubby boots were given to them, with keys to an old technicians' hovercraft. Instead of their body armor, the Rangers would only wear soft armor vests. Vu'Duc instructed them to bring in the three directors within four days of their arrival on K'Halon Prime. "Treat them with respect, especially the landowner aristocrat, Director Hu'Wit. His family has a long history of loyalty to the Empire. All three directors are presumed innocent at this point, and must not be harmed."

Steph'N asked, "What if Director Hu'Wit or the other men refuse to voluntarily accompany us?"

"You may subdue them to expedite your mission, but do not harm Hu'Wit. A director's meeting will be held at the New Tomorrow Holding Company in four days. Take care not to be seen subduing any of them. Utilize extreme stealth. You are authorized to use deadly force on any other persons attempting to thwart your mission objectives," Vu'Duc replied.

Steph'N acknowledged their orders, and they flew to K'Halon Prime. He and Dan'L flew in an unmarked shuttle to downtown Centralia, landed on the parking site on the top of the assigned hotel, and checked into their suite. The hotel was adjacent to the office building where the headquarters of the New Tomorrow Holding Company was located. There, he and Dan'L planned their attack in detail. The Rangers changed into plain clothes, clipped the police badges onto their belts, and casually strolled the hall outside the main conference room.

The directors meeting inside the big conference room began as usual, with twelve board members present. At the first meeting break, the members went to the restrooms. Director Hu'Wit was led into a side office for an urgent call by Dan'L, masquerading as a plain clothes police security officer. The Director was shot in the back of his neck with one of Dan'L's stun injection pens, and carefully laid to sleep on the sofa. He was wrapped in a special body bag, and an oxygen mask was placed around his mouth and nose. Dan'L shot him with a six-hour sedation injection.

The second man never made it back to the meeting room from the restroom. Steph'N got his attention, sprayed him with stun gas and put him in the side room with Hu'Wit. Dan'L put his sleeping body into his special body bag with an oxygen mask, and sedated him, too. Noticing two of their board members missing, the directors called a security team to search for the missing men after half an hour's wait. Steph'N brandished his police badge, and offered to guard the conference room while the security team searched for the missing board members. Then he whispered to Dan'L over his comm link, "If anyone comes into this room and discovers our targets, kill them. Do not stun. Understood, Ranger Dan'L?" Dan'L acknowledged, and concealed his two targets and himself as best he could in the small side office, and waited.

"Sir, there may be more than these three men conspiring against Emperor P'Lau. Their corporate security teams are heavily armed, and appear to have military training backgrounds. They are searching the corridor and offices across the hall. We have not been discovered. We have stunned and sequestered Hu'Wit and the second man in a small office down the hall. The third target's apprehension may require use of force, Commander Superior," Steph'N whispered.

Vu'Duc responded, "Succeed at all costs, without harming the three targets." So, he or Dan'L were expendable, but their targets were not. Steph'N watched the security team split up and check every adjoining room in the long hall. He knew Ranger Dan'L was an experienced warbird pilot with several kills, but the young Ranger had never killed anyone fact to face. Even a split second of hesitation could result in your own death. Keeping to the shadows, Steph'N followed the two security men checking the adjacent rooms. Dan'L's room was next.

"Anyone in here?" The brawny security guard asked as he opened the small office door. His guard partner told him to enter, turn on the lights, and check inside. The two men looked around the small office. When the brawny man opened the closet door, Dan'L thrust his knife into his throat. The second guard raised his laser pistol to fire, but Steph'N grabbed his mouth and sliced his throat. Two more guards entered the small office in a few minutes, and both Rangers took them out with their knives without making a sound. Steph'N removed the guards' comm links and tossed the small devices out the window. The corporate security team was now missing.

The directors' meeting was abruptly adjourned and everyone quickly headed for their shuttles on the building roof. Still wearing his police officer's badge, Dan'L "helped" the third target into the stairwell, and subdued him. He and Steph'N moved his heavy, overweight, unconscious body down the stairs to the next floor. Dan'L rolled out the cargo cart containing the unconscious bodies of Hu'Wit and the second man, and the overweight man in his special body bag was stuffed on the bottom compartment. The Rangers put their dirty coveralls on over their suits quickly. The three unconscious men were covered with laundry bags and wheeled out through the service entrance, into the rear service entrance of the hotel next door. The Rangers rolled the loaded cart into the lift, moved their targets up the ramp into their shuttle on the hotel's roof, and flew away with them to the military transport base. Then, they loaded the three men into Steph'N's ES warbird, and flew them to Home World quickly.

Director Hu'Wit and his co-conspirators plead guilty to all charges, and confessed to processing "donations" for Duma Wat. But the men had no knowledge of the originating source of the funds. Bags of gold credits would be delivered by masked, armed guards ad hoc, and left in a coat room on the lower conference room floor. A recorded message to Hu'Wit said only, "Your cleaning has been delivered," the signal to pick up the bag of gold credits and process them into funds for Duma Wat.

With his Special Inquest Commission members assembled in his private, Royal Court, Emperor P'Lau said, "We are making progress, my Rangers.

Your vigorous work has produced better results in a few months than anyone else has accomplished in years of investigations." M.C. Steph'N received a commendation and a bonus for successfully completing his mission.

Then Emperor P'Lau rose up in his levitating throne and announced, "Our Faithful Son has fought the Rebels attacking our Imperial Command Battle Cruiser and defended us well. Today, he is acknowledged for his first successful mission as our Borgund Ranger assassin. We congratulate Commander Dan'L for blooding his knives!" The Emperor proclaimed loudly. The senior Rangers cheered and applauded Dan'L. His proud Mother Javette and C.S. G'Rosk smiled broadly on the vid screen, and joined in the applause, both at the Royal Palace on K'Halon Prime.

New-Commander Dan'L received a private call from Kayla later in the evening, congratulating him on his promotion. "Thank you, Kayla. I appreciate your call. You were the first from our class to be promoted to Commander. I finally caught up," he said.

She smiled and asked, "Will you be reassigned now? Sometimes we get sent off to solitary postings after a promotion, you know," she reminded him. "There are no electronic dance music clubs on Ban'Ti," she teased, and they both laughed.

Dan'L shrugged his shoulders and replied, "No, I'm still assigned to shadow Master Commander Steph'N, and go on whatever special assignments he volunteers us to perform. I'm working at the Palace, under the spotlight. It's so political, Kayla. You've got the whole Army base, and all those men to yourself!"

"The Imperial officers and troops I interact with are all dedicated, excellent soldiers. But none of them are in the top tiers of our warrior class, Dan'L. We owe it to ourselves, our parents, and our future children to choose partners from our own tier. I'm sure your Mother would agree," she said.

"Yes, I know she would agree. Mother told me the same thing when I was a boy. But so many women are looking to 'date up,' Kayla. They make it difficult for a man to stay within his own tier," Dan'L said, with a roguish smile.

"Especially when he's such a handsome flirt," she responded, aiming her comment directly at her best friend. They laughed and talked a little longer, then signed off.

Kayla stood and looked out her room window. The Xau base was expanding rapidly, with hundreds more Imperial Army officers and troops arriving weekly. New buildings were constructed hurriedly, and a large landing site complex would be completed next month. She recalled Dan'L's words, "All those men to yourself." He knew she was still mourning Nat'N, and was only trying to cheer her up. Dan'L had been her best friend in their early Royal Academy education, and throughout Phases 1, 2, and 3 Training. They'd been through so much together. She could talk with him about anything, and he confided in her.

Kayla closed the window blinds and sat at her desk. After a few minutes she leaned her head back, and stared at the ceiling. The Imperial Army and Space Cadre men were perfectly safe from her; she had no design on any man. The pain of Nat'N's death was less acute, but ever-present. She felt emotionally disconnected, as if a part of her was forever gone. She would carry out her assignment on the Army base to the best of her ability, and continue to throw herself into her work. Forward was the only direction. It would be a long time before Kayla let any man get so close to her again.

Commander Kayla was now a full-time, regular fixture on the Xau Imperial Army Base. The troops and officers treated her with courtesy, and felt honored whenever the Shi'Lon Ranger helped them with a project, or participated in meetings with them. The number of personnel assigned to the base grew from its paltry forty-two to sixteen hundred officers and troops over the next six months. Private citizens were moving there, too. A small town grew around the full-size base, to support the troops assigned there, and provide entertainment, shopping, and other facilities for its personnel.

The Imperial Army Base Xau was now under the watchful eyes of a Shi'Lon Ranger. Commander Kayla flew her ES-519 on patrols every day, learning the moon's terrain, and keeping the Rebels at bay. She was the eyes and ears of Emperor P'Lau, his Beloved Daughter and Emissary, and she obeyed and enforced his will at all costs.

EPILOGUE

The underground river flowed lazily along, emerging into the high cave, and gently following its curved banks. Small boats were moored on the docks, full of laser rifles, shoulder missiles, ammunition, and grenade launchers. Eight monks in yellow robes sat around a fire, chanting, "Ya-Oa," and filling the cave with their voices.

When the older monk D'Ridi shook a large, dry gourd full of seeds, the chanting stopped abruptly. D'Ridi said, "We are now eight of the expected twelve monks who will make this mountain on Xau our new home. Convert others to our cause, if possible. But do not reveal us. The monks in residence at the Temple here are loyal to the Emperor, and cannot be trusted or bribed to keep silent, like our brothers on M'Wati. We twelve must keep our own company," he cautioned.

One of the other monks asked, "When can we expect the fighters to arrive? Where will they stay? Every room in this Temple has security cameras. We will be seen helping the Rebel fighters, and storing their arms for them, Brother D'Ridi." Many nodded and murmured in agreement with him. "Spy satellites and drones are everywhere!"

But D'Ridi raised his hand to silence them, and answered, "No satellite or drone can see inside this mountain. No armed Imperial Army trooper would dare violate the Temple of the Creator, and risk eternal damnation in the Afterlife. Do not concern yourselves with these trivial matters. Arrangements have been made. Powerful allies on K'Halon Prime have designed the plan to minute details, my brothers. The moon Xau and our Temple will come under their protection when the final uprising begins. We have their word. This river flows for many kilometers, with more than a few caves to provide shelter." He spread out his arms wide, and looked at each of them.

"Besides; one is on his way who will occupy the minds, hearts, and energy of our brothers and priests here. Our resettling will be a mere trifle in comparison to his incredibly public arrival. A very special 'welcome' has been planned for our esteemed leader," D'Ridi said, with an evil smile. "His arrival will be remembered for decades to come!"

"No harm will come to him, I pray," another monk whispered. "It would be sacrilege."

Brother D'Ridi stood and raised his hands to quiet them. Then he stated, "The Creator will decide his fate. Our contribution will help bring a punishing end to the oppression of the Empire. The time is nearly at hand. We will be well-rewarded for paving the way for our Lord Duma Wat, the Savior of the People!" The monks rang bells and shook gourds.

Rafts full of Rebel fighters made their way to the docks, and the monks cast the boat lines to them. They tied the mooring lines of the boats full of arms to their rafts, and slowly made their way down the river, and out of sight. The eight monks began chanting, "Ya-Oa," and climbed the winding, steep stairway up into the main hall of the Temple of the Creator.

www.ingramcontent.com/pod-product-compliance
Lightning Source LLC
Chambersburg PA
CBHW030248130626

46549CB00002B/449